Siya's passion for writing and storytelling began early on in childhood when she read and imagined stories for her siblings. From a family of poets and storytellers, she was born in Karachi and came to the UK as a two-year-old with her parents. She was brought up in Manchester and moved to London to study Biochemical Engineering, followed by Sanskrit at the University of Bonn, where she also taught English as a foreign language. A passion for understanding how the mind works led to a part-time degree in psychology back in London, all the while writing poems and short stories.

After a long winding path as a student, teacher and art therapist, she started her first novel, *The Last Beekeeper*, at the age of 40, when the idea for the book was born in a writing class that was a gift to herself after finishing her Master of Art Therapy.

She loves escaping into stories and being in the natural world, and is currently writing her second novel set in fifteenth-century Spain.

siyaturabi.com

 twitter.com/SiyaTurabi

 facebook.com/SiyaTurabiAuthor

THE LAST BEEKEEPER

SIYA TURABI

One More Chapter
a division of HarperCollins*Publishers* Ltd
1 London Bridge Street
London SE1 9GF

www.harpercollins.co.uk

HarperCollins*Publishers*
1st Floor, Watermarque Building, Ringsend Road
Dublin 4, Ireland

This paperback edition 2021

1

First published in Great Britain in ebook format
by HarperCollins*Publishers* 2021

A catalogue record of this book is available from the British Library

PB ISBN: 978-0-00-847288-7
TPB ISBN: 978-0-00-850955-2

Printed and bound in the UK using 100% Renewable Electricity
by CPI Group (UK) Ltd

For Saif

&

Hana

Arif

Qaia

A knowing comes when I sit alone under the trees
where the humming is constant from the timeless bees

Part One

Harikaya village in Harikaya state

Sindh Province, Pakistan

Chapter One

August 1974

The train had been too fast or the deer had been too brave.

A blackbuck deer with horns like waves. And it was dying. Hassan recognised it from lessons at school. Or was it a hog deer, or a gazelle? It could be an Indian gazelle. No, it was definitely a blackbuck deer. It had white fur on its chin and it was too big for a gazelle.

The train came to a stop, puffing and clanking as Hassan stood and looked down at the animal, thrown a few metres away from the railway line.

Groans and shrieks came from full carriages. People on the roof stared at the deer. Some climbed down metal ladders at the side of the train and crowded round Hassan. Baluchi, Punjabi, as well as local Sindhi speakers from the northern parts of Sindh on their way to work in the fields and factories of Harikaya. Dialects from neighbouring provinces flew around him.

'These are Mir Saab's deer,' one man said, his Sindhi hat shaped like an upturned boat.

Some shook their heads, some sighed, but no one looked as flustered as the driver who came up, scratching his head. 'Accidents aren't illegal,' he said.

'Bound to happen. He lets them roam as they please.' That was another man, small and shirtless.

'What if we lose our jobs?' another asked.

Hassan stepped back; they stank. Not surprising after a day's travelling in a hot, cramped train.

'The jackals and vultures will eat it overnight,' someone said.

The deer stopped breathing. Death was an opportunity in Harikaya. Flies were gathering around a clean gash in the deer's white chest. The evening heat was still strong enough for decay to set in.

The guard put his whistle to his mouth and blew. Hassan flinched. The crowd hushed but people finished their cigarettes before they got back on the train.

'Mir Saab's one of the good ones.'

'But he's a strange one. You know what happens when one of his rules is broken.'

The last few passengers on the ground jumped back on the train, which started its engines and then lurched forwards. Groans. More clanking and puffing before the train moved off through the sandy flatlands, reaching its normal speed and vanishing.

Everything was quiet again. Hassan stood by the deer.

That humming was in his ears again, soft and like a low whistling, almost a tune, that landed right inside him. He tried to ignore it and looked down at the deer.

This was a male one, framed by cigarette butts. He had only seen deer from far away before, or in books at school, never one in real life or up so close. Did a dead one count?

There was movement ahead. He looked up. On the other side of the train tracks, still a few metres away but coming closer, was the dark outline of a man, cradling a jar, with the orange sky and dark forest behind him. The humming stopped and Hassan didn't know whether to laugh or cry. His mother's words came back to him, 'When you find your father, bring him home.'

His father gripped the front legs of the deer.

'The jackals will eat it. Why don't we leave it?' Hassan asked.

'Mir Saab might see it,' his father said. 'He'll think we killed it.'

'But the train killed it.'

'The new law.'

Hassan took the back legs. The deer was heavy even when both of them pulled it over the dusty ground. Blackbuck deer weighed more than a grown man, but they were at the river in less than a minute. One final shove and the deer was behind the tall grasses. His father ran backwards, sand flying as he kicked the dust about to cover the drying blood.

'The jackals can eat it there,' his father said. 'I hope it didn't suffer too much.'

'It did.' Hassan wished he hadn't spoken.

Baba looked up at him, his eyes narrow. 'How do you know these things?'

'Well, it's obvious, isn't it? All of us suffer when we're dying. Mir Saab introduced this deer into—'

'Come on, we have to get out of here,' Baba said.

'You're telling me that?'

In normal families, fathers brought sons home, not the other way round. Anyway, he didn't want to think about that now.

They set off back to the village on the dirt road, tramping between the fields and the river and then between tall bamboo. His father held onto the clay jar tightly with both hands.

They turned a corner and Hassan heard a motor coming up the track from behind them. He turned to see the mir's flag on the bonnet before he was pulled backwards through the reeds. He landed on the earth in a field of corn. A man in the field with two bony oxen and a cart was staring at them. Hassan waved.

'That was close,' Hassan said, back on the road.

'Too close.'

'If you did what you were told...'

But his father never listened to him or anyone. They carried on, each in stubborn silence right until the village boundary.

Hassan stayed by the coconuts, stacked high on the ground, as his father headed to the few stalls round the side of the wall, with his jar of forest honey. There were other men with other goods. His father was the only one stupid enough to go into the forest now but all of them looked as if they were in trouble with someone or about to be. It was always the same.

Hassan faced the forest, at least a mile away now. The sun was just about to vanish before the sound of crickets filled the air. There it was again, that low humming. It only normally happened when he went near the forest to look for Baba. He'd been hearing it for a couple of weeks now, maybe more. But why it happened or why he heard it, he had no idea.

This time, it seemed much closer, a different tone, but the same melody. It was too close. He tried to shake it out of his head but the sound was getting stronger. He turned around. A woman was sitting behind a spinning wheel, quietly humming the same tune. She was looking down at her hands, folding thread.

'Are you afraid of that sound?' she asked.

'Why should I be afraid?

'You'll be watching another kind of spinning one day.'

'At the factories?' he asked.

'Another kind.'

Only the ridge of her eyebrows and the round tip of her nose were visible but her head rose just enough for him to see the edges of her lips turn upwards into a mischievous smile. The kind of smile he used himself, when he knew something that no one else knew.

'Won't be long now, before they start to use you.' Her green eyes studied him.

She was probably drunk. He went nearer to her. She smelt of coconut oil.

'Who?'

'If you please them,' she said.

'Who?'

'Hassan, I'm ready.' Baba's voice.

'Be careful, boy. Keep your head down,' she hissed.

Crisp lines spread over her face. She turned her head to the side, her lips twisting into that smile again – a seductress with wrinkles. He laughed.

'Give me a coin. I know you have one.'

He was reaching into his pocket when he felt his father's hand on his shoulder. The woman laughed now as they walked away.

'She makes the dolls,' his father whispered.

Hassan had found a wooden doll about two months ago on the doorstep of their house. Made out of wood and clothed in black wool that smelt of musk, a smell he could have lost himself in, but that was what its maker wanted. For you to bury your head into its softness. Its cheeks were scratched out and tinted with light-red powder. Just a dab. Wind-beaten face. Black eyes narrowed around a secret gleam – his father's smile. Whoever had made it must have studied his father's face and chipped at the tree bark while it was still fresh and living.

His mother had snatched it from his hand and had thrown it down the street where they lived. 'Throw cursed dolls away; every child knows that,' she had said. 'Let the dogs tear it apart.'

'Who made it?' Hassan had asked.

'That doesn't matter. They want to scare us.'

The next day Baba had fallen and broken his arm. No more work at his job with the local newspaper for six weeks.

'That doll,' his mother had said, 'is working.'

His father had only laughed. 'Please don't believe in these things.'

'Should I believe in socialism like you?'

'That's not a belief.'

'Isn't it?'

'It's a system that works for the equality of all.'

'Why do they want to curse you if you believe in the same thing as them?' She shook her head.

'They're trying to make me write what they want,' Baba had said. 'But they don't own the newspaper.'

'I just wanted to ask her about…' Hassan tried to shake his father's hand off his shoulder but the grip became tighter.

His father led him into the village. The metal letters glistened over the gates. Harikaya in Harikaya. Village and state had the same name.

'That was easy tonight,' his father said, licking his lips of any traces of the forest honey. Spillage, he called it.

Hassan looked around. Nobody was paying any attention. The law was still new. His father checked the bundle of rupees.

'Let's go to the shrine,' he said.

'But Amma said…'

'We won't stay long.'

'You always say that Baba. Every time we go to the shrine we always stay long.'

'That happens, I agree, but when the poetry begins, I forget time. You know by now that poetry doesn't belong in a world of tasks and timetables. Haven't I taught you enough to know that poetry and nature are partners? Just like honey and the bees are partners. Honey is a product of love. It can't be limited by clocks. They only feed our addiction to become, to constantly become something.' He looked around at the people. 'We need to forget time sometimes and just listen.'

'To what?' Hassan said.

'To the truth that nature speaks. When the mind is quiet and we're no longer rushing around to be somewhere, to do something or think something, that's when you can hear nature speak.' He licked his lips again for any remaining honey. 'But we're all addicted to becoming something, too busy to listen.'

With that, he laughed but only with his mouth. His face seemed to grow more wrinkles as he stepped back onto the track.

Chapter Two

The white shrine of the local saint stood tall, its dome bulging like a hump of one of the camels that sat under the date palms on the track. They said that when the saint had wandered here hundreds of years ago, his body had been buried somewhere nearby and then dug up again weeks later to be brought over to this shrine. There had been no decay at all – proof of sainthood. To Hassan it was just another story, just like the stories of the jinns, who were said to live in the forests and could be good or bad, or jadus that could live in people who were cursed. Hassan didn't believe any of it.

'Bedeel.' Hassan spoke the name of the dead saint out loud as he stepped onto the tiled area, just in case it was bad luck not to.

People were finishing off their daily meal and now the vultures, perched on the rim of the dome, had their eyes on their prize – meat – dropped from plates, spat out from between teeth or squashed under bare feet.

'Get a coconut shell for me.' Baba handed him a rupee. 'That's the only spirit I believe in.'

Hassan chose a big one and handed the rupee over to a man who was sitting on the floor and smoking a thin beedi, no bigger than Hassan's little finger. He had tried one once, and it had been over in a flash. His father was already sitting in a circle with the other poets. Hassan squeezed in between him and their friend, Ansari Saab, a poet who had brought back a chest full of books from England on the ship after his studies.

His father read the ones on Marxist theory but Hassan had picked one of those up and put it straight down again. Too many words, too many opinions. He preferred the poets. Wordsworth, Yeats, Keats. And the modern ones too. Ted Hughes. Dylan Thomas. He even read the English translations of Rumi. Over and over. Rumi's work reminded him of Ansari Saab's. The poet had never married but his poems were all about love. 'Why did you leave England?' Hassan had asked him once, but the poet had just sighed.

'Did you go to the forest again?' Ansari Saab said to Baba. He always spoke in English.

'Yes.'

Ansari Saab swished the coconut spirit about in his mouth and waited for the alcohol to reach his thoughts. 'You'll have to stop,' he said.

But Baba wasn't paying him any attention. He was drinking and watching the poets. Hassan looked around the circle too. She was there. Sami, sitting next to her father. He hardly knew her but she sat next to him in class and he had noticed her. Not because of her looks or because he was falling in love. No, he didn't believe in that. She was different from the others. She had to be, coming out here to listen to poems. There were other women there, but not girls like Sami; much older women, usually married too so no one could gossip about them. She must have felt him looking because she turned to him and smiled. He smiled back, and then kept on looking around, pretending he was looking for someone.

One of the musicians sitting in the centre of the circle, near the fire, started to drum, a soft constant beat. An oil burner was passed around until it reached Ansari Saab, who placed it on the floor, making his chin glow. He cleared his throat and looked up to the sky as if he were waiting for a tap in his head to turn on. Drips at first, in Urdu.

'The light of you.' A gentle sway of his head. 'Is the path to you.'

The audience of villagers and poets started to raise their hands. The drumming was steady.

Ansari Saab read his poetry and while everyone was looking at him, Hassan looked at Sami.

'You entered my life when I was a young bird,
Fallen from its nest.
Now I sing on that same tree,
In the hope you come back,
But that day never comes
And all I have is the memory of you.'

The others made their noises. 'Wah, wah,' they said.

Ansari Saab handed the oil lamp to Baba who placed it between his feet, careful not to let any of the oil drip. He held his coconut shell high above his head. Baba was ready.

'They tell me this is wrong.' He looked at the shell. 'Am I to cast you away and listen to their words?'

Nods of approval came from the circle of poets. He took a sip from his shell. The drum beat quickened.

'The wise ones, I bow to you in gratitude.' His father turned towards the musicians.

'You bring the sound that never dies.
Carried on thin notes through reed, skin, and string.
It is the sound of truth, a law, dropped to the earth.
It is no accident.'

Baba stood up and began to sway, only a little at first. His arms were rising. Another poet stood. And another. Soon, a handful of poets were up, ready to sway to the sound carried behind the music. Hassan stayed where he was. He was sure Sami was watching him. The drum beat was speeding up but he still didn't stand. His father was speaking again.

'How long will it be before stones and rocks are all we have, and the snow melts and the desert plants bleed dry? How long will it be before the farmers become the travellers and can no longer plough their fields because old laws say one man is better than thousands?'

This wasn't poetry anymore. Hassan looked over to Sami. She was staring at Baba. He wanted to pull his father down, all puffed up as he was with coconut spirit.

'The forest is forbidden to us because of Mir Saab's new law,' his father said.

He was at the centre of the circle now and his face was lit by the small fire. The poets began to mutter.

'Mir Saab made the law to protect the animals,' an old man said, perched with his hands on his stick in the front row. 'It's more than what the government does for us.'

'I understand that,' Baba said. 'I'm not saying the government has the answer to this problem.'

Some of the audience started to shuffle or step back.

'We need those forests,' Baba said.

Ansari Saab was shaking his head. 'Dangerous talk,' he muttered.

'Mir Saab has done a lot to help us. It's not right to criticise him.' That was another poet.

'Mirs belong to the old world.' It was Sami's father.

'Yes, the old systems are on their way out,' Baba said.

There were gasps in the crowd. Some of them started to shout.

'Mir Saab is a good leader.'

'How dare you?'

'We've used the medicines of the forest for generations,' Baba said. 'We should let Mir Saab know we need access to the forest.'

The drum beat was erratic. People were coming to join the circle of poets to see what was happening.

'A vote. That's the fair way of doing things. Those of you who want to do something… to change this law, come over here. Join me. We can have a peaceful march.'

No one stepped forwards. His father looked around the crowd and then his eyes rested on Hassan. Hassan sighed; he had to do it. He held his breath and, without looking at Sami, he stepped close to Baba, who put his hand on his shoulder.

'He's got his son into this now.'

'There'll be trouble for both of you.'

Just then, Sami's father stepped forwards into the circle. Sami looked on, her expression unchanged, and Baba raised his arm to the sky.

'Someone saw you coming back from the forest today,' a man said.

A hush fell over the crowd.

'I wasn't doing anything wrong,' Baba said.

'The new law says you were.'

'And why were you trying to hide a dead deer?'

'Come on, Baba, we have to leave.' Hassan pulled his father's arm.

'Tell us what you were up to.'

'That was Mir Saab's deer.'

'Mir Saab needs to listen to us.' His father was still trying.

People began to shout. The voices fell like sticks and Hassan felt hot. He wished his father weren't so drunk.

'We have to leave.' Hassan stood in front of his father.

It worked and Hassan looked back just in time to see Sami and her father leaving through the crowd on the other side.

'They're all held captive by him,' his father said, looking up at the fort.

They were on the track back to the village again. The noise of the crowd was still buzzing in Hassan's head. His father stopped and grabbed his arm so tightly that it hurt.

'The black honeybees. I wanted to take you with me to find

them but now…' He looked into the distance, across the fields and scrub land, towards the forest.

'We could go one last time,' Hassan said. 'Together.'

'I've never been able to find them. They're much deeper in the forest than the other bees.'

Hassan thought of his mother and the doctors she had seen for her eyes.

'Baba, you've always said the black honey is medicine. It could help Amma. I want to go with you.'

For a second the tiredness and worry left his father's face. 'Perhaps it'll be different if you come with me.' He let go of Hassan's arm.

When they got home, Hassan's mother was on the floor of the living area, waiting for them. 'He has his exam today,' she said, pointing to Hassan's room.

'The scholarship.' His father covered his mouth with his hand.

Hassan took off his clothes and lay on his bamboo bed. There were still two hours to go before school started. His head was spinning with the voices of the crowd. Sami's face when she was leaving. What would she think of him now? And all because Baba read too many of those books on Marxism. Hassan rolled over. He was too tired to make any sense of it now.

Chapter Three

Hassan woke to the sound of the cock and his parents arguing. He sat up. He was sick of it.

'Promise me you won't go to the forest anymore,' his mother was saying.

'I'll only go to find the black honeybees.'

Hassan went to stand at the door.

'You could get arrested.'

'You don't understand. The black honey's special.'

'Anything could happen,' his mother said. 'That man you sell the honey to is dangerous,' she said.

'You would know that, wouldn't you?'

His mother pummelled the chapati dough in her fists harder and faster. 'That was a long time ago.' Her voice was high-pitched. 'Tell that man you won't do it anymore.' She blinked and took off her glasses. Her eyes were cloudy and puffed up. She placed the clean backs of her hands on each eye and kept them there for a few seconds.

'I'll tell him but don't worry, the black honey's not for sale.' Baba walked to the back of the house. Before he opened the door, he turned back to Amma. 'It'll heal your eyes. There's no other way. You know that.'

'The doctors...'

'The doctors have said nothing can be done.' He stepped towards her.

'We can try other doctors. I can go to Karachi.'

'Those doctors work for Mir Saab. They come from Karachi.'

'I said, I don't want you to go,' his mother said.

'This disease has gone too far.' He came closer to her and held her wrist. His voice was breaking. 'You need the black honey.'

'Not now, not with this law. It's too dangerous.'

'Meri jaan, it's glaucoma. Stop this pretending.' Baba sighed.

'Promise me,' she said.

'All right, all right, I won't go.' His father headed for the back door. Hassan waited for the sound of his sandals on the steps, then on the roof, and the creaks of the bed as his father lay down.

The dough dropped out of his mother's hands. She went over to the small table in the corner and sat down in front of the tray filled with rose petals. She lit a candle and began to pick out the dead petals and let them drop on the floor. The skin of her strong arms glowed. Her face relaxed and she was beautiful. He understood why Baba always said it had been love at first sight.

But Amma only laughed when he said that. She had had a few proposals. Proposals she let go of – no, proposals she 'sacrificed' when Baba had kept after her. He had followed her around, begging her. He wouldn't go away. She always told Hassan that 'Baba made me fall in love with him.' And she complained about it sometimes – well, often. 'He wouldn't leave me alone.' Hassan knew all of this by heart now. 'He promised to take me travelling with him – to Kashmir – to rent a boat on Dal Lake.'

His father had broken his promise and she often reminded him of it. He never took her anywhere, she told him. She was an educated girl and he'd locked her into marriage with lies. He'd said he had an important job, that he was too busy for holidays. Then why did he go travelling on his own? Leaving her behind to do all the housework and work in the factory. Did he think that just because he wrote for a paper that he was better, that he could get away with doing nothing around the house?

That was how it always went. That's why Hassan didn't believe in marriage or love or even an affair. He'd stay single all his life. Yes, he liked Sami, but no more than that. She might be interesting to talk to but a pretty girl wouldn't change his mind.

Hassan came closer and knelt down next to his mother. She had stopped complaining recently. He looked sideways at her. 'What's wrong with your eyes?'

'They're fine. You just concentrate on your test today.'

That was typical of her. She never let herself be ill or rest. That was his mother.

'This is your chance,' she said. 'Harikaya has nothing for you anymore.' Her voice carried regret, heavier than usual. 'You'll live in Karachi,' she said. 'In Mir Saab's house. You'll have a future there.'

He wanted to tell her the truth, that the scholarship was her dream, not his. That he didn't want to leave her. 'Amma…'

Banging. The door. He was on his feet. His father's steps on the roof. Words – his mother's. She was at the door before him. It was Sami's mother.

'They came to warn him this morning.' The woman's cries were desperate. 'The guards came just now.'

His father was at the back door.

'What did they say?' his mother asked.

'He's lost his job.'

Sami's father had worked at the post office.

'Were they Mir Saab's guards or the government's?' his father asked.

'I don't know,' the woman said. Her lips trembled.

Hassan stepped forward. 'And Sami?' he asked.

Sami's mother turned towards him. 'You'd better be careful. It could be your father next, or you.'

Hassan stepped back from the force of her words.

The teacher sat at the front of the class with his head buried in books. Hassan yawned. He was at the back next to Sami. She seemed more tired than he was, her eyes red and swollen, and she just stared at the questions.

But for Hassan it was different. English, maths, nature, geography. Extra lessons with Ansari Saab had made all this too easy. He finished the papers before the others. The teacher was still occupied and he wrote Sami's surname at the top of each sheet and waved his hand just enough for her to look his way. He held out the papers and she took them with a confused look on her face. Hassan put his finger to his lips and gestured for her sheets with his other hand. A clean swap.

It was the right thing to do. She would have nothing now, not after what Baba had done. But now he had to wait for the bell and it was taking forever. He started to think of last night and sighed deeply. He felt her looking at him but kept his head low. If only he could sleep. He shouldn't have gone to the shrine but then Baba would have been alone.

That was the trouble: when Baba had an idea, he'd stick to it and it was even worse after a drink. Baba had read too many books on socialism and now he wanted a revolution and he wanted to be the leader of the uprising of the poor and he wanted it to happen tomorrow. Why couldn't he just accept that things would never change around here? Mirs would always be mirs and governments would always want more. Maybe revolution happened in England or France, but Pakistan was different. Hassan let his head flop. He felt too embarrassed to look at Sami after all this. The bell rang and Hassan packed up his pen and notebook. A teacher in Karachi was going to mark the papers and they'd know the results in a week.

Hassan went to the school gates; he was too tired to stay at school longer. He'd had enough. He heard footsteps behind him and felt a light touch on his arm. He stopped. She was panting, her face tight. Perhaps she was afraid he might change his mind.

'Why did you do that?' she asked.

'It's done now,' Hassan said, walking faster. He wanted to talk to her but it would just cause gossip.

'Wait,' she said.

He stopped.

'You don't owe me anything.'

'It was my father's fault.'

Her face scrunched up as if it were in pain. Her short brown hair fell in tangles around her face. She hadn't even combed it but he couldn't stop staring at her, at her brown skin, her broad chin, and her eyes, looking straight at him. He turned to carry on walking. She dropped behind.

Baba and Amma were at home when he got back. They hadn't gone to work. Their faces were bright. His mother had already cooked for him but he couldn't tell them what he'd done, not now. 'I'm tired,' he said and went to his room and fell asleep.

The next morning, Hassan walked past the stone cutters, sitting on the floor in their shop fronts. Hammering was slow. That meant it was still early. Taps got faster all the way to noon and slowed down after that till it was time for the workers to come home. Tap… tap… tap. Slow and steady. Must be around eight o'clock. The coconut stalls were set up outside the gate but the woman and her spinning wheel weren't there.

Past his school, past the cotton mills and textile factories where his mother worked and the newspaper office where his father worked. All owned by Mir Saab. He carried on past the line of labourers on their way to the fields.

'Mir Saab wants us to build channels in dry land,' a man said.

'More hard work,' another muttered.

In the dry season everything was more hard work. Even cricket. Men sat under the banyan trees along the track – the coolest place to avoid work – and let their wives go for them instead. At least Baba went to work.

The cricket match took place in the dry river bed, at a spot not too near the forest but far enough away from the village and the factories for adults not to disturb them. A few scattered boats made good hiding places, in case someone like a policeman or, worse, one of Mir Saab's guards came past. It was also one of the few places not overlooked by the fort.

Cricket was hot that day but Hassan scored a few runs more than the four other boys. The sun made him sweat and by mid-afternoon, he needed more water.

'Get me some too,' the other boys said, handing over their bottles.

The well was in a shady corner by the track, a few minutes away from the village wall. The bucket was heavy but he brought it up and used his bottle to throw water over himself. Summer in Harikaya was like a bread oven before the rains and he was dry again in minutes.

He filled the five bottles and rested against the well.

Footsteps and voices came from the other side. One of the voices sounded like his father's. He crouched and peered over the wall to see his father carrying the jar again and talking fast to another man – the honey dealer. His father handed over the jar, looking around at the same time. Hassan began to stand up but arms grabbed his waist and pulled him to the floor and a hand covered his mouth.

'It's me,' a voice whispered in his ear in English.

It was Ansari Saab, the poet. He let go of Hassan's mouth and Hassan checked over the wall again. The two men had separated; the honey dealer was heading off between the shrubs and his father back towards the village.

Hassan nearly sprang up again. He wanted to question his father, but Ansari Saab grabbed his shirt.

'Oh no you don't,' he said.

'Baba said he wouldn't go anymore,' Hassan whispered.

Ansari Saab let go of Hassan's mouth and began to fumble about in the sandy ground. 'My monocle,' he said. 'It's from Cambridge.'

'What are you doing here, Ansari Saab?'

'What are you doing here?' the poet asked back. He had his monocle in his eye again.

'Do you know that man?' Hassan was afraid to hear the answer.

'I know he's not a good one. That's all I know,' Ansari Saab said. 'He's involved in too many things.' He sucked his lips in and shook his head. 'Too many things.'

'Like what?'

'I don't want to know. But he doesn't work alone. He has friends – let's say contacts – in surprising places. Very powerful places. Best to keep away from him. Best not to get involved.'

Ansari Saab was Hassan's favourite poet, but right now the poet irritated him. The poet took his handkerchief from his waistcoat pocket and wiped his forehead.

'Who are these friends? Who does he work with?'

'Who does he work with?' The poet often answered a question with a question. 'The ones he works with are hidden. Or rather, they hide themselves and wait.'

'What for?'

'For the right moment to take power.'

'Who from?'

'You're asking the right questions, I see.' But Ansari Saab said no more. A drop of water ran from his forehead and rested on the thick hairs of his eyebrow. 'All I know about him is what the others say. He drifts between the dark and the light, barely visible in either.'

The drop reached the poet's eyelid and tumbled onto his cheek.

'They're the dangerous ones,' the poet said, 'the ones that trick you into believing what they want you to see.'

Baba still worked for the honey dealer. And Amma… he didn't know what had happened. Whatever it was, they had both been tricked.

'I see him at the shrine sometimes. Not many people notice him but I do. That man has some kind of inner drive.'

'What is it?' Hassan asked.

'I'm not sure, but he's a patient one. I can tell. He just waits and watches. My feelings say he's seeking revenge of some kind.'

'Why?'

'That I definitely don't know.' The poet wiped his whole face and neck with his handkerchief before taking a sip from his metal flask. 'The mir is a better alternative to the government. Your father has to be careful. Politics is a dirty game.'

'But Baba just wants equality for everyone. The old systems need to change.'

'People are too greedy for that. And anyway, there are too many people to do the government's dirty work.'

'Baba would never do anything wrong,' Hassan said.

The poet only sighed.

Hassan remembered his bottles; the others were waiting for him.

'What are you doing here Ansari Saab, really?'

'This is my favourite place at the moment. Shade and peace. Good, eh?' He held up his flask.

'Will Baba be all right?'

'Who knows? Life is uncertain, my dear, especially in Pakistan.'

That didn't help Hassan.

'Are you coming to the shrine tonight? We'll make your father read his poetry. You'll see; people will forget everything that happened.'

'He said he'd take me,' Hassan said. 'It's my birthday tomorrow.'

~

'Take it,' the musician said.

Hassan's father took the drum and placed it between his knees to begin a slow beat. Poets began. Words and beats. Hassan stood up and tapped his foot, and kept tapping even when the poet stopped. It was like nothing had happened the night before; Ansari Saab was right. But Sami wasn't there. He missed her presence.

'Go on,' Baba said, pushing Hassan gently forwards into the circle.

'Yes, speak about the stars,' one poet said.

'Say something about the sun and moon,' Ansari Saab said.

Hassan wanted to talk about bees.

'The black honeybees live deep in the forest.
Their honey is a healing gold.'

Everyone was listening. His father tapped the drum with his thumbs.

'Only those who truly know the honey's worth may
receive it.
For they only listen to the ones who love them.
And for this love, the bees reveal their secret.'

One or two of the poets stood up; some of them clapped. His father beat the drum faster; all his fingers came to life.

'He's a poet,' Ansari Saab said.

Hassan sat down as another poet stood to take his turn. The humming was in his mind again, a clear steady tune. Hassan had no choice but to ask the question that he'd been thinking about these last few days.

'Can we go for the black honey?'

'You know we can't. I promised your mother.'

'You said you wouldn't sell the honey anymore.'

'I've stopped.'

'I saw you today with the jar.'

'That was the last time.'

Hassan felt his shoulders rise. His father's words were too easy.

'But you promised me too.'

His father took several sips from the coconut. He was tapping the drum, looking for a rhythm. 'All right,' he said. 'Before the rains. You know what they mean.'

'Floods,' Hassan said. The humming in his head stopped.

'They could be tomorrow. They could be in a month. When I was your age, they would have started by now.' Baba began to find a slow steady beat with his fingers. 'The weather isn't following the old cycles.' He turned to Hassan again. 'If we go, then the sooner the better. Once the rains start, there's no chance. The nests are too deep in the forest.'

Hassan had not drunk one drop of that coconut spirit but he felt dizzy.

'It won't be easy; if those black bees don't like us… We'll go in the morning before Amma wakes up.' Baba tapped the drum faster. 'You're fourteen tomorrow.' His thumb was vibrating on the drum. 'Numbers are very important.' A poem was coming. He stood up to speak. A hush fell over the poets.

'Fourteen worker bees rode their paths to fourteen
planets that lived around the sun.

They were six-sided planets that whispered strict
instructions to these workers.
Make your caves to look like us, the planets said.
The bees brought this knowledge back to the earth
where they built cities of wax.
Caves were built in these cities to be the birthplace
For workers, drones, and queen.
Time spent in the cave was different for each.
Time obeyed the law of numbers.
Twenty-one days for workers, twenty-four for drones,
and sixteen for the queen.
Workers, drones, and queen.
All because the bees listened to the planets, which
listened to the sun, which thanked the queen.'

He took Hassan by the shoulder but still spoke to the poets. 'I ask you, isn't there magic in that?'

His father sat down and took another sip of the coconut spirit. His eyes shone and he spoke quietly now.

'The worker bees brought back a secret knowledge with them from the planets, written in an invisible language on their wings. Only humans that they love can read it but these humans have to earn their trust first.'

'How?' Hassan asked.

'By giving back exactly the same amount of love as they receive. Coin for coin, piece for piece. It's not easy.'

'What's the secret knowledge about?' Hassan asked.

Here his father laughed, with his head thrown back. Then he stopped and looked straight ahead. Serious. 'It's the secret to our existence. It's the answer to why and how we're here.

The knowledge governs the law of time and numbers. It's the answer that makes us all equal.'

His poetry voice was gone. 'I'd give everything to be a holder of that knowledge.' His head hung and he was swaying just enough for Hassan to wait for another poem but none came.

'We'll leave early tomorrow,' his father said.

Another poet stood and everyone lifted their hands to a new rhythm. Hassan looked around to see a few of the circle standing up to sway. And then his gaze stopped. Someone was walking around in between the crowds, too sober and straight. The figure stayed at the edges, like some kind of spirit without a face, watching everything. Not in an interested, general kind of way. He was looking for someone. He stopped and leant against the shrine, a still shadow in the chaos that moved around him.

Chapter Four

'If the bees get too excited, we smoke them,' Hassan's father said, handing him the smoker.

The clips that held its handles were brown from rust, but the handles themselves were like mirrors and Hassan saw his own tired eyes. He turned the handles to see his father's face in the mirror, thinking hard; his high forehead was creased and his eyes, normally smiling, were glazed with worry. His father mouthed the words, 'Knife, clay pot, water,' before he put each of these into a basket. Hassan moved his lips too, 'Smoker,' he said, and handed it back to his father as his mother appeared through the bedroom doorway, a second too early. Her eyes were watering, only half open. Her soft, sleepy body tightened when she saw them.

'You can't be…' she said.

Hassan stepped back into the shadows behind his father. He knew when his mother was about to roar.

'Meri jaan,' his father said. He only called her that when he wanted something. 'My dear,' he said again, with his poetry voice. 'The poets have written verses about the black honey.'

His father was fighting for this; Hassan was still.

'Those poets give you bad ideas,' she said.

'No, this one is all mine,' Baba said.

His mother sighed and Hassan stepped out of the shadows, no longer a little mouse.

'This is for your eyes,' his father said to his mother. 'You know what the elders say too, and the holy book. The black honey is medicine. You've said it yourself.'

'I have medicine from the doctor.'

'It's not working.' His father was checking how heavy the basket was. When he had a plan, nothing could stop him. 'The bees were generous to me with the other forest honey.'

'What about Mir Saab's law?' his mother asked.

'For the black honey to work, it needs to be fresh from the hive,' his father said. 'We have to go now, before the floods.'

His father took her hand but she pulled it back. She hated to lose but Hassan wanted his father to win this time.

'The elders say that the black honeybees don't share their honey easily,' she said.

'I understand that.'

'They're wilder too.'

'I know the stories. This is a risk we have to take. They may not even allow me to take any of their honey.'

'You're not taking him with you?' She pointed at Hassan. 'He's too young.'

That was the wrong thing to say. Hassan stood tall. 'I want to go with Baba.'

His mother's face darkened and he felt the push of tears. Crying would be the end of it all.

'It's my birthday.'

Her voice was small now, almost a whisper. 'It's too dangerous.'

His father carried on packing the bag, or pretending to.

'Amma, I want to go with Baba. It's our last chance before the floods.'

'What about the animals in the forest?'

'Don't put fear into him,' his father said.

'I'm not scared.' Hassan came close and looked up at her eyes; the lids were puffy and the insides grey and cloudy.

'He's just like you,' she said.

They had won, but he didn't want his mother to feel it. Hassan pulled his ear lobes and stuck out his tongue – his new way to make her laugh – and when she did, it was a high-pitched squeal, the one that had made his father marry her. She didn't laugh today but she kissed his cheek.

He wiped off the wetness.

'Bring him back safe.'

Baba was already at the door with the basket slung over a shoulder. He looked fearless.

On the streets, all the shutters and doors were closed. It was still dark and cool and the stray dogs were the only ones awake. They came for the crumbs that Hassan always had for them in his pockets.

They marched past the factories, light-brown splodges of paint against a sky washed dirty grey. Bamboo waved along the borders; their tips didn't snap like they did when Hassan rode his bike alongside them, faster and faster. Bamboo heads shook. Snap, snap, snap. Bamboo necks sagged. He giggled and his father put his finger to his mouth. Laughter in this quiet world could wake things up and they didn't want that yet.

Further along the river bank now, ducks rested on low waters.

'Why is no one allowed in the forest, Baba?'

No answer.

Shots went off in the distance. It had to be Mir Saab, out early in the forest. Hassan's breath caught at the back of his throat but he kept his eyes on the track. Vultures appeared in the sky, heading for the village to look for scraps. Crows stayed out of sight when the huge birds visited. People said that the vultures came to observe the villagers, ever since all humans were banned from the forest. They said that the vultures were figuring out how to become people.

They approached the forest and a red sun began to rise over the tree tops.

'Watch out for snakes,' Baba whispered.

There was a sharpness in Hassan's stomach. What if a huge hog raced towards them now?

They carried on, twigs snapping, a rustle of leaves; lizards slithered in front of his feet.

'Stop it,' Baba said.

'Stop what?'

'Stop thinking like that. It's like a car horn to the animals.'

'But it's in my mind.'

He only smiled. 'You'll learn,' he said. 'The forest is the greatest teacher. If you can survive here, only then will you understand the world.'

Hassan was tired but he continued through undergrowth, over ant hills and past forest clearings that were open to the light, which was already becoming powerful. They walked round a lake where the deer that had gathered for their morning drink scattered like bullets back into the forest. They went on. A bee buzzed past – not a black one. When he was almost too tired to walk anymore, his father stopped.

'These are their trees.'

Golden leaves sprouted from branches that twisted outwards like the antlers of ancient deer.

'Acacia,' his father said, stopping under a tree, squinting, and looking up through the leaves, but he shook his head and moved to the next. Squint, shake, move. Hassan copied and went from tree to tree, arriving at each trunk with the question, 'Is this the one?' Repeating it over and over in his mind until his neck hurt.

His father was almost out of sight when he cried out, 'I have it!'

When Hassan got there, Baba's eyes were dancing.

The nest was at the top, a big lump of earth stuck to the tree. Hassan could just make it out through the leaves.

The tree was so high and the nest far, far away. Amma's words dropped on his head like mud. 'It's too dangerous.'

'They're waiting for us,' Baba said.

His father started to climb the tree with bare feet and the basket over his shoulder, stepping on branches or pulling himself up the trunk until he was a long way off the ground.

Hassan wished he could do that – climb a tree for honey. He pressed his hands against the trunk; they were trembling. His heart was loud and his throat was dry. He had to believe. A surprise wind blew, making it easier to see through the leaves. A slow, low-pitched hum reached him from the nest. Another breeze carried the humming closer. He knew this humming. Sound swept down to him and he forgot to worry for a few moments, lost in their world. Were they going to give Baba some of their honey? Hassan kissed the tree.

His father stopped a few feet below the nest. It seemed to shake as Baba inched closer. Yes, it shook. The lump began to pulse and fold like a wave. It was alive. Bees. Hundreds – no, thousands of dark bees. Some hovered, apart from the nest, darting along short invisible lines but staying close. What were they doing? It was a breathing ball of noise. Hassan felt his skin tighten around him.

Then, a glow came from inside the nest. Yes, it was a glow. Had Baba been allowed by them to go further? The movement of the nest was clear – pulsing and folding. The mass of bees looked ready to explode. Hassan's throat was narrowing. He wanted to scream to his father to come down, but he held back, gripping onto the tree. His father's shadow was nearing the nest, getting closer to the glow.

He was nearly there. Yes, he was there. Hassan almost cheered. With his small knife, Baba reached into the blackness and came out with a small square of wax, a piece of honeycomb, dripping black gold down the knife. What would that be like to taste? It went into the clay pot and in the basket. Hassan wanted to bang on the tree, to shout for joy, to say thank you. He wanted to dance to the sound of their humming but it got louder. The nest shook again. Most of the bees stayed together but others buzzed free. Were they angry?

One touched Baba's face. He waved his hand. More came away. What was Baba doing?

Baba took the smoker out of his basket with one hand and pressed the bellows. Nothing. Hassan froze. Baba had checked the bellows that morning. Baba tried again; still no smoke. The mass of bees was stirring. A small group of bees came to hover by his head, their humming louder – a warning.

'Come down, Baba.'

But he was going closer. What was he doing?

'Come down, Baba!' Hassan shouted, but his father still didn't hear. Or was he just not listening?

The humming was now a force that made Hassan's body rock but he kept watching his father, who still didn't come down. What was he waiting for? The bees didn't want to give him more. Why was it not clear to his father?

Other bees left the cluster, coming close to Baba's face. They darted near his cheeks. His eyes. His lips. He waved his hands about as more bees buzzed around his body. He slapped his chest, his shoulders, his face.

'They don't want you, Baba!' Hassan's throat was burning.

Baba turned to look down. Was he giving up? At that moment a bee stung his face, and another. Spirals of bees left the nest and his father had to use both hands against them with his legs wrapped around the trunk.

The smoker hurtled through the leaves.

'Come down!'

A wave of bees rose, reaching Baba's shoulders. Another wave reached his ears and then his head until he was in the middle of a black cloud that roared and folded around him. A final wave struck and his father fell.

Hassan covered his eyes. He heard a yell, then nothing. He opened his eyes and his father lay still on the ground, a few feet away from the tree.

Hassan ran towards him, but the bees were faster. A great cluster broke away from the nest and swooped down to gather above his father's body, curled into a ball. The dense cloud shifted upwards, a moving, humming cylinder of power between him and his father.

A groan. Was that him or his father?

Something caught his eye, behind a nearby bush. A tiny flame, where the smoker had fallen. Hassan blinked a few times and then saw that the whole thicket was alight.

His mother's voice was in his head.

Bring him back safe.

He rose to beat the flames with his shirt but his shirt became a burning rag. He let it go and shouted at the bees, 'I want to leave with my father!' He stamped his feet on the flames but the dryness of the forest floor made the fire too eager. His father was limp on the ground, his eyes closed.

That was when the leaves and bushes started to shake. Someone – or something – was approaching from behind the branches that bounced and parted for a giant of a man. The man strode to the middle of the clearing and looked from Hassan to the bees and to his father on the ground. The man took a breath in and whistled, a combination of short and long notes. His mouth made long puffs and small grunts; it was a language. He was talking to the bees and they were listening, the tone of their humming changing.

Hassan watched him. Their eyes met through the smoke and, for a few seconds, Hassan understood the power in this language. Among the sounds, a few made perfect sense, and as Hassan listened, he knew who this man was. He knew who stood a few feet away, solid and real.

The beekeeper.

His hair, the same colour as the cloud of bees that now gathered behind him, was densely matted, and reached down his back, thick and wild. Deep lines like cracks in dry earth were etched on his face and the bones of his jaw and cheeks bulged through his skin. He smelt of honey and wax and old trees. Hassan was caught in a spell of stillness.

The man turned in Hassan's direction; a nod, and the spell was broken. The beekeeper picked up Hassan's father like a sack of raw cotton. The fire was gnawing at a dry bush and soon found a tree. Hassan went towards it and began stamping but the beekeeper was moving away and beckoned to him with a nod. Hassan obeyed. He picked up the smoker, the knife, and took the basket and the pot with the honeycomb. Baba had shut the lid tight.

They all went together, humans and bees, through the forest. The bees stayed with the beekeeper up to the edge of the trees, quiet now. The beekeeper put Hassan's father on the ground and stood up straight. He turned to Hassan, then, looking back into the forest, and said, 'The fire.' He strode back through the thickets and bush with a city of bees around his head.

Baba opened his eyes after a few gentle shakes and Hassan lay with him for a while; there was no rush. Geese flew overhead in a triangle formation, going about their busy lives. Lone birds burst into song from inside the forest. The crows were loud but the humming in Hassan's head was a soft, gentle music.

'How did you carry me out of there on your own?' his father asked.

'It was the beekeeper.'

His father only smiled.

'The bees didn't want you. Why didn't you stop?' Hassan whispered, too quiet for his father to hear.

As they walked back home, Hassan thought of the nest at the top of that ancient tree. The fire, making its way to the top. The beekeeper, alone against the fire. The bees watching him. At least they were all right. And the trees. How many of them would suffer? Baba leant on his shoulder and Hassan's ankles gave way for a second.

'Am I too heavy?' his father asked.

Hassan shook his head.

A few men and women stood up from behind short grasses in dry rice paddies to look, before bending down again.

'We'll come back before the floods,' his father said. 'The bees will let me have more, I know it.'

Hassan wanted to scream. The trees. How many of them were dead? He held it all in. Inside the village, people gave them short glances; some of them shook their heads.

'They think I've been drinking,' his father said.

It was better for them to think that; the truth was more dangerous.

Chapter Five

The front door opened before they knocked; Amma was still at home and she covered her mouth when she saw them. Even when they sat down on the floor, she still didn't speak.

'The prize,' Baba said, taking the jar out of the basket and putting it on the floor.

Her face softened and she smiled; she wanted to believe what she saw. Hassan dropped his head forward and rubbed his shoulders.

'Well, come on, try some,' his father said.

She pulled out the stopper. The honeycomb floated to the top and rested on the rim. Hassan leant forward; the golden honey smelt fresh and strong.

His mother took a stick and dipped it into the jar and, making sure nothing dribbled, she touched the honey with her finger and dabbed the lower edge of her eye. She did the same to her other eye and blinked a few times – sticky blinks. She laughed that high-pitched squeal again.

'It feels good,' she said. 'Cooling.'

'It's your medicine,' Baba said, coughing. 'Now, I need to rest.'

Amma took him to their room and Hassan was left alone with the jar of honey which was sealed again, and the stick that his mother had left on the lid. He thought of the fire. How far had it gone? Had the beekeeper put it out? He scratched his forehead. Baba had gone too far with the bees, all for this small jar.

But if it worked…

He took a deep breath in. He had to do it… He dabbed his finger on the stick and brought it to his lips. Its taste filled his mouth. All the poets were right. The sound of humming played in his ears, distant and faint, and the beekeeper felt close now. Hassan sat back against the wall, exhausted.

They didn't speak of the fire that day, not even when his mother came back from work. His father rested and recovered from the aches after the fall. Hassan thought he saw sadness in his face but whatever it was, Baba did not look at him. He came out to eat on the floor in the living room on the second evening.

'It's a miracle that you didn't break all your bones,' his mother said.

That night, Hassan lay back on his bed and put all thoughts of the fire away into a drawer in his mind that had been especially made for unthinkable thoughts. With it safely closed in his head, he saw the beekeeper's face. Had he imagined the stillness he had felt in the man's presence? When the beekeeper had looked at him, it had seemed like there had been recognition from both of them. Was that imagined too?

Hassan rolled over. They had managed the unthinkable today; Baba had found the black bees. If only he had not wanted more. The by-now familiar humming was starting again but it was becoming louder, more like the noise of the cloud of bees but steadier and calmer. Sleep came and the sound became a comforting tone in the background broken by hard knocks on the door.

The knocks didn't stop. It was late.

'Open the door!'

Hassan shot up and found his mother in the main room. The air was trembling around her and his father was running about, breathing fast.

'Someone must have told the guards,' his mother whispered.

Baba picked up the smoker and the knife and shoved them into the basket together with the jar of black honey. He ran out through the back. Hassan ran after him with his heart beating fast. 'Baba,' he whispered just in time to make him turn round. Hassan opened his mouth to speak but his father was already clambering over the wall.

The guards searched inside the house while Hassan crouched on the flat roof, watching his father running through the streets. He willed him to run faster, and when he couldn't see him anymore, Hassan began humming to himself to keep unthinkable thoughts out.

The thud of heavy boots crashing on metal steps made the dogs on the streets howl.

'Stand up!' they shouted at Hassan.

His mother was following them; she rushed towards him, the smell of smoke and chapatis still on her clothes. She stood between him and them.

'He's the son,' one of the guards said – a man with a creased face, someone who followed orders. 'You were seen hiding a deer with your father.'

'He's done nothing wrong,' Amma said. 'He's only fourteen,' she said.

All three guards went to the edge of the roof and looked out onto the street but his father had gone.

'We're watching him,' the same guard said, nodding at Hassan.

That was when the blood rushed to his head and the ground seemed closer, but he kept standing.

In the early hours, Hassan opened his eyes. Black honey. He longed for that taste again. He moved to get up and realised he was still in his clothes on the bamboo bed under the sky. The guards. Baba running away. It all came back to him now. He flew down to the yard. Could his father have come back? The reeds on the floor were still in a mess. His head felt warm. He ran out into the courtyard where his mother sat under the mango tree, her eyelids drooping, their skin folded.

'Did Baba come back? he asked.

She looked up at him, opened her arms, and he sank into her.

'I didn't say goodbye before he left,' he said.

A bee flickered between them. 'See, Amma, that's a sign. They didn't get him; I know they didn't.'

'Those guards,' she said, 'were they Mir Saab's guards?'

'Who else could they be?'

'They could have been from the government.'

'Who told them?'

'It could have been anyone. Your father broke the law and called for protest.'

She sat up, pushing him away. He faced her now. She was breathing hard.

'It would have been dangerous for you if your father had stayed.' Her voice was different – hardly her voice at all, an earthy sound filled with fire that licked the walls of some deep well.

He went to the square when the sun was beginning to rise. Stallholders were bent over their goods and he held onto his satchel which was slung over his shoulder. Guards could be hiding anywhere, waiting for his father to come back. People shuffled along to the main gates to the fields, factories, or school. Nobody else's life had changed overnight.

The woman was already at her spinning wheel by the gate. The dark wooden wheel tumbled down, thread and song spinning fast. She opened her mouth to yawn at him and reached down into the piles of cloth on the ground next to her, nodding at his satchel; he moved forwards. The jar was in her lap now, shielded behind the wheel. The smell of coconut was fresh and strong from her hair and skin. He opened the satchel, a great mouth for the jar.

'He said your mother needs it.'

'Where did my father go?'

Her hands moved back to the thread and her foot pressed again, up and down. The wheel tumbled, slower.

'He gave me a message for you,' she said.

Hassan fastened the buckle of his satchel. His hands were trembling.

'Go back to the forest and find the beekeeper.'

The metal buckle caught on the skin under his nail. Pink blood the size of a pinhead welled up. 'Did he say anything else?'

She shifted in her seat, taking her foot off the pedal. The wheel came to a halt and she steadied it with her hand, taking the thread with her other hand.

'He said that you need to find it before—'

Two guards walked past. They were Mir Saab's guards, chatting, unhurried. They wore a badge on their caps, a small crown with a deer on its hind legs on each side. Hassan's heart was beating hard but they didn't stop. She grabbed his wrist; her palm was rough.

'Before it's too late for your mother's eyes.'

'Why? Why should it be too late?' He was only a few inches away from her now.

She let his hand drop but she drew near and whispered this time. 'You'll see him again when the floods come.'

'How do you know?'

She bent her head.

'Where did he go? Do you know?' He held out a coin but he was invisible to her. The wheel started again and she began humming, looking straight ahead.

He backed off down the track again until he reached the river and walked along its bank. The workers were already bending to plant rice seeds before the rains came.

Everyone was busy and there were no guards. He was walking so fast that he was panting when he reached the corner where they'd hidden the dead deer among the reeds. Pieces of flesh still hung from the skeleton even though most of the inner organs were gone. He looked around. Baba might not be far, hiding in the forest or living in some thick grouping of trees and bushes by the river, waiting for Hassan to find him.

The beating of wings made him look up. Vultures were arriving but his feet stuck to the ground even when the birds circled the air above. It was like lifting magnets from iron. The more he pushed forwards, the stiffer his legs became. He wanted to go to the forest, but it was hopeless. The vultures waited until he was moving again before they dived down into the reeds.

They ate their meat slowly as they watched him head back to the village.

Chapter Six

Six days later

The floods had still not reached the state of Harikaya yet. There were rains in the north but the Indus River remained tame. Yellow and brown brushstrokes covered the land up to the mir's fort on the hilltop.

Hassan stood at the edge of the village square, where the evening cries of prayer, the groans of returning workers, and shouts of stallholders flew around. Was his father one of them? He walked against the flow, letting his eyes drift through the heads and faces coming home. People looked back at him; any anger towards his father had turned to pity. Hassan hated pity the most but he saw it everywhere now.

He had woken up screaming one morning, two or three days after Baba had run away. Amma had come to him and taken him into his arms. 'What is it, Beta?'

'I've lost his face. It's not there anymore in my head.'

Since then, Hassan had heard her walking about in her room every night, whispering prayers on the beads.

He tapped his waistcoat pocket. The piece of honeycomb was still there, next to his heart, in a small cloth pouch, dry and shrunken to the size of a large coin, but it was all he cared for.

A bee buzzed past his face and Hassan decided to show purpose, for when he showed purpose, people took less notice. He dodged a man on a bicycle with a red cloth wrapped around his head, slid through tired bodies, trotted alongside stray dogs, and sped up past busy cricket matches. A group of boys stopped their match.

'Come and join us!' the smaller one shouted. He was no taller than Hassan's shoulders with bright eyes and his hair streaked with dirt.

'Come on.' This was the tall one, with a thin smile.

Hassan shook his head. The thin smile stood face to face with Hassan. The other three boys stood behind their new leader and Hassan backed away, keeping his eyes on all of them and waiting for the laughter. It had come a few times already. Flames down a line of oil.

'His father ran away,' the thin smile said.

'Gone to live with another woman,' another one said.

'He didn't want one who's going blind.'

Let them think what they liked. He turned away but caught his leg on the rim of a metal bucket of water, tipping it over. His shin hurt and water gushed under his feet. The boys laughed. Hassan stood up to face them.

'My water!' a woman shouted, squatting on the pavement with soap on her hands, her wet hair streaked over her face.

'Chalo!' she cried, waving her arms.

He wanted to leave but the thin smile drew closer. The boys were like a wall in front of him and he backed off, one step at a time. They didn't move and he took his chance. He turned and ran down the narrow streets, skidding round corners until he reached the boundary wall, where he rubbed his shin and opened his mouth wide. His jaw hurt.

'You'll catch a cricket ball like that,' said a man who wore the white shirt and trousers of the mill workers. Hassan's mouth snapped shut.

Outside the gate, he stooped to swipe up a date, still untouched by the ants. It tasted good. Twigs snapped under his sandals, the sound of dry heat on the track. He had purpose now – his mother was finishing work soon. Thirty minutes later, he was at the two cotton mills, set back from the track. The early evening light washed over the cracks in the walls and the peeling paint and made the buildings look new.

Inside, clouds of raw cotton lay in iron trays next to stacks of empty cone-shaped baskets. He continued past doorways that led to the metal frames lined with bobbins. They spun the yarn into different thicknesses. The voices of a few workers made him hurry on. He passed rooms full of tubs of dye before he stepped into the main hall.

Here, row after row of great wooden weaving machines stood before him with only a handful of women left working behind them. His mother was in her usual place at the back, sitting behind a machine. He went towards her, stopping a few feet away. Strands of long greying hair fell out of her plait. Her bare lower arms glistened with moisture and her long cotton shirt stuck to her muscular frame. Paper patterns that she knew by heart lay on the floor. Her feet moved up and down on the press to lift the long wooden shafts high above the weave. She pulled the wooden stick by her head in regular time to let the miniature boats, with bright tails of yarn flying behind them, sail under those shafts across the sea of weave.

Lift and sail, lift and sail. A world of shapes chugged into creation. Hassan stepped forwards. After a minute or two she stopped, and her long fingers checked the smoothness of the geometry on the cloth. Diamonds, stars, circles, teardrops and hexagons. The shapes floated up above the weave. The honeycomb from the forest was made out of hexagons. He tapped his pocket once more. Golden wax.

'Hassan.' His mother looked up and gasped.

The shapes tumbled back into the cloth.

'How long have you been here?'

'Not long,' he said.

He came closer and saw the cloudiness in her eyes beginning to come back.

'Are you using the black honey?' he asked her.

'There's not much there. I don't want to use it all.'

He bit his lips.

'I'm going to the shrine,' she said.

'You went there yesterday.'

'I need to pray.'

'Again?'

'My eyes are getting worse.'

She gathered her belongings. It was only a second, but her lips twisted into a mixture of hate and sadness. She had to be thinking of Baba.

He followed her down the aisle. Looks of pity peered from

behind the weaving machines. He made his neck look shorter by scrunching his shoulders, by bobbing his head back and then forwards; his nose became a beak that pecked at the looms, on the cloth and in the air. He was a square-headed raven. It worked. The women broke out into laughter.

'Why are they laughing?' his mother asked, turning around.

'I'm only playing, Amma, only playing.' He ran a few steps to catch up with her.

Playfulness left him as they walked through the door. Her eyes were getting worse and he still hadn't been to the forest.

At the shrine, people and vultures were taking their turns to feed and Hassan looked for Baba's face. The poets were the first to stand up from the daily meal and make their way to the sunken circular stone area to sit on the rim of steps. Ansari Saab was one of them. A poet raised his hand and a line of spontaneous verse rolled out.

'Wah, wah,' said the other poets, their heads lifting, tilting, or swaying.

Ansari Saab called him over with his hand. Ansari Saab's monocle was gone now and there was no handkerchief in his waistcoat, which seemed more frayed even though it had only been a week – not even that – since Baba had left. As Hassan sat down next to Ansari Saab, he almost expected his father to start a poem or gently push him forwards into the circle.

'Beta,' Ansari Saab said. The sound of the word *son* was soft. 'Do you want to give us a poem?'

'No,' Hassan said.

Ansari Saab never gave up.

'You know, despite everything, your father was one of us. A lover of life, of creation.'

What did he mean, *despite everything*?

'Why did they come after him? Did they say?'

'No.'

'Wherever he is, he must be careful.'

'Baba can look after himself.'

'The new government has stricter laws. Harder ones. Even Mir Saab can't change them. They've already banned alcohol. They're banning different traditions now. He must be careful.'

'He'll come back,' Hassan said, 'before the floods.'

'He shouldn't have spoken the way he did. He displeased the one that gives him his living and he has no chance then against the really dangerous ones – the government. They're just hungry to use him to serve their purpose. That's why they went after him.'

'How do you know it was the government that came after my father?'

The poet scowled and for a second looked confused. 'Your father needs to come back, make a public apology to Mir Saab, say he was wrong. Both sides will back off that way and he can get on with his life.' The poet leant in closer towards Hassan. 'You know, you're like a son to me. It's a dangerous time. The government wants spies. They don't care about what else is happening. Gangs are getting stronger. Young men are being made to sell guns and drugs for their profit. Everybody's tied in it together except Mir Saab, and he's the one your father chose to challenge.' Ansari Saab looked around the shrine. 'I worry about you,' he said. 'Your father's made you a target now.'

'No, he hasn't. He only wanted people to speak up about Mir Saab's new law.'

'He should have known the government would use that against him.'

'But it was Mir Saab's guards, not the government's that came for him.'

A few people turned towards them. Ansari Saab looked surprised for a second but then laughed out loud as if he'd just heard Hassan say something funny. It worked. They turned back to the poetry.

'Pakistan is in between countries and in between their battles,' Ansari Saab was whispering now. 'Between old and new rules. I can only see more chaos and stricter control ahead. Anybody who speaks out has to be careful.'

Hassan wanted to ask him more about it but at that moment he spotted his mother coming out of the wooden doors of the shrine. She walked towards them with a new energy in her steps.

'Someone said your father's been seen,' the poet spoke fast.

'Where?' Hassan's heart nearly stopped.

'In one of the villages. With a group of travellers. Musicians, poets, a band.'

'Who saw him?'

'I know nothing more. Tell no one.' Ansari Saab bowed to Hassan's mother as she reached them.

Hassan stood up and walked away from the circle of poets

with his mother. So, Baba had escaped. He might even be here, watching him.

'The pir said I should pray with these.' His mother held up her wrist with a new string of beads wrapped around it. Her face was soft; something good must have come out of the meeting with the pir. 'He gave me a prayer to say too, but I can't tell anyone, not even you.'

Hassan tried to stop a laugh, but it was too late. His mother had seen it.

'You don't like the pir,' she said.

'I don't trust him.'

'He's the representative of the saint.'

To Hassan, the pir was a man who sat in the shade most of the day as people brought him plates of biryani and creamy desserts.

'He can say anything he likes and people believe him.'

'You sound like your father.' She was about to say more when one of their neighbours arrived at his mother's side.

'Did he help you? Did the pir help you?' she asked.

'Yes, he gave me these.'

The woman grasped his mother's hand and held it close to her heart as if the beads were some kind of prize. 'Let's walk home together.'

'Will you walk with us, Hassan?' his mother asked.

'No, I'll stay here.'

'Don't be too late. Kulsoom's coming,' she said, walking away.

Hassan rolled his eyes, making an internal decision to be late.

His mother glanced back, and said, 'The only thing that will help my eyes now is prayer.'

The vultures left their perches and circled above. Their numbers had grown since Mir Saab's law banning people from entering the forest. The animals were growing braver. He thought back to the deer that he and Baba had dragged to the reeds. Ansari Saab had said that his father had been seen. That meant it wouldn't be too long now before his father sent him a message. There was a dull ache in his chest; he wanted to see his father again.

He shielded his eyes from the sun as he watched the black bodies of the vultures streak the sky. The moon was already visible and the sun on the opposite side of the sky had its warm evening glow. One of the vultures dived to the ground. The others hovered and watched for a few seconds before they too joined it. They chomped at the scraps of meat. No one paid them any attention.

Hassan looked around; nobody was paying him any attention either but he still went to stand in a shady corner by the wall of the shrine before he took the small piece of honeycomb out of his pocket. He wanted to feel the humming again; it made him feel closer to Baba. Baba had said he needed to go to the forest again, to find the black honey nests. But how could he do this without his father's help?

Hassan sat down on the cool stone. The screeches of the vultures faded away. The poets were at their circle now; the man in the centre stood next to the drummer and was reading poetry. His mouth moved but there was no sound.

The trees of the forest rose in Hassan's mind. The trees that stood in a circle around a clearing. The beekeeper must have made room for them, these acacia trees that carried those special nests. Little by little, the nest and the bees came into focus. The journey to them was a long way from the forest edge. And even if he did find those trees again, how could he climb them alone?

He took a deep breath in and sighed. The smell of wax and honey was at his nose again. It made him feel dizzy. The beekeeper's face appeared in his mind; it blurred in and out of his vision. The humming he had been hearing for a few months now was creeping into his head. The beekeeper's face dissolved and more images jumped out, one after the other: the honeycomb rising in the black honey to the top of the jar, the shining rims of his mother's eyes. Pictures flowed into each other until they dissolved into the constant sound of humming. There was that taste of black honey, its crumbling sweetness. He had to go back to the forest for his mother's eyes.

He opened his eyes and slowly, he began to sit up straight. Yes, there was a way. He would start by looking for the beekeeper. Hassan remembered the black cloud of bees around the man. The beekeeper could work with those bees. If the beekeeper were on his side, then Hassan could do this.

The stone floor was cold under him again. The area around erupted with the sound of laughter; children were running around playing. The humming in his head grew quieter and he knew what he had to do. The beekeeper. He had to find the beekeeper.

Hassan left the shrine, this time in the direction of the forest. Some of the vultures left too, their day over.

Chapter Seven

Dark fields melted into sandy flatlands. Villagers loved to tell stories about the forest coming to life as the sun set. Hassan didn't believe any of them but it did feel as if lone palm trees were watching as he passed. Mighty banyans with roots like giant spider legs whispered to each other. The trunks of tall sumbul trees extended outwards like the blades of fans and looked ready to spin. Were they worried for him? It was all superstition but jinns were said to hide behind every bush.

He ran past the house of lepers that stood further along the track until he reached the river and walked along its bank. It was hardly a stream now, before the rains. Hopefully it would be a good flood this year. The land needed it.

The grit in his sandals rubbed his feet and he sat down by the rushes to take his sandals off and shake out the stones. At that moment a car with blacked-out windows came along the track from the direction of the forest. It was Mir Saab's car. The small flag on its bonnet barely moved as it went past. Hassan froze. The car turned at the bottom of the hill before it started its ascent, round and round the winding road. It reached the turrets of the old fort at the top where it waited for the iron gates to open and then drove through. Hassan stood up and carried on, looking around in case there was another car, this time with guards.

At the forest edge, he stopped again. There was still enough light to search for a good hour but he was held back by some imaginary line. His mother's voice rang in his head. 'The forest is too dangerous.'

He shouted into the curtain of thick darkness, 'I'm here!'

No reply.

A lone black bee darted through the air. It danced around his face.

The smell of wax and honey. Yes, it was that same smell, again. A light touch on his shoulder. The beekeeper? He turned. Nothing. He turned back to the forest and the pictures of the fire were in his head. Trees were burning, the flames crackled. A cloud of bees, their roar. Fire and bees. He covered his eyes with his hands until the vision disappeared and only trees stood in front of him again. He wanted his father now; he couldn't do this without him. He turned and ran; his body was on fire, along the track wrapped in moonlight. He ran along the river bank, past the dark house, lit up just enough by candlelight for him to see the shadows of lepers or ghosts.

Trees whispered, 'The beekeeper is not real.'

Empty fields screamed, 'You lawbreaker!'

Factories stood like great white boulders, about to come alive in the moonlight.

He ran until he reached the boundaries of the shrine. He stepped onto the stone floor, panting hard.

His head was full. Bees, honey, wax. Black cloud rising. How would he find the beekeeper? Why didn't Baba send him a message? It had been a week already and Baba could have done it by now. Perhaps he thought it was too dangerous. Hassan tiptoed further in, unnoticed by the crowd and stood at the edge of the circle of poets. Ansari Saab wasn't around but Hassan decided to sit down anyway with the poets. It was the full-moon night; the poetry would calm him down, and the music.

'Move up.'

It was Sami.

'I thought I wouldn't see you here,' he said, making room for her next to him on the step.

'I heard what happened to your father.'

He shrugged; he didn't want to speak about it.

'You know, I hope he's careful.'

'You sound like one of the old ones.'

'Well, don't you want him back?'

'Yes, I do, but no one can keep him quiet.'

'He needs to learn to keep quiet.'

'How do you know? Nothing's ever happened to you.'

He regretted saying that. He turned to say sorry but she was looking straight ahead at the fire, her eyes unblinking. He watched the light of the flames make her face glow.

'My father will be all right. He'll find another job,' she said.

'I didn't mean…'

He was afraid she was about to leave but she just stared at the fire. More musicians came to sit next to the drummer.

Poets lifted their coconuts in approval. Men and women laughed as the flute began to play, a slow melody that built up.

'I don't need your help,' Sami said.

Her voice was quiet and he could hardly hear her. He opened his mouth to reply but didn't know what to say. Laughter crackled behind his back, out of tune with the music. Hassan turned to see the three boys looming over them.

The tall one joined them from nowhere. 'Knocked any more buckets over?' he said.

Hassan kept looking ahead.

'What are you doing with her?'

The other boys laughed and joined in.

'The two of you going to get together now?'

'Both your fathers will go to prison.'

One of the boys, the smaller one, began to play with Sami's hair. Hassan hit out but the boy grabbed Sami.

'Leave her alone!' Hassan screamed. He tore at the boy but the tall one was at him, pulling at his waistcoat, tearing it off.

The thin smile danced around with it and Hassan lunged towards him. He had to get it back. The boy threw it to another boy. Hassan was running from one to the other until he stood face to face with the thin smile.

'What's so precious about this?' The smile reeked of spirit.

In the corner of his eye, Hassan saw one of the poets free Sami from the grips of the boy who held her. His eyes and ears were white hot and his chest pounded. He tried to grab his waistcoat but the tall boy held on. Hassan pulled him to the ground and both of them rolled on the stone floor, but the boy held on tight. Too tight. Fists and feet beat his body, but there was no pain.

The roar of the bees from the jungle was inside him, filling him with a new power. His fingers clenched around the waistcoat and held on until the boy's hands opened. He had it and he was up in a second, ready to run.

'What are you doing?' a man shouted. It was the warden with a few people standing behind him, some of them poets and others too who had come to watch.

'He started it,' the thin smile said, still on the floor.

'It's all his fault,' another boy said.

'Fighting in a holy place,' a woman hissed.

'He's like his father,' a man shouted.

Hassan's face throbbed. Pain was creeping up his arms and legs and there was a taste in his mouth, cold and hot, the taste of ink and oranges, his own blood.

'All of you leave and don't come back,' shouted the warden.

'But we come here every day.' The thin one was up now.

'Not anymore,' the warden said.

'It was his fault.'

'I don't care. All of you are banned.' The warden shooed them away to the edges of the shrine. The boys left first and Hassan turned to find Sami. She was at the back with the poet who had rescued her, looking straight towards him.

'I need to speak to her,' he said to the warden.

'No, you don't. You're banned too.' The warden pointed to the track.

The boys had vanished and Hassan was careful to stay in the shadows of the trees as he hurried back down the track.

He didn't stop when he got to the gates and he didn't turn around until he reached the edge of the village where the streets narrowed and the buildings were low. The sounds of animals and children reassured him. He opened the door of his house and stepped inside.

They were sitting on a sheet laid over the bamboo leaves that covered the dry mud floor when Hassan entered. The only light came from an oil burner placed on a table in the corner. Everything was spotless; his mother had cleaned for Kulsoom. There was not much to clean anymore. The walls, where Baba's pictures used to hang, were bare. The shelves were empty; Baba had taken the tools – the smoker, his wax-cutting knife. His mother had thrown away the rest – a few small jars for honey and Baba's trinkets from his journeys along the river. Hassan headed for his room but, even in the dim light, the tears in his mother's eyes shone and he stopped.

Kulsoom was staring at him. The two sisters were so different. Everything about Kulsoom was neat; her hair was oiled and smoothed down over her scalp and formed into a tight plait. He wanted to say she was pretty but he had never seen her smile, and where his mother was warm and soft despite the hard thinness of her body, Kulsoom was brittle. He did not think anybody had hugged her ever, and if they did, her boniness might hurt.

'What happened?' Kulsoom's voice was quiet and cool. Hassan touched his face. The blood was already hardening.

'It's nothing.' He started towards his room again. He did not want to give Kulsoom anything to talk about.

'Beta,' his mother said.

His whole body hurt; he wanted to hide but he knew what his mother was thinking. Kulsoom was the only person in their family who visited anymore.

'Something's happened that's important for us. For you.'

'What?' He stood and faced them both.

'It's about Karachi. That girl who took your scholarship…'

'I gave it to her.'

'She told the teacher what happened.'

'She shouldn't have done that. She needs to get out too.'

'It's too late. You're the new winner.'

For the first time in weeks, his mother looked happy. 'You know Kulsoom is now Mir Saab's wife's personal maid.'

'I'm going back with Begum Saab in the morning by plane to Karachi,' Kulsoom said.

'Kulsoom spoke with her about you. There's a train ticket for you.'

'Mir Saab sent those guards for Baba.'

'We're not certain of that,' his mother said.

He wanted to shout at them. How dare they? But his head was hurting and he held his jaw. His mother glanced at Kulsoom and then back at him. Was there something else? His mother turned to Kulsoom again as if she guessed Hassan's thoughts; she cleared her throat, about to say something, but Kulsoom shook her head.

'I've arranged for your train ticket,' Kulsoom said.

'You want me to become a servant?'

'You know Mir Saab doesn't allow children to work. You'll

go to school in Karachi. That's what you've always wanted, isn't it, to study more?'

'I can go to school here.'

His mother turned around to face him. Her eyes, once beautiful, were glazed with worry. It was Kulsoom who spoke.

'The train ticket is on the table. Mir Saab's been very generous. He's offered you a scholarship for your education in Karachi. He wants to meet you, the new scholar,' Kulsoom said. 'And now Begum Saab says you can come early. I suggested this. It would help you settle in, get away from… all of this.'

Kulsoom was winning. Heat brimmed under Hassan's scalp.

'Amma, your eyes,' he said. 'I'll find the black honey first.' He thought he saw hope on his mother's face.

'You, what can you do about her eyes?' Kulsoom raised her hand. It flopped down.

To Hassan, that flop was like a switch, an electric current, sharper than the one that buzzed through the generator after a power cut. Anger ripped through his feet and he turned his back on them both; one whom he loved dearly and one whom he now hated.

He climbed the steps in the courtyard onto the roof and looked up at the sky. Kulsoom was trying to destroy everything he had.

There was barking below in the street. It was the stray dog that had become his friend. He broke off pieces of chapati that he always carried in his pocket and threw them from the edge of the roof. The dog's tail wagged as he munched on the bread. He thought of Sami. This was what she had been trying to tell him before those boys… The front door shut downstairs and his mother was climbing the steps. She stood beside him and they looked up together. The stars lay dense and thick over the village like a chiffon veil.

'Why did the boys attack you?' she asked.

'They tried to take my waistcoat. It had the honeycomb in it.'

'Your father caused a fire when he found that.'

He wanted to tell her that Baba had been seen but the words would not come out; it might be a false hope.

'That honey helped your eyes.'

'This scholarship is your chance,' she said.

'To do what?'

'To get out of here. It's what you've wanted for years.'

'Not like this.'

It had been his dream to leave Harikaya, to study, to become a professional, to help his parents. But not like this, not in the household of the man who had made his father run away. His mother must have begged Kulsoom to ask Begum Saab to take him in early.

'I won't leave you,' he said. The night air was still warm but he shivered. 'I'll find the beekeeper.'

'Don't make up stories; the villagers already think you're…' Her eyes opened wide; her lips scrunched up.

'I'm what?'

'Your father was always telling stories. It became too dangerous.'

'To speak the truth?'

'I can't keep you here anymore, not on my own. My eyes are getting worse.'

'The black honey can help you.'

She left him and he sat down on the floor. From here on the roof, he could see the land: the irrigation channels that Mir Saab had set up, the factories that he owned, the school that he had started. But behind all this order, there was chaos in Harikaya. Men lined up behind the boundary wall for the drink that kept them awake all night and made them fight. Women walked with heavy shoulders, exhausted after working to grow enough food and bring back enough money to buy medicines.

He let his gaze travel to the distant flatlands and dark hints of trees, the beginnings of the forest. He would go there again tomorrow and this time he'd go further. He would go every day until he found the beekeeper. And then he'd be free to leave. Not before. And not to Mir Saab. He would make his own way. Another thought dropped into his head. Even if he found the beekeeper and he did help him, what then? In the end, it was in the hands of the bees.

The dog's low growls from below made him sit up. Voices. The sounds grew louder. Nearer now, shouting.

It was those boys, heading towards the house. He crashed down the steps, threw himself inside, and locked the front door. The barking was fierce outside, growing louder. He ran around the house and fastened every shutter.

His mother's body rose easily under the touch of his hand.

She picked up her glasses and the lit candle as if in a slow-motion dream that only added to Hassan's panic. He led her by the arm to the centre of the main room.

'What have you done now?' she asked, her eyes shining like metal, reflecting the glint of the old bolt on the door.

They clung to each other in the middle of the room as the voices arrived at the front of the house. The barking died down.

'What are they doing?' his mother said.

That taste of ink and oranges was in his mouth again, though the blood on his lips was dry. There was a yelp and all was quiet. Feet scraped outside the front door for a minute. Then a thud. Was that laughter? His mother stumbled and shrieked. The footsteps ran away. Moments passed before either moved, not daring to imagine the cause behind the thud. Hassan opened the door and saw the dog was lying on the ground. It was still breathing but there was blood on its back.

'They kicked it,' he said, kneeling beside the dog. 'You were protecting us.'

Something lay next to the dog. It was a small doll, smaller than the palm of his hand, dressed in black clothes, with a mop of black woollen hair. Its body was laced with fine needles. A curse, made by the hands of the woman who had warned him.

'That's you,' his mother said. She stooped and picked up the doll and threw it down the street, like last time. 'There's nothing left for you here.'

It took only minutes to pack his bag. A shirt, trousers, pyjamas, a towel. The piece of honeycomb in its pouch was in his waistcoat pocket. When he was ready, he stood at the door with the bag over his shoulder.

'You need this for the train,' his mother said, 'Your ID card.'

He slipped the small card into the inner pocket of his bag. It was a floppy small thing that belonged to his father. His mother stepped out and he bent to pick up the dog. He carried it to the end of the street where Sami lived and stood under her bedroom window. His mother waited a few feet away. The shutter of the window was slightly open and he heard movement inside.

'Sami,' he whispered.

The front door opened and there she was.

'I need to leave,' he said. 'They've hurt the dog.'

'Those boys?'

'Yes, but I think it's bigger than that. Can you look after him?'

He placed the dog in her outstretched arms. Before he turned to leave, he had one last thing to say. 'Thank you,'

'It was never mine in the first place,' she said.

He didn't know what to say.

'I don't know when I'll see you again,' she whispered.

Mother and son walked in the darkness to the station. They would make the last night train to Karachi.

'I'll come back,' he said, 'to find the beekeeper.'

'There'll be lots to learn there,' Amma replied.

The touch of steel that her words carried pricked his throat.

In the train, he went to stand at the window. There was no glass and she took his hand through the frame.

'Promise me you'll never talk about your father to Mir Saab. Or this plan to find the beekeeper.'

A whistle blew and her hand tightened around his. 'Come back for the Eid holidays with Kulsoom. Mir Saab's family comes back then,' she said.

'But that's more than six weeks away. The floods will come sooner.'

A horn blasted from somewhere behind her.

'I'll bring you the honey.'

'The doctor told me I have two months at the most before I'm blind.'

He stumbled and his own voice trembled. 'I'll come back before the rains, and find the beekeeper, Amma. I promise.'

The train was moving and she let go. He leant out through the open frame of the carriage.

'You'll see. I'll bring the black honey to you. It'll cure your eyes.'

He bent his neck and waved hard as his mother became smaller. The train tracks curved out of the station and she was lost in the rising dust. He sat down. The carriage was full of people, busy with themselves. He let the bag drop to the ground. The engine roared as the train chugged onwards but he could only hear her last words: she could go blind in two months.

The wall of the train was cool on Hassan's back. His breathing grew heavy and his eyelids struggled with sleep. The beekeeper's face came into his mind; his dark skin glowed and he stood in the middle of a circle of golden trees. The train jerked and Hassan opened his eyes again.

The wind outside blew fine dust on his face and the old trees stood firm like great-grandfathers in inky blue jungles that stretched for miles. The forests gave way to villages bordered by banyan trees, their branches curling to the ground, hiding men and women who made them their homes. Did the beekeeper live under a tree, or did he have a house? He'd come back soon before the floods and find him. For now, he would begin this new life, do what they all wanted.

The bench under him was hard. Perhaps going to Karachi was the right thing to do. If he went to school in Karachi, he could become what he wanted and help Amma too. Baba couldn't argue with that. He thought of those guards and a shudder moved through him. He couldn't stay in Harikaya now anyway. He'd go to Karachi, show his face to the mir and be an ideal new scholar. Then he'd find a way back before school started. Kulsoom would help him. She had to. Amma was her sister after all. Hassan's breath quickened. Something grew certain in him. His father was going to come home when the rains came.

Dawn turned into daylight and he was still awake as the train rattled past larger settlements. The train was delayed by a breakdown around noon and he stood in disbelief for hours watching the men make repairs. Passengers spent the time chasing shadows made by the carriages. Once the train got going again, there were more hold-ups because of cattle moving across the tracks.

It was already evening when trees and villages transformed into the great desert plains of the lower Sindh. He had learnt about these at school. He caught an hour, or maybe more, of sleep before the outlines of buildings in the darkening sky of Karachi filled the window frame. The train made its way through ramshackle dwellings until it stopped, in its grand, old centre, like a hive swarming with workers and drones. No sign of the queen.

At the station, Kulsoom took his bag and said, 'We've been waiting for hours.'

Hassan was pleased to see Ali Noor, a familiar face from the village. Ali Noor carried his bag to the car.

'Don't get used to this kind of service,' he said with a wink.

Ali Noor drove past the railroad fence and the car wove its way through Karachi's hyperactive traffic – cars, trucks, donkeys, carts, buses, and amped-up motorcycles carrying families of four or more. Bicycles flew past and cyclists tried to look through the darkened windows of the car. Hassan ducked, but even with their faces close to the glass, they saw nothing.

The muscles of Kulsoom's face were tight; her eyes looked like shiny raisins whenever she looked at him. She bit her lower lip and rubbed her hands as if she were cold. His mother must have spoken to her. He imagined his mother standing in the village square at the public telephone, alone, her voice shaking. She would have returned, made chapatis for herself, and sat alone in an empty house.

'Khala, when did Mir Saab arrive?' He called her *Aunty*. The word felt unfamiliar to him. Ali Noor replied for her. 'Last night.'

The car slowed down. A boy came close to the car; he must have been the same age as Hassan. His hair was like straw, dried by the sun, and he looked like he was sleepwalking. Kulsoom pushed a coin into Hassan's hand.

'Give this to him.'

The skin of the boy's hand was rough. He walked away but then dropped the coin and bent down to grab it in the middle of traffic that veered off to either side of him like flowing water round a pebble. He banged the bonnet of a rickshaw that swerved too close.

There was courage here on the faces of the people who lived and worked on these streets. The dogs were different too. Tougher, going about their business in twos or threes. Life, with all its beauty, all its shades, but how did they get through the nights? Hassan stopped his thoughts there; he didn't even know what was going to happen to him. There was no question that he would be fed and sheltered in the world to which he was going now but this other world, here before him, was never far away for him, a villager. He only had to make one mistake and he could fall.

Even Kulsoom's grimness was soothing at that moment. He sat back, relieved to be in a car, to have a destination. He opened the window and stuck his hand out to feel the air. It felt more humid than the dry heat of Harikaya and made his hair stick to his skin. And there was something else that added to all of this, a new smell. It had to be the sea. He breathed it in.

The city went on forever. They drove past open shops, built in the last thirty years. Colonial façades lined wider roads like old giants with flaking and fading skin. Balconies, domes, minarets, spires, and woodwork spoke of better days, when Karachi was a much smaller town – a coastal habitat, a playground for nobility, fishermen, farmers, and fairies alike. That was before the separation. He had learnt about that too. People had flocked into stories of freedom in the new country. Old stories were squeezed into forgotten suitcases left in the shadows of their new lives.

'Tomorrow, Begum Saab's niece comes from London,' Kulsoom said to Ali Noor. She turned back to Hassan. 'Mir Saab's been very good to you. Meet him and then keep out of his way.'

Ali Noor looked at him in the mirror but Hassan looked away, out onto the road again.

Part Two

Karachi

Sindh Province, Pakistan

Chapter Eight

Hassan lay on his bed made out of bamboo, with his sheet up to his chin, opposite a window and daylight. He must have slept through the night because his eyelids opened now to morning life: the cries of a baby in another room, the creaks of a water pump, an outside tap splashing water in short bursts. And then he heard clanking music.

There was a knock on the door. He lay on his elbows. Kulsoom stood in the doorway with clothes hanging over her right arm. In Harikaya, his mother never came into his room.

'Please don't come into my room until I say you can,' he said.

'Why not?' She was inside before he could get up.

'This is not normal,' he said.

'Your mother has always allowed you too much. That is not normal.'

'My mother has never had much to allow.'

She came closer to the bed as if she was about to hand him the clothes.

'What's that music?' Hassan asked.

'What do you mean?'

'That horrible music, can't you hear it?'

'The traffic?'

The music fell apart into car horns, the brakes of buses, and speeding engines.

'Does music sound like that now in Harikaya?' Kulsoom asked.

He tipped his head back, stopping himself from smiling. 'Look, I have to get back to the forests. Baba is probably there waiting for me.'

'He's disappeared again and you think he'll be waiting for you.'

'He hasn't disappeared. It was those…' He stopped. There was too much satisfaction on her face.

'The scholarship can blow away in seconds if they find out about your father. Here, Begum Saab gave you these.'

He sat up and reached out his hand to take the clothes but she held onto them, coming closer and standing tall over him.

'You be careful,' she said. 'You'll be going back for the Eid holidays when we all go back. Before that you'll stay here and start school,' she continued, her voice softer now. 'Make sure you stay low, out of their way. They've been good to let you come so early.'

'The holidays begin in over six weeks. And school doesn't start for another three weeks. I can go and come back after Mir Saab sees me,' he said.

'I don't want you messing things up. It's my reputation at stake.'

'I have to get back before the floods.'

'You don't even know when they are.'

'That's why I need to return after I've met Mir Saab.'

'It's too dangerous for you in Harikaya now.' She spat the words out as if it was his fault. 'Forget about all that here.'

'Baba said the black honey…'

'Your father's crazy. Believe him or Mir Saab's doctors. They've done everything they can for your mother…' Her hands squeezed the clothes on her arm.

'I will go back whether you help me or not.' It was then that he noticed the seat of the chair was empty. 'Where is it?'

Her eyebrows rose and she stepped back. For a second, he thought that she was scared. He stood up, his long shirt falling down over his pants and legs.

'Where is my bag?'

'You don't need it here. Look, Begum Saab has given you new clothes.'

'You've taken my ID card.' A sickly feeling was squeezing his chest. 'You came in when I was sleeping and took my bag.'

'If you leave here and don't come back, I risk losing my job. People talk here. Your father's done enough damage. They'll say the whole family is…'

'I said I'd come back.'

'Stop this,' she hissed. 'I thought you were less of a fool than your father. It's too dangerous out there. You have no money, no status. You'll be lucky to make it to the end of the main road without someone stealing your things or attacking you. Go out there and you'll never come back.'

He was trembling. 'Go now.'

'Come to the house. They want to see you.' Her voice was softer now. She let the clothes drop onto his bed.

He stared at the window ahead.

'It's for your own good,' she said from the door. Her face was long, its skin drooped, and her eyes looked somewhere behind him.

'Take away my freedom for my own good. Are you crazy? I have nothing else.' The calmness of his voice surprised him.

'You have a good education ahead of you. Don't waste it on some myth.'

'Black honey is medicine.'

'Stop this. Can't you understand? You're a village boy. There are five million people in this city. If you go out there on your own anything can happen.' She shut the door as she left.

Hassan turned to the window. There were smudge marks on it, greasy fingers from some previous resident. A servant.

He went to open the window and its wooden handle flopped as it swung inwards. A mosquito mesh was fixed in the frame.

'This is how I will see this place until I see you again, Amma. Everything will be distant.' He spoke out loud.

Stray dogs barked outside. He flinched. The fan's motor wobbled and the old white blades spun but there was hardly any movement of air. Everything was too humid here and now he was supposed to meet Mir Saab and his wife, Begum Saab. As he lifted his shirt, he saw something black on the floor. It was his waistcoat, half hidden under his bed. It had fallen off the chair where he had put it before he went to sleep and Kulsoom must have missed it in the darkness when she came in last night. He bent to pick it up. The honeycomb was still in the pocket. He took the small, yellow piece out of its pouch and held it in his palm.

'I'll get my ID card back and be back before the floods. There has to be a way,' he whispered. He put the piece of honeycomb back into the pouch and put it under his pillow.

He picked up his new clothes – a light-blue shirt and grey trousers. First, he needed to wash and he went down the steps at the side of the building. He washed his body in semi-darkness at the communal tap. The clothes were crisp and soft on his skin and he was clean at last after a night and day of travelling.

The courtyard was surrounded by high walls. Guards just beyond the gate held steel mugs of chai, their rifles resting on the arms of their chairs. They ignored him but a crow leapt out from a palm tree nearby. It flew in circles above him, and then, with a screech, it headed in the direction of the main house, a huge, old yellow building with three floors, a flat roof, and hundreds of windows.

He followed in the same direction until he was out of sight of the guards, then he stopped and looked around. It was still dark enough and no one was about. He set one foot out in the air before him and took a leap. With his arms swinging like pendulums, he skipped. 'One, two, one, two,' he whispered to himself, as he lifted each foot. He reached the steps at the main door. One, two, three jumps and he was through the door and into another world.

Inside, everything was marble, even the winding staircase. Kulsoom had to be here somewhere. He walked to the other end of the hall and through a doorway, opening onto a room with a round wooden table as big as his whole house. It must have come into the room in parts like a cake and then been put back together again.

Someone in the village made a cake once for a wedding, out of pistachio and dates that had got caught in his teeth. Loud bubbles of hunger shot up and into his stomach. Where was Kulsoom? He would sit with the servants, be one of them, if he could just have some food. And then he would go back to his room and not talk to anyone.

'There is nothing they can do to change my mind.' English words, a man's voice from the next room. 'Had me round for dinner and told me about the cotton mills over chocolate mousse. How dare they think I'd agree to something like that?'

Another voice, a woman's, too quiet to hear. And then the man's again.

'They have the fort already and it's falling apart because they haven't kept one of their promises. Those idiots. Now they're after my factories. Not in my lifetime.'

Footsteps.

'Don't forget to tell the cook about the chillies.'

A woman came through the doorway.

'Yes, Begum Saab.' Kulsoom was following her, a little breathless.

Hassan had never seen his aunt like this before. Her lips tightened as soon as she saw him but her voice was sweet. Too sweet.

'This is my nephew,' she said.

Begum Saab lifted small glasses attached to a golden chain around her neck, and perched them at the end of her nose, which was powdered white and seemed fluffy. Her nose rose to view him better through the lenses. She looked up and down at his new clothes. Her general plumpness, wrapped in a long silk dress, softened the strictness in her lips.

Hassan dared not smile and yet, at the same time, there was a strange lack of cruelty in her. The bracelet she wore looked old: two silver snakes wrapped around her wrist. A red ruby joined their heads and their scales glinted as she moved her hand, picking up the sunlight from the window of the dining room.

'Has he eaten?'

'Not yet, Begum Saab,' Kulsoom said.

A girl rushed in from an entrance on the other side of the room; she must have been a few years older than Hassan. She stopped at the sight of Begum Saab, nearly tipping forward but managed to keep her balance on her toes.

'Is the cook in the kitchen?' Begum Saab's voice was urgent.

The girl's ponytail shook with her head. 'Yes,' she said.

'Come, let's find him. My niece doesn't eat spices.'

Begum Saab looked at Hassan again. He shifted on his feet and made his back straighter – it worked – her face became softer.

'Remind me, why did he come here?' she asked Kulsoom.

'The scholarship. He's a very studious boy,' Kulsoom said, smiling. 'His father's a poet.'

'A poet?'

Hassan held Begum Saab's stare.

'My children are around his age. Have breakfast with them

when they wake up,' she said to him. 'You can practise English with them before you start school.'

They walked away but Begum Saab stopped and took an envelope from the top of the sideboard and handed it to the maid who handed it to Hassan.

'Give this to Mir Saab,' Begum Saab said, pointing to the room from which she had just come. 'He's in his study through the living room. Tell him you're the boy with the scholarship.'

With these words, they left. Kulsoom looked back at him with a secretive, stern expression, better than anything his mother could do.

The room was bigger than his school hall and had two pillars in the middle. Long rifles hung over the sofa on one side. A snooker table stood on the other.

A head and then body caught his eye from the open door across the room. The body moved through different positions in candlelight: body standing, hands together in front of chest, body bending, body kneeling, and then on the ground with the head touching a small slab of stone at the top of the prayer mat. Whispers of words that Hassan could never remember.

The movement stopped and so did the whispers. Mir Saab got up. A door shut from inside the room; he must have left. The gold-trimmed envelope flapped in Hassan's fingers until he reached the study door. A clock on the mantelpiece faced him. Tick, tick, tick. An empty chair. A large wooden desk. The window. Wooden bookshelves lined the walls.

But it was the desk that caught Hassan's attention. A structure, the shape of a large egg and as high as his arm, stood in the middle of it. It was made of golden sticks, the size of big matchsticks, arranged in the shape of hexagons, like his honeycomb. He moved closer. The curves of the side of the desk were carved like vertical hills and were soft against his thighs. The smell of wax and honey touched his nostrils from some distant place. Only an arm's length away now, the shape was too fragile to touch. It reminded him of the secret Baba had been looking for.

Piles of paper lay all over the desk like a frothy sea around the egg shape. Different sizes, creams and whites. Sketches filled every corner – fine lines and shading like photographs, only more beautiful. Bees with body parts touched by arrows that pointed to words in sloping black ink. Nests hung from branches or emerged out of holes in tree trunks and were alive with colonies of bees.

One drawing made him stop. A bee, larger and darker than the other ones. Could it be? His free hand flew forwards towards the image.

'What are you doing?' a voice snapped.

He pulled his hand back. The envelope in the other hand dropped to the floor. A man was at the other door. He had a small and slender frame, black hair parted on one side in a straight line and large square glasses that slipped down his nose. Beneath his glasses were round, surprised-looking eyes. He wore a woollen jumper that looked so warm that Hassan started to sweat.

'Mir Saab, I was looking at…' Hassan stooped to pick up the envelope and shook himself into straightness.

'Who are you?'

'I'm Hassan, the one with the scholarship.'

'One thing I won't have is anyone uninvited in my study.'

Hassan held out the envelope, without looking up.

'I'm sorry,' Hassan said. 'I couldn't help it.' He pointed at the golden ball on the desk.

Mir Saab dropped the envelope on the chair. 'The hive?' He narrowed his eyes at Hassan before he fixed them on the structure.

'Did you make it?' Hassan asked.

There was no reply. Mir Saab picked up the camera that lay on the table at the other end of the room. He turned the camera around in his hands; its back was open. 'This thing won't go back together.'

His voice in English was like a song.

'Hand me that screwdriver.' Mir Saab pointed to a long metal stick lying near the table. 'Where did you learn your English?'

'In school and from books and films.' The television placed in the village square every week was from Mir Saab. 'And from a poet friend who studied in England.'

Mir Saab took the screwdriver from Hassan. Silver and black buttons on the camera shone through his fingers; he chuckled as if he had solved a puzzle until a shadow fell over his face. 'Oh, I give up.' Mir Saab shook his head at the camera. 'The film won't wind forwards.' Mir Saab's own voice seemed to be winding forwards like a tape recorder that was secretly chewing the tape. 'It's not clicking on the spool.' He put the camera down, leaving the flap on the back open.

Hassan took the camera and slid the loose film over the

spokes again before turning the metal handle that wound the spool with his thumb. The film was stuck. He pushed the handle back again, a persuasive press. It gave way and the film caught on the reel. His fingers moved with the same ease as his mother's at her weaving machine. He shut the back cover with a flick of his other hand and heard the buzzing sound of the film winding itself around the spokes of the drum.

'My word, you've done it,' Mir Saab said.

Hassan held the camera as if it were a living creature in his hands. His fingers had known what to do.

'So, you won the scholarship?'

'Yes.'

'What else do you do?'

'I like nature,' Hassan said, his head bowed and his cheeks warm. The truth was that he loved nature and animals, and this man in front of him, the one he hated, shared that with him.

'That camera took two weeks to arrive on the ship from London,' Mir Saab said. He picked up a roll of paper from the table, untied the ribbon around it and stood there for a minute or two, looking at the sheet, at eye level. He examined it with nods and sighs and then turned the paper around to Hassan.

It was a sailing boat – no, a ship. A great wooden boat, with sails reaching out to the sky like wings in the wind, drawn in pencil with such fine detail that Hassan could not take his eyes away from it.

'Take a picture of the boat,' Mir Saab said. 'Turn the lens until you can see it.'

Hassan steadied himself. The lens turned both ways. One

way made the drawing closer and darker, the lines tighter. The shutter snapped and his mouth opened. 'I have it,' he whispered.

Mir Saab put the sheet on the table, flattening it with his hands. He picked up a pencil and made a mark on the drawing. 'What drew you to the hive?'

'The shapes,' Hassan said. 'The hexagons were moving and overlapping each other.'

Mir Saab went to the chair and began opening the envelope.

'You're very interested in bees, Mir Saab,' Hassan said.

'What? Yes, the bees.' His eyes glowed for a second behind his glasses. 'It's their collective mind I'm interested in.' He tapped the drawing of the black bee that Hassan had nearly touched. 'Why this one?'

Hassan cleared his throat; he had to be careful. He could never forget that Mir Saab had sent the guards.

'It seems unusually big.'

'*Apis dorsata*,' Mir Saab said.

'Pardon?'

'The black honeybee.' Mir Saab took the card out of the envelope. 'Rare these days, but they still exist in the forests of Harikaya.'

Before Hassan could think of what to say, that humming sound, more like a tingling now, was inside him. Faint, but meeting him in the centre of his body. The beekeeper's face was there, so clear now in his mind that he gasped.

The envelope floated from Mir Saab's hand onto the desk and landed in front of the matchstick hive. Mir Saab took out the card and bent it back along its spine to read it. His eyebrows moved upwards to meet at the centre of his forehead. 'What's he playing at?' He scrunched the card up into a ball. 'He won't get my factories by inviting me to a wedding.' He walked out through the door at the back of the study.

Hassan was left, forgotten, but with his mind racing. His mother worked at the factory. Would she be all right? And her eyes? Fine blood lines in yellowing irises.

The picture, on the desk, there it was.

Apis dorsata.

Chapter Nine

'Amina Bibi, Begum Saab asks you to come down for breakfast.'

Hassan spoke in English but he added *Bibi* to her name to show respect. Amina, Mir Saab and Begum Saab's daughter, had the same moon-shaped face and surprised look as Mir Saab. She was a little taller than Hassan but seemed younger, her eyes wide and timid. She nodded from the other end of the bedroom that was as big as his whole house and backyard together.

It was the girl kneeling on the stone floor with her back to him that had his attention. Her long hair was not tied back like Pakistani girls' hair. Her movements were sudden and sharp, like the little bolts of lightning that sometimes played in the sky on a monsoon night in Harikaya. She threw open a suitcase lying in front of a bed as big as his whole room and took out presents. So, this must be Maryam, the niece from London. She looked about the same age as him.

'That's all Zain wanted.' She put a box of chocolates on the bed.

Maryam stood up and turned to face him.

'Who's this?' she asked. She stared at him from behind smudged glasses.

Amina came up behind her and said, 'He doesn't speak English.'

'Yes, I do, Bibi,' he said.

'I'm Maryam. I'm fourteen and I'll be doing eleven subjects when I go back.'

'I'm Hassan. I'm fourteen and I…' He stopped.

She was smiling. He looked down.

'Pleased to meet you,' Maryam said.

The edges of her lips disappeared into her cheeks when she smiled.

'That's Kulsoom's nephew.' Amina spoke in an accent that reminded Hassan of old films. 'Baba's offered him a scholarship to study in Karachi.'

'Are you from London?' Hassan asked Maryam.

'Yes, I live in Partridge Way.'

'She came here on a plane,' Amina added.

'Flew over like a partridge in a pear tree.' A boy walked in; he was thin and tall with floppy black hair.

'That's Zain,' Maryam said. He must have been a year or two older than Maryam and probably Amina too.

'A partridge in a pear tree,' Hassan whispered to himself.

'A partridge is Pakistan's national bird,' Zain said. 'Pears are delicious. We have a pear tree at our house in London.'

'It's still night-time in England.' Maryam skipped to the wooden doors that led to the balcony and opened them to let the light pour through. The others joined her behind the mosquito netting that was fitted over the balcony wall. Maryam turned to Hassan. 'You too, come and take a look.'

He saw the yellow wall of the courtyard, a line of trees and then land, stretching out to a distant boundary wall. Three men lay on top of it like cats with nothing to do. Behind them was the city.

'How long have your family lived here?' Maryam asked Amina.

'Ma says two hundred years. It used to be a hotel.'

'I can see it as it was then. Women wearing saris and men with long jackets to their knees over trousers. They're on holiday here. Can you see?' Maryam pointed down to the courtyard, her nose pressed against the netting.

'Maryam, you're finding your stories again.' Amina clapped.

For a second, Hassan saw those men and women too.

'Look, can you see the poets sitting on chairs in a circle? They're making up poems,' Maryam said.

'Go on, tell them the one you made up last night,' Amina said.

Maryam placed her hands on the netting and began.

'It's all over, all this will be gone in a day, the wife
said to her lover.
No, he replied, his lips in the air.
But there was no return for his ready kiss.
Make the days longer, he said, in anger.
But time cannot be altered, she replied.
Time is the ruler.

Change time, he ordered. Change it.
What can I do? she said. Time is the ruler.
The lover sat back on his chair, grumpy, disobeyed,
and soon to be forgotten.'

Maryam stopped. Amina clapped.

Hassan thought of the bees. He thought of Baba's poem, the time lines, sent from the planets, brought down by the workers. The number of days in the hexagonal caves. Twenty-four for the drones, twenty-one for the workers, and sixteen for the queen. 'Everything has time in it, everything rests on time, but why should time be the ruler?' he asked.

'Go on,' Maryam said.

All three of them were looking at him. He had said too much.

'Please go on,' she said.

He looked down onto the courtyard. Traces of saris and long coats. Wicker chairs and dark drinks. Wife and lover.

'If time rules you, it's only because you allow it
To swallow you up, to rush you, to limit you.
A rushing stream or a still lake.
Time depends on how you see it.'

He pointed to the courtyard below. 'The poets. The wife and her lover.' That word, *lover*, was strange, soft. 'They want to play with time.'

'But that doesn't answer the wife's question. How can she make the days longer?' Maryam asked.

'The lover plays with love,' Hassan said.

'What do you mean?' Maryam asked.

'It's not real. It's only a thought. Like time.'

'But love is real,' she said.

Hassan thought for a second. 'If love is truly real then there's no time to play with,' he said.

He pressed his hand against the netting, to get a better view of the courtyard. How could love be real? Love between people. It only happened in films or stories. His hand slipped through the mesh and he stumbled. The netting was loose. Maryam grabbed his elbow. It was the first time a girl had touched him. He moved his arm away.

'Come on, let's go down,' she said.

Two pieces of metal lay on either side of the plate – instruments for cutting. This was the first time in his life that he had used a knife and fork. He had heard about them in his lessons – that people in some countries didn't eat with their hands. He watched for a few moments. Metal clanged on plates. He picked up the instruments, clutching one in each hand. The others held the instruments in a lighter way than he did. He stabbed he fork into the small chunks of meat and with the knife, he cut the eggs. This was not too bad.

'They're in the wrong hands.' That was Amina.

He stopped with a piece of meat a few inches from his mouth, his face warming up.

'You can use your hands if you like,' Maryam said.

Her words felt like a poke from that pronged thing

dripping juice into his hand. He put the fork down and wiped his hand with the napkin.

'It's all right, I can manage,' he said.

The others started talking again but Maryam still watched as he picked up the fork with his other hand and put the food in his mouth. Hassan ate slowly, turning his fork around to scoop up the rice. She smiled at him and carried on with her own meal. Pity was in that smile.

After the meal, he offered to take the dishes and the cutlery back to the kitchen. His stomach rumbled in front of the kitchen doors. They wobbled – heavy, floppy, and transparent like plastic jungle leaves – when he walked through.

The air was humid in the kitchen, sticky with oil and spices. He spied baskets of fresh ginger and garlic, glass jars of cumin, cardamom, cloves. He breathed in the smells. Huge spoons and other tools stood in jars on the worktop. There was nothing he didn't recognise, but something wasn't right.

He put the dishes next to the other breakfast plates on the sideboard. The crows in the yard were loud through the open back door. Chickens clucked in the background, like in the street outside his house. He stood in the doorway; the yard was huge, nothing like home.

Servants squatted or sat on low stools around the stove with plates of food in their hands. Some were smoking or holding cups of hot chai; a few of them were from the village, talking in Sindhi. Others were silent. They ate meat and eggs like the family inside but here they ate with their hands. Like his mother and father. Baba had told stories over plates of daal, breaking off warm chapati and scooping up the daal.

Those meals had been the best. Amma had never spoken much at meals.

In the courtyard, nobody bothered with Hassan. It was best that way. He was one of them and also not, someone who ate breakfast with the family but yet was not one of the family. He stepped backwards. He heard chewing sounds.

'Nice of you to make your way here.'

Hassan spun around. It was a man, stepping out from behind the back door. He wore a white apron and a thin smile that ran straight across his face, hinting at gaps in his teeth. It had to be the cook. He had been there all this time, in the shadows.

'You're the kid from the village,' he said.

Hassan moved back towards the door flaps, but the cook stepped forwards to pick up a teaspoon of sugar from a pot on the sideboard, blocking Hassan's way. The man dropped the cube into a cup. With his free hand, he took a cigarette from his pocket, placed it in his mouth, and lit it. The cook blew out smoke and dropped the burnt matchstick on the floor.

'Had breakfast with the family?'

'Yes.'

'Enjoy it?'

'Breakfast?'

'Being with the family?'

'Yes.'

For a moment, their eyes met. The cook took another puff of his cigarette. Everything about this man was neat. His hair, longer than normal and slick, was tied back. His face was clean shaven and he looked at Hassan as if he could see through him. Even his clothes under the apron were crisp and hung on his tall, straight, and bony form.

'You won't remember me. I knew your father.'

'How?'

'We were friends.'

His father did not have many friends. 'Keep reserved,' he used to say, and, 'Don't let people know your business.' When he had spoken poetry with the poets, he had called it, 'Nature's voice, not mine.'

'Your father left around the time of the fire,' the cook said.

'I don't know about any fire.'

Hassan turned to head for the door flaps. Something clattered on the floor. It was the teaspoon.

'Don't worry, you're safe here.'

Hassan picked up the spoon and held it out. The cook's fingers touched his for a second, warm and cool at the same time.

'A shame about those guards. Mir Saab's guards, weren't they?' The cook shook his head. 'He'll be back.'

'I know he will.' It was not a secret that his father had left but Hassan felt his breath quicken.

'The question is when. It's too dangerous now.' The cook's smile reappeared. 'It's all down to you now, isn't it? To be the man that your mother needs you to be. She's going blind.'

'She won't go blind. I'll find the black honey.' He had said too much.

'As I said, you're safe here. I could tell you a little about your father, if you like.'

Hassan's feet were stuck to the ground.

'It'll come.' The cook sucked at his cigarette. 'You don't have much time, do you? The rains are coming anytime now.'

Hassan found himself nodding slightly.

Out of the kitchen again, in the dining room, the air was hot but clear, with no stickiness, no smells of spices or smoke. But that man, the cook, Hassan had seen him before but he couldn't remember where. His old life in Harikaya seemed so far away now after only a night here; this was another world. A world where a mir lived, a mir who had sent guards after his father. He crouched down on the ground. He had to remember where he'd seen the cook, but the more he tried the more thoughts and images inside his mind blurred.

Just then, footsteps burst through from the direction of the hall and he looked up. Maryam was at the round table, her hand on the back of one of the chairs. When she saw him, she came and knelt on one knee in front of him.

'What's wrong?'

'Nothing, Bibi. I was just tired.'

Amina and Zain came in. Maryam took him by the hand and helped him up. She told the others to go ahead and stayed with him.

They took several steps before he spoke. 'Thank you,' he said. 'I'm all right.' He didn't need her kindness.

'Come with us for a walk.'

'Where to?'

'To the back of the house.'

The guards greeted Maryam by standing up. Their gaze followed Hassan as he walked alongside her. He wanted to say something to them, to tell them to stop looking but he held his mouth shut. He was a boy; she was a girl and he wasn't one of her lot. Maryam saw nothing except the way ahead. The guards' chatter started again once they were past them, busy again with a card game.

Two paths lay before them. One to the main gate across the bare land. The other edged around the inner wall. They took this one. The ground here was dry, like in Harikaya, but the soil was redder and the trees and bushes had been planted in patterns. Palm trees stood around a stone water-fountain with dry leaves in its trough instead of water. A buffalo, standing under a banyan tree, stirred. Further on, the land became wilder, more natural, the sandy floor dotted with shrubs and trees.

'When will you start school, Hassan?'

'After I find—' He tripped over a root and his words stuck.

They turned the corner of the wall and about forty metres ahead was what seemed like a forest. Amina and Zain were near the trees.

'Wait for us!' Maryam shouted. It was hard to keep up with her march.

They all walked on a twisting, overgrown path between the trees. Hassan's footsteps fell as heavily as theirs on bramble and weeds. He reached out to touch the trunks of acacias, palms, and eucalyptus, names his father had taught him.

There was a clearing, and in the middle stood a structure. Hassan walked over to it and found that its walls reached his shoulders. Grass sprouted up between broken sea-blue tiles on its floor. It was too big to be a water tank.

'A swimming pool,' Maryam said.

'It used to be for parties,' Amina said.

'Baba's friends came from all over the world,' Zain said.

'Poetry.' Maryam waved her hands for the others to be quiet. 'I hear it,' she said. 'Wait.'

A breeze shook the leaves and the crows chattered, as though in a gush of applause.

'Tiger, tiger burning bright. In the forests of the night,' Maryam said.

The others laughed. Poets and friends, imaginary or real, it didn't matter. Zain was the first to move into the forest again; it was cooler under the canopy of trees. They walked on to another clearing, a bigger one. Dozing birds shot upwards in panic.

'That's the masjid,' Zain said.

A small building stood in the sun's rays that spread around its dome like the fingers of a giant hand. Winding weeds clung to broken orange and turquoise tiles. Flakes of paint from the timber frame dusted the ground. The building was alive.

'Baba listened to poets and scholars here. Our grandfather was one of them. We called him Nana,' Amina said.

'I called him Dada, because he's my father's father,' Maryam said.

All those people were gone now. Had they been chased away or simply blown away by winds too delicate at first to notice until too many tiles had chipped? A flake of paint drifted to the floor. The grandfather, this building, was dying in front of them.

'What's a scholar?' Hassan asked.

'Someone from the olden days who told stories and read a lot,' Zain said.

'Why did the parties stop?' Maryam asked.

The others just shrugged. Maryam walked over to where Amina and Zain stood at the bottom of the steps. Hassan stayed at a distance. This was their place, this building; it belonged to those who were part of Mir Saab's family. The building stood solid like a grandfather should stand. Theirs, not his; he had never known *his*. Yes, this building was a grandfather.

'Why are all the tiles hexagons?' Maryam asked.

'Six is a special number,' Hassan said.

'Why?' Maryam asked.

'I don't know why but it's special for the bees.'

'Father designed it to look like a beehive,' Zain said.

There was row after row of hexagonal tiles; the walls were like sheets of honeycomb.

'Each hexagon is a cell for a young bee to grow in,' Zain said. 'Sheets of wax hexagons make a nest.'

'A city of hexagons,' Hassan said.

Zain was already on the bottom step and he swung his arms in the air as if waving a sword. 'Be careful of bird droppings.' He was laughing and jumping up the steps in twos to the wooden doors.

Hassan wanted to copy him, to join in with the play, but the wish only made him tense, stiff.

Zain pulled one of the doors and stopped. 'What's that?'

Hassan went nearer. It was a humming sound, but this one was outside his own head. Zain raised his hands up to tell them to stop. Hassan took a step back but Amina and Maryam carried on. They were following him up when a bee appeared from inside the masjid through the open door. Another came and then another.

'Go back,' Hassan said.

'What is it?' Amina asked.

The sound was growing but still faint.

Another bee came through the door. Three became four, then five, six; more came out in pairs and Hassan lost count. Amina covered her face with her hands as a cloud of bees gathered at the top of the steps. The humming was loud and strong; Maryam screamed and waved her hands. It was the wrong thing to do; the bees approached her.

'Keep still!' Hassan shouted.

Maryam screamed again and jumped down the steps, followed by Zain and Amina. Maryam was shouting something at him, but he couldn't hear above the humming. All three of them ran across the clearing and disappeared behind a tree. The bees moved now as a cluster after them, like a slow thunder cloud. Running was useless. Hassan stayed at the bottom of the steps. Maryam's head poked out from behind a tree. The long shirts of Amina and Zain flapped even though there was no wind.

Hassan took the honeycomb out of his pocket and held it between his palms, close to his heart. His eyes were open but the beekeeper's face was clear in his mind. Behind the face was another clearing, the one in the forest where the nest of black honeybees lived. The beekeeper's mouth was moving and Hassan began to copy it. It was the same language that had saved his father's life – a series of puffs, growls, and gargles. His lips came together to whistle both high and low tones. Mouth opening wide. A sharp puff. Then another. Wider. A grunt and then a long, low, throaty sound.

The swarm stopped at the line of trees and Hassan moved to the top of the steps.

The bees paused and changed direction, faster now, heading towards the masjid until they stopped, hovering above the bottom step. The cloud was spinning, becoming wilder, a potential invasion. Spinning faster and faster, the cloud rose, a flying wave coming towards him. It circled him and explored his presence, but Hassan was neither food nor threat and the bees had a choice: to attack or show mercy.

The humming changed. It was just as loud, but softer, less angry. He was lost in their sound, his body still, the movement of his breath steady and deep.

The bees became a cylinder of humming that expanded and contracted around him, in and out. His body sang to their sound. His being merged into theirs and the bees became part of him.

He was a statue with head bent and arms folded across his chest. Every cell in him hummed and his heart opened to their power. Nothing mattered except the sound, the humming. It was part of him. It was him.

The bees started to retreat, one by one at first. When the final bee had left him and made its way back inside, the spell of stillness broke apart and the inner sound was gone. He wanted to follow the bees but some kind of force, emanating from inside the building, stopped him.

'I'll be back,' he said to the bees, and shut the doors to their world.

Silence.

He placed the honeycomb back in his pocket and went down the steps into the strong sunlight that pricked his skin. The others were waiting for him behind the trees.

'What happened?' Maryam asked Hassan.

She was trembling; Amina and Zain were shivering.

'You saved our lives,' Zain said.

All three of them came towards him with their eyes and mouths open.

'How did you do that?' Maryam asked.

'I don't know.'

The heat was heavy but Hassan trembled on the way back.

They walked in single file at a pace that made him out of breath.

He was at the end of the line and looked back from time to time, not out of fear, more out of a hope, that one of the bees had followed.

Chapter Ten

What had happened? He was pacing his room without end. Had it been real? Bees filled his mind. That cloud of bees so close. Part of him was still there at the masjid with them. He paused in the middle of the floor and waited for any signs, but there were none: no humming, no image to make him feel whole again.

He wanted to go to school, to be like them, like Maryam, to tell stories and laugh. He would return home briefly with Kulsoom to find the beekeeper and the honey and then be back for school if everything went well. He sat down and took the honeycomb from under his pillow. He held it with both hands. Yes, Baba would be happy with that plan. And when he went to look for the beekeeper, maybe, if it were meant to be, maybe he would find his father in the forest too.

A crow screeched on the sill, its black eyes watching his thoughts through the netting. And now this with the bees. What would they all make of it? He placed the piece of honeycomb in his waistcoat pocket. His lips were dry and his head pounded; he had to find water.

He crashed down the steps into the blanket of heat below. From the shade of the wall, he braced himself to run across the courtyard but a car drove through the gates and stopped at the main house. Ali Noor jumped out to open the back door for Begum Saab. Kulsoom got out of the other side and hurried to help Ali Noor take the shopping out of the car as Begum Saab went into the house. Hassan stepped back into the shade to wait until Kulsoom was gone. He still had to speak to her about returning. He would try and find her inside.

The water in the fridge in the dining area was cold. Drops splashed on his chin and neck as he gulped down half a bottle, paused and then drank the rest. That was better. The air filled with the sounds of sandals slapping on the floors and Begum Saab's instructions that echoed around the rooms. Suitcases thudded as they were pulled up the stairs in the hall.

Two women came in carrying bundles of knives, forks, and spoons and dropped them with a loud clatter on the side table. The women ignored him as they chattered and sang. He slipped into the living room where it was quiet and cool; the fans worked hard to blast the air around the room. He noticed some photos lined up on the mantelpiece to the side of him.

Carriages, uniforms. Mir Saab, as a boy, on a horse. Mir Saab with his father. Other men sat on thrones in front of palace doors, round men with round heads and decorated coats. Men on horses, men and women smoking cigars, jewels, rainbow silks, and lavish cushions. All with the same faces as Mir Saab but that's where the similarity stopped. Mir Saab was small, modest even – at least he appeared to be. But no, actions were reality; that was what Hassan told himself. Mir Saab had sent the guards after his father. But he loved the bees. How could someone who loved bees and drew them so beautifully be heartless?

He walked over to the open doorway of the study. The clock was ticking. The shutter was open and the golden hive structure, a skeleton shaped like an egg, seemed like it was on fire. He stayed at the door. What if he had to leave because of what had happened?

Mir Saab came through the other door and faced the table at the other end of the study. He did not notice Hassan and picked up the camera, humming to himself. A minute passed. The hive glowed.

'You can practise with this.' Without turning around, Mir Saab stretched out his hand for Hassan to take the camera.

As Hassan went to take it, voices came from outside, getting nearer.

'Where's that tiger poem?' Maryam asked. Amina and Zain came in behind her.

Hassan brought the camera to his eye and aimed it at Maryam, his finger over the button. She smiled, almost half a laugh, pleased to see him.

'Closer,' Mir Saab said. 'Portraits should be taken up close.'

Bravery was easier behind the camera. Her face was nearer now, in focus.

'Yes, that's close enough.' Mir Saab's hands were raised and his fingers were spread. Maryam's smile became stiff and her eyes narrowed behind her glasses.

'Now,' Mir Saab clapped.

The black button clicked and the handle turned under Hassan's finger.

'I wish I could have taken a photo of Hassan surrounded by the bees,' Maryam said.

Hassan nearly tripped but he gripped the camera more tightly. All eyes were on him.

Stumbling in their words, talking all at once with their expressions changing fast, Maryam, Amina, and Zain explained what had happened, like three buzzing bees loud and close. He laughed.

'There were thousands all around him,' Maryam said, 'like a wall.'

'I'm never going back there,' Amina said.

Mir Saab watched him. His eyebrows rose and fell until he said, 'That's impossible.'

'How did you do that, Hassan?' Maryam asked.

'It just happened,' Hassan said. He wanted to tell them that in the middle of the swarm, his own body had not mattered anymore. That he had been one with the bees, that—

The sound of tea cups.

Kulsoom came in and put the silver tray down on the table in front of Mir Saab before she headed out again, giving Hassan a questioning look.

'Did that really happen?' Mir Saab asked when she had left.

'Hassan saved our lives,' Amina said.

Mir Saab was thinking. His eyes narrowed, his lips were slowly moving, and he was muttering to himself. It was too many words. Hassan didn't trust words. For a moment the smell of honey and wax and old trees touched Hassan's nostrils.

'I knew a man once. He had a special connection with the bees,' Mir Saab said.

'Who?' Zain asked.

'An old beekeeper.'

There was a deep longing in Mir Saab's eyes, as if he were opening a locked treasure box containing some old secret that was only now ready for sharing.

'Where is he now?' Maryam asked.

'Twenty years ago, the beginning of this country meant new laws. The old beekeeper went to live in the forest with his wife and son. Father taught son in the forest, and I left for boarding school in England. I heard the old beekeeper died a few years later and so did his wife.'

'What about his son?' Amina asked.

'The summer I finished school, when I turned eighteen, I tried to find him.' Mir Saab was sitting at his desk now and touched the golden hive. 'We travelled in jeeps to the edge of the jungle and then went in on foot with the guards every day. I tried again after that a few times when I was back for good, before the rains.'

'Did you find him?' Amina asked.

'I found nests.'

Hassan could see the black honeybee nest high in the tree and feel the cool shade of the trees at the forest border with his father; he smelt the smoke on their clothes and in his hair.

'Bees, bees, bees,' Mir Saab said.

So, Mir Saab had found the beekeeper too.

'But I never found him.'

'Why not?' Amina asked.

Mir Saab picked up a picture and held it a few inches from his face. 'These drawings are the only way I have into their world now.' He put the paper down too quickly. 'Anyway, what about you? Where did you get this skill from?' Mir Saab bent over and stroked the egg. 'This knowledge?'

Whatever he meant by this, Mir Saab looked like a child who had had something snatched away from him, something that should have been his. Hassan stayed silent. They were kind now, but that could change in the blink of an eye. The clock ticked.

'Hassan, how did you do that?' Maryam asked.

'I don't know.'

Everyone leant forwards, except Hassan and Mir Saab. There was a look in Mir Saab's face that made Hassan hold back. Only a hint, but it was there, like in the faces of the boys when Hassan had won at cricket.

'I'm not sure I believe you,' Mir Saab said.

Was this some kind of trick to make him admit what had happened? Moments passed.

'Perhaps this is your path,' Mir Saab said, 'to come to know the answer to that question.'

No, this was not his path. It was a job he had to do, to go back for the black honey and then start school here in the city so he could leave Harikaya; that was his path. He opened his mouth but Mir Saab spoke, 'That's enough for now. The tea must be getting cold.'

'Can you read the tiger poem for us, Baba?' Amina asked.

'We heard it in the masjid,' Maryam paused. 'At one of your old parties.'

She and Amina laughed, two conspirators sharing a secret memory.

'I'll read it to you, and the next time, one of you will recite it to me by heart.'

'Hassan's father's a poet,' Amina said. 'Mother told me.'

Amina brought over the poetry book.

'Sit down everyone,' Maryam said.

Hassan dropped to the floor.

'On a chair, silly,' she said. Hassan looked over to Mir Saab. He had sat at the dining table with them but he hesitated. Villagers did not sit at the same level as the mir or his family.

'Yes, yes,' Mir Saab said, and reached for the hive structure again.

Amina poured the tea. The milk went into her cup first from a small jug. The brown liquid was the colour of the Indus river when it was still low before the rains.

The chai his mother made was always darker. She made it in a big pot for all the neighbours on special days: birthdays, death days, and holy days. He enjoyed squeezing the cardamom pods from the bottom of his cup after he drank the chai. Their black seeds were soft and warm in his mouth. Softer than when he had eaten the pods raw every morning until his mother put the jar away. But Baba would always give him a handful here and there. 'They're good for you,' he would say.

Maryam began.

'Tyger, tyger, burning bright,
In the forests of the night;
What immortal hand or eye,
Could frame thy fearful symmetry?'

A cry came from outside the living room. It was Begum Saab. 'There you all are! Come upstairs for the gathering.'

Hassan stayed seated.

'You too,' Mir Saab said. 'Go on, with the others.'

'What?' asked Begum Saab, looking from Mir Saab to Hassan.

'He put himself in danger for the children,' Mir Saab said.

Taking off the camera strap was difficult. Hassan had got used to it around his neck.

'No, keep it for now. Take pictures. You know what to do,' Mir Saab said.

'Thank you, Mir Saab.' He made his way out of the door with the camera hanging around his neck. Before he slipped out, he turned to see Mir Saab picking up the picture of the black bees and closing his eyes.

Hassan followed the sound of sandals on the stairs. His shadow fell on the steps before him. All was quiet. He held the camera tightly in his hands as he turned the corner of the stairwell. Almost at the landing now, he saw the double doors of the girls' bedroom slam together and then swing, the two pieces of wood clapping against each other until they came to a rest. Next to their bedroom, light seeped through the gaps under the closed doors of the prayer room – old doors with decorated glass. Hassan brought his foot down onto the landing. One of the bedroom doors opened. Maryam stepped out. He jumped.

'Got you.' She was right in front of him with a camera to her face.

'Maryam Bibi.'

'Shh.' She brought the camera down without pressing and pointed to the other set of doors.

They went into a room soaked with incense. Zain, Amina, and Maryam were sitting on the carpets. Begum Saab flapped her hand and gave him a nod, keeping her eyes on the book she held. He stayed at the door. Her large reading glasses were perched on the tip of her nose. She licked her finger and turned the book's yellowing pages. The thread barely held the sheets together anymore.

She began to sing. Quiet sounds. Throaty notes. Her voice had to be warming up. A train of words fell out of her mouth to form a melody that was painful. Begum Saab was singing high notes and low ones in some kind of tune.

He looked around. Zain rubbed his forehead. Amina rolled her eyes. Maryam hugged her knees to her chest. She looked ready to bury her head behind her knees but she beckoned to Hassan with her hand, looking at the space next to her. Instead, he shut the door and sat down in front of it with his legs folded, ready for a picture.

So, this was a family gathering. To Hassan it was beautiful. The glow of candlelight made it even more magical. His body relaxed for the first time since arriving in Karachi and he let go of the camera to let it rest on his lap. He knew he had to be very careful because all of this could fall apart at any time, destroyed with just a few wrong words about his father.

And then he caught Maryam looking up at him, a sideways look.

He took hold of the camera again, lifting it to his eyes and pointing it in her direction, and pressed.

Chapter Eleven

The next morning, servants rushed in and out of the main house, propelled by Begum Saab's orders. Around mid-morning, Hassan entered the dining room with the camera hanging from its strap around his neck and found Amina and Zain sitting at the table with school books. A man, who must have been their tutor, sat with them.

'Will you join us, Hassan?' Zain asked, but Hassan backed up, out of the room. He lifted up the camera and took a picture. He bashed his heel on the door frame and disappeared back into the hallway to the sound of giggles.

He went back up to the long balcony outside his room. Water splashed and then stopped; he peered over the wall. Ali Noor was at the tap below near the steps; his children were playing on the swings and they waved at him. They, like him, were being sponsored by Mir Saab. The mir was supporting them all, even the beekeeper that he had not found.

He wanted to see the bees again. He walked to the top of the steps by the balcony and then stopped and went back down. There was still too much to think about and understand: the language of the bees, he had used it and they had understood; his knowledge that Mir Saab had talked about; the secret knowledge that Baba wanted to hold; the bees' knowledge...

A door opened and shut. Kulsoom came out of her room a few doors down and stood by the balcony wall. He stepped back into the door frame of his room and watched as she adjusted her dupatta around her shoulders. The sun fell on her bare arms and head, making her skin and hair glow. The camera was at his eyes now. His finger froze. Through the camera lens, the movements of her head and arms were tiny but they didn't stop. She touched her face, wrung her hands, and moved her head, looking down at the courtyard as if searching for something or someone. After a minute or so, she turned and walked away and down the steps at the other end of the balcony.

Dinner was still a few hours away and he thought if he went down to the house he might be able to catch her now. She was in the hallway, standing beside a woman who was thrashing a broom in corners of the room to beat the cobwebs. They both had their backs to him.

'They're putting up the tent in Harikaya,' the woman told Kulsoom.

'Is it big?' Kulsoom asked.

'Yes, and people from other villages are coming too for the gatherings.'

They were eleven days into the month of Sha'ban now. In the new calendar, September would begin in three days. He pictured the tent with the people flowing all around, doing what they always did, whatever that was with their songs and gatherings. He always stayed away from them, preferring to walk around Harikaya, leave the track and run along the river banks. He did that every year as the water rose slowly at first and then more steadily when the rains were in full force. That's when his father used to disappear for his travels.

'The tent will still be up when I get there for Eid,' Kulsoom said.

'Mir Saab says it's important to remember the ancestors just before Ramadan too, not only at Moharram. He says it brings us together more,' said the other woman. 'Mir Saab's a good man.' She started making her way towards the stairs, thrashing her broom across the floor in time to her steps and singing to herself.

Big crowds would make it easier for him to slip away to the jungle. He stepped forward, trembling, 'I want to go back now. I've done what I needed to do. I've met Mir Saab.' Kulsoom turned around, surprised to see him.

'You're starting school here in Karachi.'

'I can come back before then.'

'Why?' She pretended to laugh.

'You know why.'

Kulsoom looked towards the woman. 'He's a good boy. He misses his mother.' She turned back to Hassan. 'We'll visit her for Eid.'

'That's in two months.'

Hassan was losing his balance. The woman carried on thrashing the floor with her broom.

Kulsoom came closer to him. 'You're doing so well here. I don't know how you've done it but you're even joining them for meals.' Her voice was low and her breathing shallow. 'Don't spoil things.'

Raisin eyes were upon him, only a few inches away from his face. He was picking up the smell of camphor perfume mixed with the sweat from her clothes. They sold small bottles of camphor at the shrine, pretending it was blessed. She had to be pretending too. The song from the woman on the stairs continued. Hassan stood firm. Even if Kulsoom always won with his mother, she would not win with him.

'I need to go back for the black honey.'

Her face was tight and serious. Her warm breath carried the taste of chai.

'You're just like your father, charming your way into families.' She stepped back again. 'He always got what he wanted. He played people well.'

There was a distant look in her eyes, some memory that she resented. 'But forget his foolish dreams. They're dangerous.'

Before he could think of a reply, she said, 'Your mother and I have never been lucky with our men.' The skin on her face creased into fine lines and she walked away.

He hated her at that moment.

Outside again, the air was thick, and not enough. He needed air and wind and space. The sun beat down on his body, dripping with sweat; he had to shade his eyes with his hands. The gates were open and the guards were hot and drowsy in the shade of the wall. They only glanced in his direction. He followed the same path through the shrubs around the wall, grateful for the shade of the trees. Past the forgotten swimming pool and the ghosts of Maryam's stories that made him feel better for a second, but he didn't stop until he was at the edge of the clearing.

He could hear only the sound of crows. They were watching from the trees at the edges of the clearing. He stopped in the middle. His clothes were soaked with sweat, but he stayed where he was because it was there again: the smell of wax and honey and the face of the beekeeper.

He climbed the steps. The doors of the masjid were heavy but they opened with ease. Light fell from behind him onto the floor of a small chamber with six pillars, positioned in each of the corners. Air came through openings that lined the tops of the walls under the dome. It was a six-sided cave, a honeybee cell for a human.

The sound of humming reached him. He closed the door and walked into the darkness to a pillar on the other side. The volume of the humming changed: a human body was in their space. His body. The sound peaked, the bees' interest steady and clear.

The pillar was a support for his back until his eyes could see outlines and then more. Six openings were at the top of each of the six walls, and above the walls was a ledge. The dome rested on the ledge and rose up to a small, flat hexagon at its highest point. The tiles on the walls and pillars were positioned like spirals, round and round, smaller and smaller to simulate the effect of being inside a cone. They rose up the wall in waves to meet at the top of the dome at the central hexagon. Was this like the inside of a hive?

The sound of humming became low and steady, softening his body. Then he found it, the source of the sound: a lump, a nest, hanging from the curve above the ledge. Bits of wax combs glowed amber behind a thick coating of bees. The walls of the combs grew down in soft, endless waves, like upside-down mountains.

The whole mass of bees came into focus. A few bees hovered a little way from the nest while a few more broke away. All around the nest was a mass of steady activity. Bees came into the space through the openings; they were workers returning home, some of them loaded with nectar. Baba had said that was for feeding the young and building the comb. Sound reached down and wrapped his body in an invisible blanket.

And then the picture changed again, blurring into a black blob. Seconds, minutes, perhaps even hours passed as the sight and sound of bees held him tight in this ebb and flow between one big mass and the separate bees. Their humming, its highs and lows, was the switch; the bees had full control over what he saw of them.

This was a temple of sound, the humming rose now, spiralling upwards along the walls. It swept down towards him, then it was inside him. This chamber was an extension of their nest. The humming vibrated in his head, in his arms, in his torso and legs. His eyes closed under the weight of the sound and he had a vision of wax cells, stacked around him with an overall order and symmetry – unending rows of cells. Could it be that he was actually in their nest? The humming was deafening, closer, as if he was one amongst a thousand bees. He became part of their world, and, even though he could not see them, they had to be here.

Then it happened. A feeling stronger than any words could have prepared him for. Joy. A flash of light lasted for less than a second but it was long enough for him to see the cells, and they were all gold. Shining gold joy, and he was part of it. Some of the cells were closed and some open.

But there was no time to think, to doubt, or to ask. He wanted to go further but an invisible force stopped him, blocking any movement. The humming grew quiet; a growled warning shot past him. Its sound alone was enough to block his way, and it was stronger than any wall.

He opened his eyes and the chamber came back into focus. Light poured in from the openings in the dome and the bees were humming above in the nest.

But just the memory of the inside of the nest was enough. For now. Hassan's loneliness gave way to a deep, spacious stillness. That golden fluid power that he had been allowed to see and hear was part of a truth greater than him, greater than anything he had heard or thought of before.

He might have been with the bees for hours, but outside again, the sun hadn't moved much. Its light was like fire and he ran into the shade of the trees and stopped in front of one with large roots like the toes of giant elephants. He settled himself in between two of these roots and spread his arms on each one of them as if he were on one of Mir Saab's armchairs.

He had just been inside their inner world. They had shown him what was happening in there. Baba had told him that eggs grew inside those closed hexagonal cells. The queen laid them. Baba's poem came back to him.

Workers, drones, and queen.
Time in the cave was different for each.
Time obeyed the law of numbers.
Twenty-one days for workers, twenty-four for drones,
and sixteen for the queen.
Workers, drones, and queen.

The caves were their cells. The number of days for each was the time it took for the workers, drones and the queen to emerge.

Baba seemed closer now after what had just happened. Kulsoom was wrong about him. There had been good times before his father left – his father dancing in colourful clothes, beating the drum, reciting his poetry. He had made music from ordinary objects he picked up, even the clay bowls that children played with. Baba had made an instrument for Hassan out of a pumpkin once. He had attached it to a wooden rod with two strings made of steel and played a soft tune with words from one of his poems. Amma had listened when Baba played that tune. That instrument was gone now, but there was no time to think about that. The world of the bees and their light had been a brief taste. He wanted more.

Hassan went to pick up the water for dinner.

'It's good you're becoming friends with the family,' the cook said. 'Just be careful.'

What was he trying to say with that? Hassan went to fetch a jug from the shelf, reaching out to it with both hands.

'You'll never be one of them.'

'I don't want to be.'

The cook put down the knife in his hand; its metal blade was coated with wet green leaves. Coriander. The smell was sweet.

'Your father had a strong character, just like you.'

Hassan stayed where he was. This man did know his father.

'Once he made a decision, there was no going back,' the cook said.

Hassan could lose nothing by listening.

'He was taken from you too soon, wasn't he?'

'He's coming back.' Hassan bit his lip but stayed still.

'He was a good man. Wouldn't hurt anyone.'

'Were you friends?'

'Yes, I told you that.' The cook looked hurt. He picked up a wooden spoon and dipped it into the pot and stirred. 'What are you hoping for, then, from the family?' he asked, still leaning over the steaming curry.

'Nothing.'

'Come on. No need to hide anything from me.' The cook smiled as if he had been saving something special for Hassan. 'I heard that your father was sighted.'

Hassan froze.

'Who did you hear that from?'

'No one.'

Hassan shrugged, just as he'd seen villagers do when they talked about the dry weather or the smelly sewers. 'Oh well,' he said. 'What can we do?'

'You know, I can help you.'

'To do what?'

'Look, you want to get back to Harikaya. You said it yourself.'

'So?'

'The rains haven't started yet.'

'How do you know?'

'I had word from the village. I asked someone to send me a telegram. You have a little time.'

'Why did you do that?'

'Just like your father. Always suspicious.' The cook tapped the wooden spoon on the sides of the metal pan. The sound was sharp. 'There are plenty of ways to make money. Pay for your ticket back.'

'I'm not interested.' Hassan stayed where he was with the jug in his hands.

The cook put the spoon down and faced Hassan, 'Do you want to make a deal?'

The cook was almost friendly now, softer. Hassan backed away.

'I can arrange your trip back to Harikaya if you do something for me, a small errand.'

'No, thank you.'

'Nothing hard. Just give me information about what you see when you're with Mir Saab. It'll be easy. They like you.'

'No.'

'It'll be easy. Just tell me what he says. What he likes, or doesn't like. What views he has.'

'Why?'

'You're a curious one, aren't you? Don't worry about that. Look, think about it. If you help me, I'll help you. Our kind, we need to survive. What else do you have?'

It was difficult to get through the heavy door flaps with the jug and glasses on the tray.

The cook was there before Hassan could turn around. He held one of the flaps open for him. 'Let me help you,' he said.

Hassan slipped backwards through the door.

That calmness from the temple was gone now and Hassan wanted it back. He did want something from the family but it was not what the cook thought. The tray rattled in his hands. If helping the cook was the only way to save his mother's eyes, then what else was there to do? The door of the living room was closed. Footsteps and voices entered the hall; it was Maryam.

'I'm curious about you,' she said, opening the door for him.

'Don't be.' He stopped himself.

'What are you thinking about?' Maryam walked around him, almost skipping, 'Don't tell me, I'll guess.'

He waited for her to guess his thoughts. That he was wasting his time here, that she would go back to London and everything would continue just as it always did for her. That Amina and Zain would forget about him as soon as she was gone. That Mir Saab had sent the guards and he could never forgive him.

'Are you thinking about the bees?'

He made a slight nod.

'Told you I could read minds,' she laughed. 'Come on.'

Her words irritated him. He was tired of all this pretending. He left the tray on the smaller dining table in the living room and they walked towards the voices.

The study was filled with activity. Amina and Zain sat on the chairs, reading. Two young women sat on the floor. They were from the village and talked to each other in Sindhi. Around them must have been ten reels of film. One of the women was holding her hands up, her fingers looping the thin, plastic film that the other one was winding onto a reel. They finished off and started to pile the reels into boxes.

'Everyone, come and sit on the carpet.' Mir Saab pulled down the screen in front of the shutters. I'll switch the projector on,' he said.

The machine rattled and chugged. The silhouette of the golden hive rose onto the screen in the bottom right corner. The reel on one side of the projector began to spin, its film flowing onto the empty ring. The film started.

Harikaya. The fort from below, the view from the winding road leading up to the fort. The village wall, the well. An old film in black and white with no sound; Hassan didn't want it to end.

From the top of the hill, the camera swept across the landscape to the shrine, standing alone at the beginning of the flatlands, and then to the factories.

'My father was the cameraman,' Mir Saab said.

A new scene with trees and gardens that went on forever in the background. The camera zoomed in to focus on a box. No, a clay pot, like one used by the villagers for water with a hole in its lid. There was nothing for seconds until a bee crawled out of the hole onto the lid. Another one joined it. Two or three more moved out, and then back in. A hand lifted the lid, a strong hand with veins that stood out, and the camera moved back to show the rest of the body and the face of the man.

'Is that the old beekeeper?' Maryam asked.

Even with the camera on him, his face remained still and stern, the way Hassan remembered this man's son.

'Yes, he brought the bees for my birthday,' Mir Saab said.

'Where was his son?' Hassan asked.

'In the forests. He never left. He was always busy with the bees,' Mir Saab said, 'and climbing trees.'

The camera moved forwards, looking down onto the swarm of bees.

'That colony moved to an arch in the fort,' Mir Saab said. 'I wish I had a film of that.'

The door flew open; it was Begum Saab. 'Amina, Zain—' Her words stopped in mid-air as her eyes landed on the two women on the floor with boxes around them and reels of film still in their hands. Begum Saab looked like she had just lost at cricket and she didn't like it.

'The tutor. Five minutes,' she said. A shadow crossed her face as she glanced at Mir Saab and left.

Hassan saw the silhouette of the golden hive on the screen as it shot up again.

'There are far fewer of those black bees left today than there were twenty years ago,' Mir Saab said.

'Even the rains are coming at different times of the year.' Hassan remembered his father's words.

'You've noticed that, have you?'

Hassan shrugged. 'It's hard not to.'

Mir Saab sat down on the chair and picked up his pencil. Soon, he was lost with his back to them. He had drawings of nests and tree tops in his hands and he was speaking to himself, 'That's where I'll find it.'

'Look what I've found,' Maryam said, putting her hand on Hassan's wrist.

His whole body stiffened. She had a large book in her hands with a bee on its front cover. The picture was blown up, larger than his hand and the bee's glossy oval-shaped eyes on either side of its head stared at him. The three small middle eyes were like tiny black hills in a forest of hair at the top of its head.

On the first page was the queen with a long yellow and black body, lined with fine hair. What would it be like to be touched by those hairs? The antennae were long, and poked out of either side of her head. Her wings were drawn close to her abdomen. Everything about this creature was perfection.

'The female workers are smaller than the male drones,' Maryam said.

She turned the page. A man was climbing a tree with his bare hands.

'That's what my father did,' Hassan said.

'I'm curious about that,' she said. 'Was he a beekeeper?'

'No, but he went—' Hassan bit his lip. He needed to find a

way out of this. 'Mir Saab, are Pakistani bees the same as English bees?' he asked.

'Pakistani bees are different from all the rest. They're the "in-betweeners".' Mir Saab spoke without turning around.

Hassan wanted to ask him what he meant but Maryam was quicker. 'In between what?'

'East and West,' Mir Saab said. 'But the black honeybees, or *Apis dorsata,* they're unique and quite rare.' He picked up the picture he had been studying. 'About two centimetres long and ferocious, but with good reason.'

'Why?' Hassan asked.

'To guard their honey. It's said to be very healing, and hard to get.' Mir Saab's lips sank as if he had a bad taste in his mouth. 'There was someone only a short while ago. A honey hunter who caused a fire.'

'He wasn't a honey—' Hassan caught his breath. He glanced at Maryam; he had slipped again.

'What happened to that honey hunter?' she asked.

'I don't know,' Mir Saab said, scratching his chin.

'Hassan, what's wrong?' Maryam said. 'Are you worried?'

'It's nothing, Bibi,' he said. 'I was just thinking about the forests. They must be beautiful.'

'That's why I keep the people out,' Mir Saab said, 'for the sake of the animals.'

Or was it to keep the black honey to himself? Hassan bit his lip. He stopped himself from clenching his fists. These people had no idea. Mir Saab created a law without thinking about the rights of the villagers.

'And to keep the jinn out,' Zain said, getting up. 'Come on, Amina.'

'The jinn?' Mir Saab laughed. 'That's what the villagers think.'

'I don't think that,' Hassan said, his voice quiet.

'I think we have some in the house,' Zain said at the door before they left.

'Nonsense,' Mir Saab said. He turned to Hassan. 'And your father. He was a poet?'

'Yes.'

'So, he understands the laws of nature.'

What did Mir Saab mean by this? It had to be some kind of trick.

'Where is he now?'

'He left Harikaya.'

'Why?

'To visit friends in another town.'

Mir Saab turned back to the drawings and picked up his pencil. Maryam went to stand by him, her elbow on the desk and her head in one hand. She sifted through them with her other hand, her thick curls falling around her shoulders in no order. 'That's the beekeeper's father.' She held up the picture – a drawing in pencil of his face and neck. 'If his son is still in the forest, that would make him...'

Mir Saab lifted his head.

'The last beekeeper,' she said.

'Do you think he's still alive?' Hassan asked. He had to find out what Mir Saab knew.

'Baba never found him,' Zain said.

'That doesn't mean he's not there,' Mir Saab said. 'I found his house again a while ago.'

'Where?' Zain asked.

'Deep in the forests. Very different to when his father was alive.'

'What does it look like?' Hassan asked.

Mir Saab shook his head; that treasure was not for sharing.

'That means he's alive,' Maryam said.

A glimmer of hope flew through the air. Hassan caught it for a second before that hope hardened into something quieter and infinitely strong. Mir Saab moved to the desk and smoothed his fingers over the sides of the frame.

Chapter Twelve

'Zain, stop it,' Amina said to her brother as all four of them sat on the floor around the board. It was noon and Hassan's third day in Karachi.

Zain had written words in each corner of the board and placed a glass at the centre. They were here to test Zain's theory that the upper floors were haunted by jinn, but Hassan was more than just curious. To the others it was a game, at best an adventure. To Hassan, this was dangerous, but it was too late to go back.

They were in one of the many upstairs rooms that had been empty of human life for too long. Hassan thought of all the invisible stories from before Mir Saab's family had lived here. Were the characters of these stories walking between the furniture draped in sheets that had aged like old teeth?

'Stop what?' Zain asked.

'Stop moving the glass.'

Hassan blinked; the glass was trembling, almost alive.

'I'm doing nothing,' Zain said, waving his hands in the air and bringing them down again in a second.

The glass wanted to move; Hassan could feel it. The room felt cooler but the air was changing. And so was the light.

'Come out if you dare,' Zain said, looking around the room.

Maryam giggled. Amina frowned.

'A jinn only comes out at night.'

'How do you know that?' Zain asked.

'I feel cold,' Maryam said.

The shutters of one of the windows began opening and closing. A light breeze touched Hassan's face. The banging continued, becoming louder until the shutters clapped for a final time before they shut.

'Let's go,' Amina said.

'Yes, we've seen it move now,' Maryam said.

'The glass has not moved yet.' Zain sounded calm, but he looked scared.

'What if the jinn doesn't want to be disturbed?' Maryam asked.

The sound of heavy rain outside made them all go quiet; the sky darkened behind the mosquito netting and there was a clap of thunder.

'Now look what you've done to the weather,' Amina said. She was about to stand up.

The changes in the weather, the breeze, and the darkness were too quick. The thunder crashed a second time; the lightbulb swung and the room darkened. They were all too scared to speak now. There was another burst of thunder and the glass swept across the board to Hassan's corner.

'That wasn't funny, Zain,' Maryam said.

Zain's mouth was wide open.

'Stop it, Zain.' Amina smashed her hand down on the board, making the glass jump.

Zain held his hands up but it happened again. This time the glass moved back to the middle of the board in a smooth sweep.

'If you're not doing anything, what's moving the glass?' Amina whispered. Her face looked like the sheet behind her. They all stared at the glass. Zain's fists were clenched, as if he was holding onto all his courage.

'Somebody, ask a question,' Maryam said.

Zain brought his mouth close to the glass and said with a loud voice, 'Left for yes, right for no, and shake for don't know.'

The glass moved to the left slightly and Zain nearly fell back.

'I'm not asking a question,' Amina said.

It had to be a joke, one done very well by one of them, but there was a small flame growing inside Hassan. If it were a jinn here with them, it may know things. The flame burst into a fire. Hassan wanted answers.

'Where is Baba?' he asked.

Nothing. The glass shuddered. That was a shudder. Everyone was silent. He carried on, his throat burning.

'How is Amma?'

The glass moved a few centimetres to the left. Everyone gasped, including Hassan.

'Is Amma managing without me?'

It moved more to the left. Nobody moved this time.

'Are her eyes still all right?'

This time to the right. The floor under him shook. Hassan swayed.

'Where is the beekeeper?'

The glass shuddered.

'Will the beekeeper help me?' His hand was on his mouth and his voice came out muffled.

All heads turned to him but only for a second before the glass moved again, neither left nor right, but with a full sweep straight off the board. It landed on the marble floor and crashed into pieces.

The shutters clapped; they were laughing at them.

'There's a jinn in here,' Zain said, his voice trembling and high.

Everyone stumbled to the door as if there were no oxygen left in the room. Out on the landing, one of them started screaming and the others joined in. They carried on screaming down the stairwell, one behind the other until they went through the front door to the outside world again.

Amina nudged Maryam with her elbow. 'Everything's dry,' she said.

They all panted in the sunlight until Amina and Zain walked over to the swings by the wall.

'How did you do that, Hassan?' Maryam asked. She looked frightened.

'I'm sure one of us moved it,' Hassan said.

'I don't think so.'

'Maybe I did move it.'

'Maybe you did it with your mind?'

He laughed.

'What about your mother?' She came closer to him. 'And your father?'

'They...'

A shadow spread over them.

'Hassan, give this to Begum Saab. In the living room,' Kulsoom snapped.

'Later,' Maryam said as she left. A tiny smile broke out from behind her eyes at first and then it spread to her lips.

Just before the front door of the house, he stopped at a puddle. It had rained. It had really rained. His feet itched to run back, to find Kulsoom, to demand that she give him his ID card, buy him a ticket now, tell her that she was blocking his way, but he held back.

The clouds in the marble on the living-room floor slowed Hassan's thoughts down. He didn't believe in jinns. But the answers. The glass. All correct. Yet he still didn't believe. The shapes turned into bees; silent, caught in mid-air. Even if he wanted to give the cook any information about Mir Saab, what was there to say? He could feed him scraps. That could be the answer to everything. Just give the cook enough to get him to buy him a train ticket, a return, from Harikaya to Karachi. He wouldn't be hurting anyone that way. A stone scratched the skin under his heel and he tipped his foot upwards. The stone rolled under his toes. He shook the front of his sandal side to side until the stone was under his big toe. He pressed. It hurt.

'This is about the Prime Minister and you. Go and talk to him at the wedding.' Begum Saab's voice was urgent. 'It could save our cotton factories.'

The door was open.

'In the wrong hands, those factories...' Mir Saab stopped.

'He might block the bill if you talk,' Begum Saab said. 'He'll be in a good mood at his own child's wedding.'

The piece of paper slipped out of Hassan's hand and floated to the ground.

'He wouldn't dare nationalise the factories,' Mir Saab said, 'but he's done it to so many businesses – nationalised them and then neglected them. Flops, all of them.'

'You might change his mind. You've known him for years.'

'That's precisely the problem.' Mir Saab's voice carried sadness. 'Sibling rivalry...'

Hassan didn't hear the rest. Begum Saab came into the living room.

'Oh, you're here,' she said.

Hassan bent down to pick up the piece of paper and held it out. Begum Saab took it and hurried away.

Hassan waited at the door before Mir Saab glanced at him and nodded. He approached the desk where Mir Saab stood before the golden egg, looking at it as if it could give him answers to some urgent question. His hands moved fast to open a wooden box with a small key, as though he were running out of time. 'Everything is governed by a pattern of numbers that allows life to unfold,' he said.

Mir Saab lifted a golden stick out of the box and held it to the window. A ray of light fell on it. He took another stick and attached it to the first – a ball and socket. 'I had these made in Harikaya. Wooden sticks painted with gold paint,' he said. He cleared the papers to the side and placed more sticks flat on the surface of the desk.

'What is this pattern of numbers, Mir Saab?'

'It's a code that makes shapes happen the way they do. It's a law of nature that makes forms unfold with symmetry and balance.' He took another and did the same thing. A few more sticks and he'd made a flat hexagon.

'Now for the tricky part.' He continued, building on the hexagon with six sticks pointing upwards. 'The bees use the most space-saving shape to build the cells.' He then joined these six vertical sticks together with flat sticks to make a hexagonal unit on top. He placed it next to the large egg structure, and Hassan saw that it was made of at least fifty of these smaller units.

'Building bricks,' he said. 'Structures obey the code by building up these single units into different forms.'

'An instruction?'

'Yes, an incredibly simple one. It's a ratio that governs everything. From the whole to the large…'

'And from the large to the small,' Hassan said. This was the first time he had seen Mir Saab smile.

Mir Saab opened another drawer and brought out more drawings. Spirals, shells, hexagons, a honeycomb. 'Magic and mystery. That's what the world is built on,' he said. 'Everything is connected by numbers.'

Mir Saab picked up a black spiralling stone from his desk. 'Look at this fossil.'

He held it out to Hassan. It was heavy.

'It curls like so many forms in the world, unfolding under the same code that instructs the positions of petals on a flower, the shape of a wave, the turning of spirals, the formation of shells, or the branches of trees.'

'A honeycomb,' Hassan said.

'Yes, the honeycomb.' Mir Saab narrowed his eyes at the large hexagonal egg. 'I had a chance to be with the bees and I gave it up.' He put his hand lightly on the egg. 'They never allowed me into their world again.'

'But they did they allow you into their world once, Mir Saab?' Hassan asked.

But Mir Saab only sighed and, as if he'd suddenly forgotten that Hassan was there, he walked away through the far door. Hassan stayed by the desk. He looked at the hexagonal egg and then at Mir Saab's drawings. The code had to be connected to the knowledge that his father had spoken about, the knowledge that the bees had taken back to the earth. Mir Saab and Hassan's father loved the same thing.

It was hard to walk away from the structure but he did, and he went through to the living room. He stopped in the middle of the floor. A ball of paper lay, abandoned, under the sofa. He saw Mir Saab's crumpled ink marks. It was easy to reach and he opened it up to see a sketch of a large wooden sailing boat. It was beautiful. Would Mir Saab let him have it? He'd ask him later. In the meantime, he'd look after it. He folded the sheet of paper into quarters and then again until it got smaller and smaller and his hand closed around it.

Out in the empty courtyard, he put the drawing in his waistcoat pocket and took his sandal off. A stone fell out onto his palm, small and sharp, and he let it drop at the gates. He put the sandal back on and walked past the guards who ignored him now that he wasn't with Maryam. He turned the corner and stood in a patch of shade by the wall. Everything was calm here, away from the world. He walked through the forest and was at the clearing again at last; the ageing masjid stood against the sun. He leapt up the steps and opened one of the doors. The sound of humming was around him like a dancing rush of wind. He closed the door and walked to the middle of the floor.

A bee flew towards him and hovered in front of him. It came closer to his chest; his fingers moved to brush it away but he stopped. He let it explore his presence and it stayed with him until he moved and sat down by the same pillar as before. Another bee came to him – on his skin this time; it crawled along his forehead, over his hair and onto his neck. Its humming was growing louder and Hassan's body tensed but it flew away. He leant back against the pillar. He wanted to be there again, to travel to their inner world. Bees came and went but nothing happened. Stillness, that was what he needed – the stillness again. Had Mir Saab got this far too? The bees had to give him more. The longer he sat, the easier it became to ignore the cold, hard floor under him.

The activity of the nest was steady. Workers buzzed through the holes in the walls, in and out. The male drones were too busy falling in love with the promise of the queen. That was what his father had said: drones and workers lived very different lives, just like the men and women in Harikaya. His father had written a poem about them. What were the words? *All of us, part of the same jigsaw, some pieces faded and overused.* Nothing was different here. Everyone was part of a jigsaw, even Mir Saab. Maryam, though, was different. Or was she? He couldn't be sure.

Up there was a big hanging heart, a single organ made up of thousands of bees. Humming floated out towards him, joining with his own breathing. In and out. The bees belonged to their colony; loyalty and duty was their nature, each bee having a part to play. Hassan had never been part of anything but now he ached to merge with the whole, to be another unit in their world. His breath moved in and out. Their sound, his chest, became one. In and out.

Humming soothed his whole body, wrapping around every part of it. There was no more trying. The humming wrapped around his own heartbeat and pulled him deeper. Pulsations of sound became his guide as he sank deeper into a vast darkness. And then, with no warning, he began to hurtle through a tunnel of light and dark. Objects were flung to the sides of his path until he finally stopped.

Stillness was held together by some distant murmur of life. Short and long tones rang from near and far and made up some kind of background language. It was the call of the bees.

Two or three dark spots approached, turning into blobs of light. They grew bigger, were about to engulf him, but then vanished leaving just a flutter in the air, the memory of a wing. Then there came the beating flurry of more wings.

A light began to flicker in the distance; it sent joy out to him as if some distant star had finally reached him, an ancient star that was still alive. The joy had a distinct scent. Whispered words came into his mind: *The queen…* It was the scent of her; a beautiful scent from deep within the hive.

It was as if a switch was turned off too soon and he was back in the world again, breathing hard, his throat dry and his lungs tired, as though he had been fished out of water onto a stone floor. He wanted to be there again, to stay longer. He fell to the ground, lying for several minutes in the memory of their world, his body numb.

That light, the source of the joy, was the home of the queen. How could he reach her? Blood flowed around his body again and he moved his legs. He let out a laugh. He had no control in their world. They brought him in, showed him what they wanted and then let him go. Baba had talked about their love. He had said that to win their trust, he had to equal their love, to balance it with his own for them. Was it the bees that had stopped him going further? Or perhaps he did not have enough of this love to give them. The floor felt colder, hard. Perhaps he would never have enough.

He bolted the door and started to walk back.

In his room again, he took out the honeycomb. It spoke in pictures: the beekeeper, the jungle, the forests of Harikaya, a moon disappearing behind rain clouds above tree tops, the beekeeper calling. Yes, he was calling; the beekeeper was waiting. The call was a slow song from a clearing, deep in the forest. It would be his homecoming.

Days of drifting around without his father and trying to forget were coming to an end. His will had stirred and was waking up. It was the same will that had carried him and his father to the forest in the first place. It was the same will that drove his father to find the bees again and again.

There would be no hesitation when he reached the forest.

It was all so clear now.

When he found the beekeeper, he would also find himself.

Chapter Thirteen

The humming was still echoing in Hassan's ears, like a steady rumbling. It was nearly dinner time. Servants walked around the courtyard, their day coming to an end before the evening meal. The guards chatted at the gate.

'Where have you been?' It was Maryam. 'Did you go again?'

The humming suddenly vanished and he nodded.

'Did anything happen?' she asked, coming closer, her voice lower, her eyes searching his for answers. 'Can we go together?'

'Not now, the guards.' Hassan turned to the gate.

'But last time...' Maryam said, tilting her head.

'Last time, we went with Amina and Zain. Pakistan is different. People talk.'

'But we're friends...'

His heart raced. Her words were kind – more than kind.

They were true, but standing in the middle of the courtyard, just the two of them, was drawing more glances.

'It's not so simple. I'm a...' The word *villager* stuck in his throat.

'Come inside,' Maryam said. 'To the study.' She went ahead.

It was different in there. It was another world, the world he wanted. Maryam had already taken out the book on bees from last time. She was turning the pages and he came to stand next to her. The warmth of her body touched him even though they were a few inches apart. She stopped at a photo of a honeybee swarm leaping into the sky from a row of hive boxes. In the picture, a line of female beekeepers stood by the boxes, all with their faces hidden under dark nets that hung from their wide-brimmed hats.

'That'll be you one day,' she said.

'I'm not sure,' he said.

She turned to him. 'Why not?'

'I'm going to school, and then...'

Zain and Amina came in and, without a word, came to stand by Maryam to look at the open book. At the same time, the back door opened. Mir Saab entered and said, 'I have to write that reply now or I'll never do it. The wedding's tomorrow.' He reached out for a steel ink pen. 'Two blackbucks, the symbol of Harikaya,' he said, pointing to the top of the letterhead paper. 'They'll protect us against the government's intentions. The factories will remain mine.'

The dead deer by the train tracks... Its wounded flesh, the skin, the lifeless head framed by cigarette butts...

That was the image in Hassan's head.

Mir Saab's metal pen clinked as he laid it down on the table and the dead deer vanished.

'That's that,' Mir Saab said, tossing the card to one side. 'They'll get this before the wedding.' The dark shadow on his face disappeared as he stood again, pursing his lips and scratching his chin. He took the large roll of paper lying on the table, unfastened the ribbon that held it, and stretched it out on the table, shuffling some weights onto each corner. 'I have it,' he said, picking up the sheet. He turned to the children and waved them nearer. 'I know what the boat needs.'

Mir Saab added lines to the huge sailing boat, making the sails bigger. 'This boat may be our only choice one day if the machine they're running on grows too big,' he said.

'Who's running on?' Hassan asked.

'The government.'

'What machine?' Hassan asked.

'Political greed. It eats up everything around it: people, land, livelihoods. The weather too.' Mir Saab looked at his drawing, bringing the sheet closer to his face. 'I've had this dream for a long time.'

'How long?' Maryam asked.

'Ever since I had to make a choice between them waging war on me or me handing them my sovereignty of the state of Harikaya.'

'Why did they want you to do that?' Maryam asked.

The shadow came back over Mir Saab's face. 'So that it would become part of the new country, Pakistan. They argued for the cause of unity.' He swallowed. 'I wanted to believe them but they cornered me well and truly.' He sighed and looked up. 'It's a long story. The first government was fine –

good intentions and all that. The second was all right. After that, things changed. The third government told me it could be two ways. A peaceful takeover or a violent one.' Mir Saab frowned. 'It was nineteen fifty-three. The partition had happened a few years earlier. Six, to be precise. And the population of this new country was growing. The folk were traumatised. I'm not blaming anyone. During the split into two countries, there were huge casualties on both sides.'

Mir Saab put down his pencil.

'People who had once lived side by side with their differences suddenly called each other enemies. They had to move from their homes and rebuild their lives. Many of them suffered so much.' He hung his head. 'Much too much. When the second government decided to make Harikaya part of Pakistan, the new land, and not a separate state as it had been for hundreds of years, they threatened me with war if I didn't agree. I could not fight back.' He pursed his lips. 'The people had gone through enough.'

'So, you gave them what they wanted,' Maryam said.

Mir Saab looked relieved that someone else had said those words. 'I had to believe in the goodness of some of the original sentiments that were behind the birth of this nation. They promised to pay for the upkeep of the fort and the village services in exchange for my loyalty.'

'You had no choice, Baba,' Amina said.

'In truth they wanted total power. They haven't kept their promises as they should have done. They say money is scarce but they live in opulence.'

Everyone fell silent. Hassan pictured the factories if the government got control – quiet, lonely. His mother's job could vanish because of the whim of a Prime Minister. More and more people would be coming to Karachi to work in the factories and the tiny shops he had seen on the way from the airport. Those would be the lucky ones. They wouldn't have the protection of a home like this. Hassan shuddered. He looked towards Mir Saab again. His eyes were wide. He seemed to be somewhere far away.

'I suppose nothing lasts forever,' Mir Saab said.

'Why a boat?' This was Hassan.

'Things are so uncertain. The population is growing too fast. The pollution in the air and soil is destroying life. The trees are being felled to make way for more people. The weather is changing. I'm worried the floods will become out of control.' Mir Saab started to shade in a corner of the boat.

Something rustled. No one else noticed. Only Hassan turned. Someone was behind the open door.

'I'll teach you all how to sail,' Mir Saab said.

'With the wind?' Amina asked.

'How else?' Zain asked.

'And when there's no wind, we'll float,' Maryam said.

The rustling was there again. It might be someone listening or it might be nothing; Hassan wanted to go and look. Was someone there, eavesdropping?

'There'll be room for animals too,' Mir Saab said.

'Hassan can look after the bees,' Maryam said.

'They'll help us find dry land,' Zain said.

Maryam clapped her hands.

'Yes, they'll send scouts out to search for land. They'll be led by the sun to the scent of the flowers,' Mir Saab said, 'and when they find them, they'll come back and dance.'

Just as Hassan was about to say something, he saw Kulsoom approaching the doorway, her hair falling out of her plait and shiny drops of water on her forehead.

'The estate manager,' she said, out of breath.

'Oh no, I'd forgotten,' Mir Saab replied.

The dream dissolved in front of Hassan's eyes and Mir Saab rolled up the sheets before departing to greet his visitor.

Hassan left the others in the study and went to look behind the door. There was no one there. No one in the hall either. The male voices from the drawing room became louder as Hassan approached, and he picked up words about the factories and the new bill.

'I don't understand.' That must have been the estate manager's voice, quiet and unsure. 'Why does the Prime Minister want your factories?'

'Because they're mine,' Mir Saab said. 'He's always hated me. I laughed at him in public a few years ago over a new law he brought in. He wanted to look more conservative, to make alcohol illegal. And yet he won't give up his whisky. Now he's stripping away the rights of minorities. Calling it religious purity. The new trend. Preposterous! All to please the conservatives, to get their vote. Very dangerous, I'd say. This country was built on tolerance. Anyway, I made him look small.'

'And now he's looking for opportunities to hurt you,' the estate manager said.

'They started by taking away the funding for the fort,' Mir Saab said. A glass came down on a table. 'And the fort's crumbling.'

'Talk with him at the wedding. You are going, Mir Saab, aren't you?'

'I'll go, but…' He paused and sighed, and it came out as a long, hard blow of air. 'For the sake of the people.'

Hassan turned around. He heard footsteps but the hall was empty. Had he imagined it? He listened for more. In the dining room perhaps? Nothing. He tiptoed to the entrance of the living room; nobody was around. No breathing and no echoes of tapping sandals.

Chapter Fourteen

The afternoon nap had been Begum Saab's idea. No, her order. It was better that way, and now he felt light, just in time for the wedding. Maryam had insisted he accompany them. The white cotton shirt and trousers embroidered at the edges in sky-blue thread were a little loose but so soft against his skin – a gift from Begum Saab. This was a different world, their world, Maryam's world, and he laughed. What would his mother say? Before he left his room, there was one last thing. He put on his waistcoat; it was old, but it was part of him.

On the balcony, Kulsoom's door was slightly open. If he asked her about returning to the village while he was wearing this suit, she might listen to him. He knocked but it was quiet. He went to the main house. Nobody else was around yet so he braved the kitchen; Kulsoom might be there. Nobody seemed to be inside, so he went through the flaps of the door. It was a mistake. The cook's thin back was bent over the counter at the other side. His shirt was stained with dark patches of sweat.

The cook threw him a dark look over his shoulder and turned round. He pulled out a cigarette and lit it. 'So?' he said.

'What?' asked Hassan, looking at the door flaps. It was too hot in here.

'Stop playing games. What do you have?'

'They don't speak much.' Hassan scratched the back of his head. He had to be strong.

'Neither do you,' the cook threw back at him.

'All right. I'll tell you something.'

'I knew you'd see sense. You're a true businessman like your father.'

'Mir Saab loves animals.'

The cook laughed. 'That's not enough for me to organise your trip back.'

'What more do you want from me?'

'What more do you have?'

'I told you what I have.'

'I'm watching you. You're walking a dangerous path.'

'What do you mean?' Hassan was well aware he had walked into the fire.

The cook came closer now and Hassan stiffened, keeping his arms pressed against his sides. Strength stirred in his legs and he found himself taking a step back. That taste was back in his mouth. Ink and oranges, like at the shrine.

'You've got the best job in the house.'

'I don't have a job.'

'You hear everything. You give me what I ask for, and I'll

make sure you get what you deserve. Enough for a quick trip back.'

The cook leant forwards.

'I want more,' the cook said, tilting his head,

A hot, sharp pain gripped the back of Hassan's neck as if someone was squeezing it, and he rocked back on his heels. 'No,' he said.

'Come on, kid, stop pretending you're one of them.'

'No.'

'Don't be a fool. You're using them too. I'm just more honest about it.'

'You're the fool,' Hassan said, edging towards the door.

The cook wobbled on one leg as he bent down and took off a sandal. 'Get out of here then.' He lunged forward, throwing the shoe at Hassan who jumped back through the door flaps just in time. The cook lost his balance and toppled over. He lay on the floor with a crazed look on his face behind the plastic doors.

Hassan ran all the way to the hall and outside into the early evening sun. The light was mild at this time of the day. Ali Noor leant on one of the two cars in the courtyard; he was chatting with the other driver, Muhammed. The cook's words floated into Hassan's mind again and he tried to push them out as he walked to the cars. He'd be able to go back to see Amma, to pay his way. But that man, the cook... there was definitely something familiar about him.

The drivers saw him and carried on talking; he nodded at them in greeting. Soon the family would be out. How could he, even for one second, have considered that money from that man might be a good thing? Was it that cursed doll that the boys had left at the door? Was it starting to work?

What a stupid idea.

He dragged his feet; he was no better than the cook. He looked down at his new clothes. The smell of kitchen oil had touched their crispness and they seemed to sag.

After a few minutes, Mir Saab came out with Begum Saab. He wore a black suit and she, a red sari. His face was like a small child's, scared but full of eager hope. They both disappeared into the first car.

Hassan sat in the back of the second car in his own little corner, feeling like a prince. The last time he had been to a wedding was in Harikaya, when the guests had danced in the village square until the early hours.

In the coolness of the car, it was hard to be as calm as the others. Every time they came to a standstill, Zain opened the window to see the city without the dark glass in between. Countless rickshaws, cars, trucks, and decorated buses with people hanging onto outside rails, seemed to be on the same journey as they were.

Thin, old donkeys pulled heavily laden carts on their way to the bazaars. Families were balanced on bicycles or scooters, weaving expertly through the flow. Traffic lights were there to be ignored and horns were indicators. Whenever their car stopped, women in burqas, old women with dupattas, or young children appeared with outstretched hands at the windows and Ali Noor handed out coins from a pouch.

'Why does he look like that?' Maryam asked. A boy staggered from one car to the next. He looked straight ahead, seeing nothing, even when he tripped and got up.

'Opium,' Zain said. Hassan was uneasy. On the one hand he was glad he was in the car, safe. But this could slip away so easily and he could find himself on the other side of the glass. He was a pretender here.

A woman in a full burqa walked right up to the window of the car next to theirs. A man's arm reached away from the steering wheel but Hassan could not see the face; the woman grabbed a note from the man's hand but stayed where she was. The hand and arm moved slowly, finding their way under the burqa. The woman was patient. The traffic light changed and the man's arm went back onto the steering wheel. Hassan blinked in disbelief. The others had not seen. Karachi was a strange place.

They took shortcuts through narrow side streets strewn with bits of paper and plastic, where children stopped cricket matches to let them pass. Wider roads opened out before them, bordered with walls. Broad, leafy branches reached out over the walls and behind them were glimpses of flat-roofed houses.

'Look, the Jinnah Mausoleum,' Zain said, winding down his window at the front and pointing at the white building shaped like a huge box with a dome.

The car crawled past the sign that said 'Founding Father'. A shopping complex came next; a girl got out of a car and walked into a glass-fronted shop.

'She's wearing jeans,' Maryam said.

Amina laughed. 'Yes, that does happen.'

Hassan wished he had a brother or a sister, or even a cousin to listen to him. There was no one to do that for him, but there was no time to think about that now. The car went up the hill and stopped. They had arrived at the hotel. The air was fresher here and mingled with the salty sea air blown in from the ocean below. Flags were strung from tree to tree.

Ali Noor winked at Hassan as he stepped out of the car and Hassan smiled back kindly as he had seen Maryam do, which made Ali Noor wink again. Men in long white jackets and fan-shaped hats lined the steps of the hotel entrance. A tall, thin man with a round eyepiece rushed down to Mir Saab's car. Another man who was scowling followed more slowly, flanked by a wall of guards. His grey silk jacket was buttoned from his neck to his knees, and worn over stiff silk trousers. His hair was jet black and streaked back over an empty scalp while his stomach was puffed out like a pregnant dog on the streets of Harikaya. He had a cigar in his hand and he flicked it just before he reached the bottom of the steps. Mir Saab stepped out of the car.

'Your Highness,' he said to Mir Saab with a quick bow of his head. 'It's an honour.'

'That's the Prime Minister,' Maryam whispered.

They followed him into the hotel. Glass doors to the marquee were swept open for them. There were at least a thousand people in there, or were there ten thousand? They stood or sat on chairs around tables and their loud chatter became a low lull as their group appeared. Mir Saab and Begum Saab disappeared with the Prime Minister into the corner of the marquee while Amina, Zain, and Maryam made their way further into the hall. Hassan took a deep breath and followed them.

The waiters ran around, weaving in and out of the shiny people. Hassan checked his waistcoat; it was straight. Maryam was a few steps away on the rugs, whose diamond shapes overlapped so that a sea of geometry rippled towards him. Someone like his mother had woven these carpets in a very different place surrounded by very different sounds. The shuft, shuft of the loom in his head formed a bubble around him and turned the chatter into a distant droning. From here he was safe to watch.

A man entered and stopped at the end of the red carpet.

'That's the groom,' Amina said.

Behind the groom were three men – friends or relatives, he supposed. The band of musicians stopped tuning their instruments and started playing as the groom made his way to a platform where he sat on one of the two thrones. Under the garlands of white flowers around his neck and face, it was hard to see what he looked like.

A waiter appeared in front of Amina with a gentle smile. He carried sweet desserts in small clay bowls and handed one to Amina, one to Zain, and one to Maryam. When he reached Hassan, he paused, holding the bowl in the air.

'Do you want one too?' he asked.

Hassan froze. The man had used *tum,* the informal *you,* whereas he had called the others *aap*.

The expensive clothes had failed to hide who he was, especially worn under his 'villager' waistcoat. He glanced sideways at the others who all had their hands full. They acted as if everything was normal, but they had heard the waiter. And everything was normal for them. If Amina and Zain spoke with him in Urdu, they would do the same – call him *tum*. Amina and Zain spoke in English to help him learn more. It had made him forget his place. He was the fool, to think they wanted to treat him as an equal, no different to them. It was all nothing but charity. They only let him sit at the same level as them in the house to make them feel better. The scholarship, the conversation, even this trip. Everything was to make them feel better. And he had fallen for it, for their conversations and the pity disguised as kindness. Even the poetry with Maryam was pity. The overlapping diamond shapes in the carpets were all he wanted to see. The waiter walked away.

'What's this called?' Maryam asked him.

The shiny, sticky doughball looked so good. 'Gulab jamun,' he said without looking up.

'Don't you like them?'

'I do.'

'Have mine,' she said. 'Too sweet for me.'

How could she not like gulab jamun? He covered this perfect ball of syrup with the napkin before he put it in his waistcoat pocket.

'It's hard to be different, isn't it?' she asked.

So, she had understood. The mischief that made her dark eyes shine was gone and she looked tired, as if she had been on a long journey.

'Yes,' he said.

Amina came up to them with a handful of petals. 'To throw on the bride.'

'Where is she?' Maryam looked round.

'This is Karachi. Everyone's at least an hour late,' Amina said.

Maryam took Hassan by the elbow to the edge of the red carpet. Everybody leant forwards to stare at the entrance. Finally, the bride appeared in red and gold, with two women on either side of her, each holding one side of a thick book above her head. The bride walked down the carpet like a box on wheels under heavy silks.

'Why isn't she smiling?' Maryam whispered, looking in the direction of the entrance.

'Because she's getting married,' Amina replied.

'But that's supposed to make her happy.'

'The bride never smiles,' Zain said.

Words flew into the air from the people around them.

'The silk of her dress is from their estate,' came a woman's high-pitched voice.

'Sindhi Textile,' said another.

'Supporting the cause,' a man's voice added.

'I thought he said he was a communist.'

'A socialist.'

'He doesn't behave much like a socialist.'

As the bride passed, people clapped. Near the stage, Mir Saab was in deep discussion with the Prime Minister. Neither bothered to turn to watch the bride walking up to the groom. They didn't even look when garland after garland was laid over the shoulders of the bride and groom until they were buried under roses.

'Can they breathe?' Maryam asked.

The crowd spread out again to sit or stand around the

tables. Rose petals were scattered on the floor and Maryam raced to scoop them up. She came up to Hassan with her face buried in her hands.

'Smell them, Hassan,' she said. Their scent seeped into his head. He saw his mother, the stars in Harikaya, and the view of the fort on the way to the factories. The fields and the forests. Yes, he was a poor villager, but none of the people here had those pictures in their heads.

'My mother crushes these at home for perfume,' he said.

'What's wrong with your mother's eyes?' she asked.

The glass on the board flew across his mind. She had remembered.

'The doctor calls it glaucoma.'

Maryam nodded, and he went on, 'The medicine isn't working.'

'You already knew about the black honey when Mir Saab was talking about it, didn't you?' she asked. 'Can it help your mother's eyes?'

'Yes.'

She had pieced it all together. 'Why were you able to calm the bees?' she asked.

'I don't know.'

'And your father, where is he?'

He shook his head. 'All I know is that my mother will go blind if I don't get back home before the floods and find the beekeeper.'

'Why don't you go back?'

'It's not that easy.'

They stood in an invisible bubble together until a voice shot through from behind.

'Come and meet the Prime Minister.' It was Begum Saab.

As they got nearer, a twitch in the corner of Mir Saab's lips appeared from nowhere. His eyes hung like heavy clouds; he looked old.

The Prime Minister was shaking his head with a smile stuck on his face. 'Living proof that nationalisation is a good idea. Give the resources back to the common people, I say,' he said, pointing at Hassan's waistcoat. 'Surely, you believe in people and equality.' The Prime Minister took a puff of his cigar.

'Of course. That's why it's important to be careful. Look at the other industries that have been made public,' Mir Saab said.

'Are you saying I'm not doing a good job?' the Prime Minister asked, puffing faster on his cigar.

The thin man with the monocle approached and, with a quick bow and a few steps, this man moved forwards and Mir Saab backed away.

Hassan stepped forward, a companion for Mir Saab. Mir Saab raised his hand; he had had enough and he turned to leave.

Hassan trailed behind the others, his cheeks burning even though everyone was looking at Mir Saab, not at him. Mir Saab walked fast, alone on the carpet, a river of red. The crowd fell away at his every step.

Everyone was quiet on the journey back. The streets were a distant, silent screen now. The guards stood to attention like frogs with bloated chests as the cars rolled past them. Once inside, in the living room, Begum Saab lay on the large sofa, propped up by several cushions. She flicked her rosary beads over and over. Her fingers moved fast; prayers joined with the beads which raced with her lips which blew out prayers like kisses. She stopped, whispered a longer prayer, closed her eyes and, holding the tassel at the top of the beads, moved her hand up and down along the beads until her prayer stopped and she gripped a bead. She then counted the beads in threes back to the tassel.

'It's not good,' she said.

'What did you ask?' Amina asked her.

Begum Saab just looked towards the closed door of the study and carried on turning the beads.

'What's your mother doing?' Maryam asked.

'The beads,' Amina said, 'she gets answers from them.'

The study door opened and Mir Saab came out. 'We shouldn't have gone,' he said. 'It's even worse now.' He sat down with his fists clenched. 'They'll go ahead with the bill. They're determined to turn my factories into state property.'

'We thought he'd change his mind,' Begum Saab said.

'Change his mind? Change the mind of a feudal ruler who's kept his own lands but thinks it's all right to plunder everyone else's now that he's Prime Minister?' Mir Saab's voice was louder, but it was sadness, not anger that the words carried. 'He's always wanted what's mine. Ever since we were children.' Mir Saab put his head in his hands, 'He'll close the factories down, just to spite me. How can I look my people in the eye if that happens?'

The speaking stopped but the leftover silence pounded the room like a drill.

Outside, there was another power cut in the city but it was too late for candles now. The sound of the generator soared above the traffic as Hassan washed under the tap and found his way through the darkness to the balcony outside his room. There were only a few stars here, unlike in Harikaya where they hung so thick that sometimes he thought he could pluck one out of the sky with his fingers.

Inside, the sound of snores from the other rooms made him feel safe. He placed the gulab jamun wrapped in the napkin on the window sill inside his room. His hands still smelt of rose petals.

They reminded him of his mother. That was a job that the villagers did in this month; they made garlands of rose heads, piles and piles in silver trays for the platform where the speakers sat. If the factories got into the wrong hands, his mother…

What would happen to her?

He refused to think about that. It couldn't happen.

He checked for the honeycomb under his pillow; it was safe. He took off his clothes and lay down in bed but it was hot without the fan. He got up and opened the door, being careful to close it again because of the mosquitos.

Out on the balcony, the movement of a point of light from below caught his attention.

Someone stood behind the floating amber point.

It was too dark to see who it was until the clouds shifted and a bright full moon lit the courtyard. It was the cook, and he was smoking and looking straight up at Hassan.

Hassan's hands stuck to the top of the balcony wall. The clouds started to cover the moon again and the cook gave a faint nod, before his body faded. The point of light moved up and down a few times, until it flew to the ground and the cook walked to the gates and vanished.

The cook's words from before the wedding came to him: 'You're walking a dangerous path.' Hassan went back inside and huddled in bed; he was so far from home.

He thought back to that morning when his father had leant on his shoulder on the way back from the forest. Labourers had seen them but why would any of them care? And then he remembered there had been someone, as they approached the shrine, someone sauntering along, in no hurry. Tall, and thin, with his hair tied back and a cigarette in his mouth. Hassan felt as if he'd been punched in the chest. The cook. The honey dealer. They were the same man.

The cook must have seen the smoke above the trees even if the beekeeper had put it out. He must have told Mir Saab's guards. Hassan wanted to go out and yell at the cook from the balcony but he stopped himself. He had to get back home. If he had to do an errand for the cook, would that be so bad? Baba had sold honey to him, after all. He heard his mother's words: 'That man is dangerous.' Ansari Saab had talked about him too. And the cook had told the guards; it must have been him.

But Hassan was desperate. His mother didn't have much

time and the floods would start in a few weeks, three, four at the most.

Hassan nestled deeper under his sheet. For now, he had to pretend he suspected nothing about who the cook was or what he might have done. He reached for the comb. He thought of the beekeeper, then of Maryam. He felt his eyelids closing; sleep numbed him.

Chapter Fifteen

The moon was framed by the open shutters when Hassan woke to noises in his room. A crow again. It looked like the same one as before. It hammered the window frame with its beak and tore at the mosquito mesh. The bird stopped when there was a hole big enough for its grey beak to poke through but it could not reach what it wanted – the gulab jamun from the wedding.

The crow and Hassan looked at each other.

Hassan got out of bed and, keeping his eye on the bird, picked up the camera from the chair. He tiptoed to the window. The bird looked back at him with a curious look. It was then that Hassan noticed a white mark on the right side of its head.

'Here you are.' He unwrapped the gulab jamun and crumbled a piece, holding it within the bird's reach. It stared at him while he lifted his camera. The crow and the gulab jamun were in the frame and something else.

The square of paper, still folded up. The boat plans.

He had forgotten to tell Mir Saab that he had them. He took the paper between his fingers, keeping the camera on the bird. The crow started to pick at the crumbs. This was the moment.

'Got you.'

He pressed the button. The paper dropped to the floor.

Outside, the water pump creaked as cold water splashed on his squatting, naked body. Finally clean and fresh, he dried himself off. He thought of the wedding. Maryam knew everything now except that his father had been the honey hunter. Or had she worked that out too?

Nobody was around as he went over to the gates; the guards were playing cards and their sleepy comments were dotted by quiet laughter. He loitered by the wall, unnoticed by them. Their sameness and satisfaction… he wished he had that. A figure made its way down the track from the main gate; it was too far away for him to see who it was but he recognised the walk and the tall, thin body. When the cook was about halfway down, Hassan slipped behind the wall, but with the top of his head and eyes peering round. The cook was coming nearer and so he slid further behind the thick creeper on the inside of the wall. The cook walked past him into the courtyard, stopped, and took out a cigarette. His dusty clothes stuck to his body as if he had been walking the streets all night. He looked thin and tired even though his hair was still neat. He blew smoke out of his mouth and headed for the servants' building.

There was still another hour before the house woke up. Hassan left through the gates, went past the guards, around the wall, and stopped to empty his sandals one by one, leaning with his hand against the wall. The sand was already warm on his toes.

That was when he saw the hole – more of a large crack in the wall. It was covered by weeds and probably just big enough to heave himself through.

An oval black eye. One on each side of a head. A million dots turned into three small eyes in the middle of the head. Two antennae, covered in fine black hair, moved closer. The antennae grew bigger. Hairs touched him. The long body of the bee came into view. Its outline shimmered and merged with Hassan's own centre. He was being absorbed into the body of the bee and taken into their nest once again.

Fine outlines of open cells were above him, all lined up in a row. Each cell was the texture of light. Row upon row of empty hexagons made up the wax walls, stretching out into infinity.

Some of the cells were incomplete; some broken and some broke off into space. It was a building site, the border of a great city. He could sense the activity of invisible bees moving deep in between the walls. His senses moved or floated along, taking him deeper.

Behind him was the sudden beating of wings and moving

shadows of what could only be bees. He turned again and again. There must be hundreds of them: workers not ready to show themselves to him. Or was he just not ready to see?

He moved through corridors, both open and closed. Winding pathways. Flashes and blobs of light darted about like last time, only more distant. The bees were sending messages. The temperature became warmer in one area and the flashes more urgent. His presence here was questionable. He turned around and wandered through dark tunnels. The energy of industry was all around him and it carried him. The sound of humming was a motor. But there was something else now; a feeling. He was being watched.

The walls of hexagons came to an end and before him was a gap. Darkness was all around, and then, suddenly, flashes were everywhere, like stars in the night. A platform made out of light appeared in the space and a bee flew in and landed on the platform. Its appearance must have been the signal for more bees to gather and watch this incomer. The space grew brighter and the humming was steady but excited.

The bee in the centre, the incomer, started to follow an invisible path of a figure of eight on the platform, its body vibrating as it moved. Then it stopped and traced an invisible line that cut the two circles.

The line pointed in the direction of the sun. Somehow Hassan remembered this. The bee then wiggled and spun, and then stopped, at an angle to the line. It was showing them the direction of the flowers from which it had just come. The angle the bee's body made from the central line was the direction in which the other bees should travel to find the flowers. This was the waggle dance his father had told him about. This area was a welcoming platform, a dancefloor. Some bees left the area, in search of the flowers. He too wanted to follow, wanted to be one of them, but instead, he found himself on the floor of the masjid, in his body again. He wanted to be in the nest more than anything now. Maryam had talked about love but this was different. The love between lovers ended. This could not. He just knew it. But a love equal to the one that was in the hive, how could he ever find that?

And yet, somehow, he knew what it would mean to find that kind of love. It would mean the death of everything he knew. There was no way he could do that. Surely the bees did not expect that? When he found the beekeeper, perhaps he would ask him to get the black honey for him. They liked the beekeeper. They trusted him already. His love had to match theirs.

Hassan sat, waiting for the others to come for breakfast as Mir Saab paced the living room. Dark rings hung under Mir Saab's eyes. Begum Saab's beads lay in an abandoned pile on the couch and the room felt airless even though the shutters were open. The bees and their dance seemed far away.

Mir Saab ushered him into the study and opened the box of golden sticks. 'Come on then, make yourself useful.'

Hassan took a stick, and then another. He laid them on the surface of the table, slotting them together. Both of them worked, quietly, side by side for several minutes.

'The code acts through our hands when we do this,' Mir Saab said.

'Did you make the wall in the masjid look like spirals because of the code?' This was a risk but Hassan had to take it. Small steps to the question about going home that he had to ask.

'You've been in there?' Mir Saab stopped with his hand in mid-air, a small golden stick between his fingers. At that moment, the sunlight burst through again; it had been stuck all this time behind a rare, stray cloud. The large hive structure was lit up, its shape reflected in Mir Saab's glasses as tiny sparks of light. 'Were the bees in there?'

'Yes.'

Mir Saab continued joining sticks together. The familiar shape was unfolding, growing into a small hexagonal ball. He picked it up in both hands and held it out to the sunlight. Hassan had finished his structure. He also held it up to shine in the sunbeam.

Mir Saab pointed to the sticks. 'More. I want a larger hive this time.'

They carried on together. So much was in his head. His father. The bees. The beekeeper. All the lies he was telling. No, not lies; he was just keeping secrets. Necessary secrets. Building this hive, next to the man who made his father disappear, was calming. He would have laughed if he had been told this would happen when he first came to Karachi. And the bees… that was even stranger, yet it didn't actually seem strange. He continued to slot the sticks together.

'The bees, they make these structures without thinking. Their whole lives are products of the instructions,' Mir Saab said.

Hassan's hand slipped and he knocked a stick against the small half-made egg. It wobbled but did not collapse.

'See? Perfect balance,' Mir Saab said. 'There's strength in balance.'

Mir Saab picked up some of his papers and began looking through them. He brought the face of the beekeeper's father to the top of the pile.

'Why didn't you find the beekeeper?' Hassan asked, just as Maryam came in and stood next to him.

'The forests grew so much over the years. He could have been anywhere.' Mir Saab laughed. 'Perhaps he didn't want me to find him.' He picked up his pencil.

Maryam nudged Hassan and mouthed the words, 'Tell him.'

'Tell me what?' Mir Saab asked, looking up.

The words seemed to slip out of Hassan's mouth. 'The black honey in the forest is healing.'

Maryam's eyes widened. 'Go on,' she mouthed.

'I need it for my mother's eyes.'

'The forest is out of bounds now,' Mir Saab said. 'For the sake of the animals. I thought you knew that.'

'But if he finds the beekeeper…' Maryam said.

Hassan dug his nails into his palms as Mir Saab stared at him.

'Would you allow me to look for the beekeeper?' Hassan asked, his heart beating loudly.

Oddly enough, there was something about Mir Saab's stillness now that reminded him of the beekeeper. 'What do you know about the beekeeper?' he asked. There was that look again in Mir Saab's face, like a cricket match. Loss.

Hassan cleared his throat, 'I keep being drawn to the bees.'

'I'll have my doctors look at your mother's eyes. I'll get someone to send a message to the clinic in Harikaya.'

'The doctors have already seen her.'

'And?'

'They say there's nothing to be done.'

'The forests are forbidden.'

Hassan felt his stomach sinking.

Mir Saab was already too deep in his examination of the drawings again. There was a cloud of sadness around him that made being angry with him hard.

'At least we have these ship plans,' Mir Saab said. 'One day, it'll be built.'

Hassan thought about the rest of the people and the animals, the ones without a ship, or even a dream of one. His mother, the poet, the beekeeper. What would happen to all of them?

Maryam must have been thinking the same thing. 'What happens to the bees if there are floods?' she asked.

'Bees are good at learning,' Mir Saab said.

'Learning what?' Maryam asked.

'They adapt to change and can make new nests anywhere. I wish humans were more like bees; bees work together.'

'Humans work for themselves, too afraid to lose what they have, too greedy to share. Instead, they hate each other.' Hassan thought of the people in Harikaya, the ones who had shouted and jeered at his father.

'Not all of them,' Maryam said.

'Enough of them,' Hassan said.

'The government can do what it likes when the people are divided,' Mir Saab said.

Mir Saab sat up straight. 'I'm afraid of what could happen to the people if the government takes over the factories.' He clenched his fists and slammed them down on the desk. 'Slaves, that's what they'd all become,' he said.

Hassan crept out through the hole in the wall behind the servants' building. Apart from a goat, there was no one around. The goat stood in the open sun, munching on a tuft of dry grass, and watched him walk on to the corner of the wall.

A few crows landed on the ground around him. 'I have nothing for you,' he said to them.

She should have been here by now. What had he been thinking when he agreed to meet her here? Maryam was from England; it was different for her. She could do what she liked but the servants still talked. Under their silent looks were tales and lies. He stamped his foot. These thoughts had to go.

'Are you trying to magic me up?'

There she was, right next to him.

'Yes, and it worked,' he said.

'Good, you're a magician.'

They walked into the forest, side by side, the crows screeching louder than when he was alone and the sun beating down.

'This is where the magic starts,' she shouted and ran ahead of him, turning around and running backwards.

He caught up with her. 'Can you imagine if anyone knew what we were doing?' he asked.

'Is it very bad?'

He laughed, 'You and I, we're different.'

'That's what you said before.' She pretended to yawn.

'Well, I'm sorry.' He started to run. 'Catch me if you can!'

She ran after him, through the forest. She was coming close, but he was faster. They ran past the swimming pool and through the trees beyond, until they both stopped, side by side, as if some invisible line had been drawn up. Her panting was louder than his.

'There's magic around here,' she said. 'You feel it too, don't you?'

'Come closer with me. It's all right,' he said to her. He wanted to take her arm and guide her to the masjid, to show her the bees.

They took a few steps forward. She stopped and took a step back.

'I don't want to go there.'

'Why not?'

'I'm not you, Hassan. Not everyone can do what you did.'

He stood watching her. 'I don't know what you mean.'

She laughed with her eyes. 'I think you do.' She became serious again. 'How will you get back in time?'

'If I'm truthful, I don't know, Bibi. Perhaps this is all a crazy dream. Even Mir Saab…'

'No. Don't lose hope.'

He waited for her to say something or to start moving again but she seemed lost in thought. She didn't even notice how long he looked at her. She came from a different world to his. She could snap her fingers and be on plane back to London when she wanted. He couldn't even take a train without begging and—

'What's Harikaya like?' Her words cut through his thoughts.

'It's a crazy place.'

'Like Karachi?'

He laughed. 'Harikaya is a tiny village. There's a main square where the market is. And then there are the streets and a wall that runs round the whole village. There are gates too with the words "Harikaya in Harikaya" over them.'

'I want to go there one day.'

'It's nothing special, Bibi.'

'And your mother, where does she live?'

'She lives in a house with a small yard right at the end of the village. If you go to the roof you can see for miles.'

'The forests too?'

'Yes.'

'How big are they?'

'People say they go on for miles and miles.'

They looked at each other for a few seconds. He wanted to tell her more about his home, about the stars that were so clear at night time, about the stray dogs that were his friends, about the river and the bamboo that snapped as he rode past on his bicycle, about the trees that people were scared of because they said that jinns lived in their branches. No more questions came. Instead, Maryam turned and started to head back.

'You go on your own,' she said, turning to him again. 'This is your magic.'

There was truth in that but he wished she was there in the

empty space beside him as he reached the masjid. He stood outside and watched a bee leaving through one of the holes, followed by another. Both were larger male bees. They hovered in the air for moments before a few more came out. Others joined them but this time from the forest or from behind the masjid. It was becoming a gathering of drones. There was something about the sound of their humming that was different, unbalanced. These bees seemed to be in competition with one another; he was sure of it. By now hundreds of bees had come together but their attention seemed to be pulled by something still inside the masjid, and they stayed close.

A drop of water fell on his hand. And then another. A few drops came down on his head and he moved back under the tree. It was a short shower but the bees only cared for one thing.

And then she appeared.

A new queen, with her formidable bulk, guided their passion on the path of her scent. The humming grew more intense; the males were eager to please her, to be her partner, to be the father of her brood.

Then the struggle began in earnest. The drones raced to reach her, ready to make the ultimate sacrifice. Only one touched her; it beat all the rest. The queen and her new mate were in freefall.

The audience of drones hummed quietly. Wave upon wave of sound turned into a joyful dance. His joy or the bees'? It didn't matter. His whole body was laughing. The two lovers were wrapped in their own destiny, and then they separated. It was over in seconds. The impregnation of the queen. The other bees drew back and the queen returned to her nest to lay her eggs in the empty cells.

Hassan took the steps of the masjid two by two and opened the door. Inside, he sat by the same pillar as last time. No bees approached. He searched for the beekeeper's face in his mind. He searched for any sign at all. Nothing. Words rose in his mind. He spoke out loud, 'What will happen to my mother if they take the factories?'

He thought of home. He pictured his mother's smile when he arrived in Harikaya – it would be a homecoming. The rains would begin in Harikaya in a few days, or a few weeks. This was his fourth day here.

'Twenty-one for the workers, twenty-four for the drones, and sixteen for the queen.' He spoke out loud.

In twenty-four days from today, there would be young bees in some other nest while the rest of their colony was preparing itself to swarm. Swarming always happened later in Harikaya than in Karachi. That was what Baba had said. He still had time. He would find a way back before the floods.

Thinking about all this made him tired.

A gentle breeze touched his face. He felt his body again on the cool floor, saw the light streaming in from the holes in the dome, heard the sounds of the bees, and smelt the honey and wax from the hive. Order and goodness reigned here. The invisible pulsations of the bees' dances travelled and touched him from inside the hive.

He stood up and felt the dancing beings watching him from their home, from their collective body. Yes, the nest was their body. One desire governed them and at this moment, it governed him too. It was the one force that brought all the bees together in unending service. Dance. Its language became one with his being and his arms began to part from his body to become like wings.

Bees approached him from their home, travelling along lines of light that radiated from the nest. His arms lifted higher; his palms rose upwards. Cradled by the humming, he no longer needed to understand. Even the questions that were burning in him faded now. The answers would come when they came, if they came. The world of thinking, of needing to know, and the need to become anything, were far away. The smell of their joy was enough and he closed his eyes.

He gave in to the spinning that propelled his body.

Infinity spoke to him and there was no rush towards it. The spinning was a language understood by the bees. They spun with him, floating around his arms. Together. Humming and silence. Flight and stillness. Arms stretched out like wings opening, and then they pulled in, close to his chest. Over and over, out and in, caressed by the floating bees.

The presence of the queen was behind all of this, a force from deep within the hive. He may never meet her in there but her presence… her presence was real and that was enough, simply enough. Would he deserve her love? Could he match it with his own as his father had said was necessary?

At that moment, it was all he wanted to know.

The cook's lips held onto a burning cigarette over a large pot that he stirred with one hand on the kitchen stove. Ash threatened to drop into the pot. Smells of spices and smoke competed for dominance.

'Are you looking for your aunt?' the cook asked Hassan as soon as he entered the kitchen.

'Yes.'

'You won't find the girl here either.' The cook leant further forward.

'What girl?'

'From London, isn't she? Nice.'

'I don't know what you mean.'

The cook laughed. 'Come on, you're almost a man.'

Those had also been his father's words before they had entered the forest.

'Look, I'll be straight with you. I've been thinking. We can make money, you and I,' the cook said, continuing to stir.

'What did you say?'

'Your father was a businessman. He knew what was good for him.' The cook banged the spoon against the side of the metal pot. 'Well, most of the time.'

Hassan stood taller.

'People like us, we've got to look after ourselves. Nobody else will.'

Hassan had seen and smelt many times that same hunger for money that sweated out of the cook's pores now. He had even seen it in his father, but only sometimes. The stench crept up his nostrils. The blades of the fans were feeble against it. The idea of grasping for money in this way stank, but still, the cook had a point. Money. It was interesting.

The cook seemed to understand Hassan's silence.

'You need money, like all of us?'

The cook took the cigarette out of his mouth and smiled as if he had eaten a gulab jamun, then licked his lips. 'You spend a lot of time with the girl, don't you?' He winked. 'I won't say anything about that.'

This man knew too much.

Hassan was about to turn around, and walk out at that second but his feet were stuck to the floor.

'I'm glad you're beginning to see now,' the cook said. 'For people like us…' He started to stir the pot again. The long line of ash that had grown on the cigarette fell onto the floor.

Footsteps.

Kulsoom came through the door.

'What are you doing here?' she asked Hassan.

'Looking for you.'

He went up to her and she took a step forward. She was watching the cook and, for a second, her look softened. He must have imagined it.

'Nice boy, your nephew. We're getting on very well.'

The cook winked at him. Kulsoom's face was back to being stern. He waited for her to ask him why he was looking for her. Instead, she said, 'The family's waiting for you.'

He slipped away.

Chapter Sixteen

This was Hassan's first time in the drawing room. He sat on the long couch with Maryam, Zain, and Amina. Swirls and spirals were everywhere, carved into the wooden furniture and stitched into the soft furnishings. Maryam was very close to him and he inched further away without being noticed. Mir Saab was moving the pencil in his hands, round and round.

A car rolled into the courtyard and stopped. Moments later, the doors of the drawing room were opened by Muhammed and he announced, 'The estate manager.'

The man stood with arms at his sides like a soldier standing to attention, and bowed. He nodded politely at each of them but ignored Hassan. Yes, he was definitely ignoring him; it was an automatic reaction, but it made Hassan want to become invisible. He sank into the sofa behind the others.

'Yes, yes,' Mir Saab waved him down and the manager sagged into an armchair. Muhammed offered him a glass of lemon water on a tray. The manager took the glass without speaking. The lemon water formed a froth on his thick moustache and threatened to drip down one of the curls that hung at either side of his mouth.

'Your Highness, it is very difficult for me,' he said, putting the glass down on the glass table. Glass touched glass too quickly and water splashed.

'As you know, the Prime Minister has decided to go ahead with the bill.' The manager breathed heavily.

'They have no idea about how to manage the factories,' Mir Saab said. 'They want to destroy the whole of Harikaya state.'

The manager's face turned grey.

'I gave them control of the state,' Mir Saab continued. 'They forced it from my hands.' Mir Saab's veins stood out blue and purple on his round face. 'Even Jinnah, before he died, told me to be careful. He said, "Have faith in our new nation." I thought they'd look after the fort. I thought they'd value our common heritage. But they're hell bent on destroying me, all for the sake of power.' Mir Saab took a sip of water. 'Doesn't he have enough land himself?'

Hassan thought of his mother and the women working at the looms. He conjured up the smell of the oil used in the weaving machines and the swish of the cloth on the floor. His mother's hands checking the weave before she let it go. He looked down at his hands, searching for hers in his.

'I set the factories up for the men and women,' Mir Saab said, 'so they wouldn't need to depend on charity.'

'We'll have to trick them in some way,' Maryam said. 'In

the best detective stories, there's no difference between the detective's level of intelligence and the criminal's.'

'You could pretend the factories don't belong to you,' Amina said.

Hassan thought of the fort, ever watchful over each one of them. How many times a day had he been reminded that nothing belonged to any of them and everything belonged to the mir?

'Charity,' Mir Saab said. His lips tightened. He blinked fast as if he was seriously trying to understand what the word meant. 'They can't take over a charity. That's the law. I'll make the factories into charities that don't belong to me.' Mir Saab leant forward. 'In name at least.'

The manager sat rigidly unmoving, his mouth open.

'What on earth will they make of that?' Mir Saab asked.

Back in the living room that evening, around the dinner table, everybody was smiling – including Mir Saab. His whole body was lighter and he was looking at Hassan, about to say something, but Begum Saab got in there first.

'Have some more food,' she said, and handed him another portion of the sauce.

Despite her efforts over the last week, Hassan remained thin.

'We don't want you to look like a skeleton,' she said.

Hassan raised his hand in polite protest with his mouth full of cauliflower but more food appeared on his plate. He could see Maryam grinning at him as he gave in at the sight of the second helping. It tasted good even though the cook had made it. His body would never gain the fat by which Begum Saab measured the success of her hospitality; his thin return to the village was guaranteed.

'Your mother will think we haven't been treating you well,' Begum Saab said as she left the room.

'When will you see her?' Maryam asked once they'd all finished.

'I don't know,' he said, putting down his knife and fork. He was getting used to eating with them now but he still preferred hands. Before he could say any more, Mir Saab got up and headed for his study; he waved to them to follow.

The door creaked as they went in. Mir Saab went to the bookshelf and stopped at the section full of his notebooks. He came back with one that was frayed at the corners. He turned the yellowing pages of ink drawings.

'Have you seen all of those birds in the forest, Baba?' Zain asked.

Mir Saab nodded. 'There it is, the honeyguide. Very rare. The old beekeeper taught me the honeybird whistle.'

Mir Saab lifted his jaw, pursed his lips, and whistled. Softly at first, though the sound was shrill and echoed in Hassan's eardrums. The whistle became louder, until everyone put their hands to their ears and Mir Saab stopped.

'It led me to bees' nests, up in trees and in mounds on the forest floor,' he said. 'It didn't lead me to the current beekeeper as I'd hoped, but I still broke a little earth off a mound to say thank-you to the bird.'

Begum Saab was at the door. The tutor had arrived and Maryam, Zain, and Amina went for their lessons. Hassan was left alone with Mir Saab. This was his chance to change the mir's mind.

'I saw a queen and drones outside the masjid.'

'The nuptial dance?'

Hassan nodded. 'I think it was a queen from another nest, not the one in the masjid.'

'So, you went again,' Mir Saab said. There was no judgement in his voice. 'This means that the hive in the masjid may be ready to swarm soon. There will be grown ones in there keen for more space.'

'Yes.' Hassan was desperate.

Mir Saab put the notebook back on the shelf and stood in the middle of the room.

This man, the Mir of Harikaya, the man who looked down from the fort and made new laws like others made bread, shared the same love of bees as Hassan's father. The man who had sent the guards after Baba shared so much with him. One day, Mir Saab and Baba would meet. And when they did, Mir Saab might understand that the forest fire was an accident. A foolish accident.

It was time to say what he needed to say. 'I know the bees will be swarming in Harikaya later than here,' he said. 'I need to get back to the forests before the floods.'

'Too dangerous.' Mir Saab was shaking his heard. 'I've said that already. We can go for Eid.'

'Mir Saab, that's too late. I need to go back now.'

'Prayers,' Mir Saab said, as if he hadn't heard. He headed towards the door at the far end of the room.

Hassan had been blocked. If there had been less anger inside him, he might have used his clenched fist to swipe at all the papers on the table. But his anger wanted to break the hexagonal shapes, to scream and throw them at the window.

Instead, he dug his nails deeper into his palms. He walked out into the courtyard. It was darker now but he made out Ali Noor coming through the gates, hurrying towards the car with the car keys in his hand. Hassan quickened his steps and met the driver just as he opened the car door.

'Take me to the station,' he said.

'What?' Ali Noor straightened up.

'I need to get to the station.'

'I have a task to do for Begum Saab.'

Ali Noor put his hand on Hassan's shoulder but Hassan drew back.

'I would help if I could.'

'Please.'

'It's dangerous out there. You know I come from the same place as you. I've heard about your mother. We all have.'

There was no pity in his face, just an openness.

'You have to accept it.' His voice was kind. 'Wait till Eid. I'll make sure you see your mother then. I'll drive you personally. How about that?'

'It'll be too late.' Hassan turned. He didn't want Ali Noor to see the tears.

That night on the balcony, Hassan looked out on a half moon. He thought of Harikaya. When he got there, he'd slip away to the jungle unnoticed. He rested his hands on the balcony wall to steady himself and took a deep breath in. Baba was watching the stars too, he just knew it.

He went into his room and lay down on the bed. He must have fallen asleep in his clothes because when he awoke it was still dark, and he felt the longing to be with the bees in the masjid was growing. He closed his eyes and heard humming. The moonlight bathed his eyelids and the beekeeper's face appeared in his mind. The humming was steady. The bees were calling. The sound grew louder and louder until he covered his ears with his hands.

What was he thinking? It was the middle of the night. At that moment, a bee entered his room and Hassan bolted upright. It must have come in through the hole in the mosquito mesh. The bee's humming was steady but getting faster. It hovered at the end of the bed at first but made its way forward, filling the room with its sound.

The bee came closer, so close now that Hassan stared at its face, its antennae and its black eyes framed by golden hair. This was a worker, come to find him. The bee darted one way and the other, just an inch or so from his body. He stood up and opened his bedroom door but the bee stayed inside. It circled under the fan and moved back towards the window but didn't leave. Hassan went out onto the balcony and the bee and the humming vanished.

Downstairs, the bee was there again, waiting. Hassan started forward to leave through the main gates but stopped. It was still too dark; the guards might stop him. Instead, he slipped behind the trunks at the back of the servants' building, and was through the hole in seconds.

Snakes and lizards came out at night. Out here, alone in the moonlight, with the trees before him, he had a choice: to answer the call or go back. He ran into the forest, leaves brushing against his ankles. He stumbled once or twice but he got up and ran hard, a wild animal through the trees. He was free.

The masjid with the crescent moon at its head looked like a form from another planet, like a temple that could take off. It was the home of the bees. Inside, he bolted the door behind him. It was dark and he felt his way to his usual pillar and sat down. A bee landed on his finger – from nowhere – and when it launched into the air again, it was followed by a thread of light like silver shots of electricity in the dark. The bee came close to Hassan's face, close enough for him to see the three tiny eyes at the top of its head between its two larger eyes.

Tremors. He felt tremors in the darkness and he was no longer on the stone floor. Instead, he was inside their nest and he could see with a new vision. The cell walls were vibrating like piano keys played by the bees' feet. He moved on between the walls. Previously empty cells were now closed white ones, with curved lids for the male drones or flat lids for the smaller female workers. They were brimming with life, yet to be born. More tremors, this time louder, but there were patterns to the tremors as if the bees were sending messages from one part of the hive to another through its very framework.

He arrived at a place where he felt the touch of air and the brush of wings. A bee flew in, landing on the dancefloor. He was here again. The bee brought with her the scent of flowers from the outside; purple and blue, the colours of that scent, danced in dappled light on the hexagons. Another bee came down and landed next to the first one who opened her mouth and kissed this second bee. Chewed nectar was being transferred from one mouth to another. Two bees kissing.

The receiver bee continued with the chewing and stirring of the nectar in her mouth now. Once she had finished, more bees flew in to watch and the nectar was transferred to yet another mouth and then finally into an empty cell in the comb wall. The cell was then covered with a thin, transparent thread that came out of the bee's body like the weave emerging from his mother's loom.

More bees came in with their cargo and nectar was passed from mouth to mouth. Nectar was chewed. Nectar was stirred. Mouths kissed and nectar was dropped into the empty cells. It was a production line, efficient and steady. Smacked kisses. A steady rhythm. Tap, tap, tap. Like the stonemasons in Harikaya tapping with silver hammers. Tap, tap, tap.

He was back in human shape, neat and compact on the floor. There was a taste of honey in his mouth. Why was all this happening? The bees had allowed him in once more, to be part of them, and in there, everything seemed familiar and new at the same time. He didn't know what that might be or if it was all his imagination, but it was as if the bees were preparing him for something. He still had a lot to prove to the bees but he was becoming more and more sure that he belonged with them, that he was one with many. Yes, he was human, but in their world; his body, his name, his memories were left behind. It was just him, without form. And he liked that feeling.

He opened the door of the masjid to early morning

birdsong and stood at the top of the steps. He had been in the nest for a long time, absorbed in their comings and goings.

Humming rang out from behind him. The door of the masjid was still open. He jumped back and held the edge of the door in his hand as he listened. The humming was strong and steady; he breathed in the fragrance of the hive. What had just happened had brought the flowers into the hive. The flowers were part of them, separate but part of their body; their nest and the bees made love to the flowers. The bees had allowed him to watch and learn. They were carriers of nectar, builders of cities, weavers of homes, and they were also his teachers who turned the flower's gift into gold.

Hassan closed the door with care. The world of people was different. Greed and politics were different. There was no harmony there. The knowledge of the bees seemed far away.

He stopped on the top step. There was no sound from inside the hive now. The traffic was far away but he heard it now, faint but always there. He took another step down.

He had to get home to see his mother and to find the bees in the forest in Harikaya. The errand for the cook was the only way.

Chapter Seventeen

Hassan came to a halt in the dining room. An unknown smell was emanating from the living room, and it wasn't breakfast. The smell was fragile at first but steadily increased in strength until it stuck in Hassan's nostrils. Someone was smoking, but the smell was more acidic than usual, like flowers and buffalo dung mixed together. Mir Saab didn't smoke. Guests only smoked in the drawing room. Mir Saab's mother was arriving in the afternoon so hopefully the smell would go by then. He put his hands to his nose as he was about to sneeze.

Sounds of chatter came down the stairs and Maryam, Zain, and Amina approached the doorway that led to the living room from the hall, but their voices came to a halt at the door like a record forced to stop. The three of them disappeared inside the room without seeing him. He hesitated for a moment and then followed.

'George, pass me the lighter. The cigar's gone out again.

This thing's hardly worth smoking.'

It had to be Mir Saab's mother. She must have arrived early. The accent wasn't as English as Mir Saab's, but only his mother called him George, in honour of the then King of England who had visited the family after Mir Saab's birth in a place called Eastbourne. Hassan took a few steps through the door. He had heard all about it in history lessons and here it was, living history, right in front of him.

'It's far too early to make conversation,' she said to Zain and Amina and then, to Maryam, she said, 'Hello.'

They were her eager audience but Hassan started to retrace his steps very slowly, hoping that no one would notice him by the time he was at the door again.

A sound distracted his concentration and he looked in the direction of Mir Saab's mother who was now holding a glass bottle and sucking at a drinking straw. The cigar was resting on the rim of the ashtray, smoking on its own. She looked up and her lips seemed stuck in the shape of a circle that fitted perfectly around the straw. Hassan kept his mouth tightly shut. She was looking straight at him with big, dark eyes, outlined with black liner and made darker by the creamy whiteness of her powdered face and deep-red-painted lips. All of it was framed by jet-black hair tied back loosely so that spiral curls hung like earrings behind her ears. Her real earrings hung even lower and shone in the light like her necklace. Hassan wanted to make himself invisible but the cigar smoke had dried his throat and he coughed instead.

'Who's this?' she asked.

'This is Hassan, Mother.'

'Who?' she repeated.

'He's a nephew of one of the staff,' Mir Saab said.

'You're always so kind to people, George.'

Hassan longed to be back in the masjid. He had washed before he came down for breakfast but he wished he had put on the wedding clothes again. Mir Saab's mother was like a queen.

'This boy is quite different,' Mir Saab whispered.

Maryam nodded in the direction of the sofa. 'Come and sit with us,' she said to him. He was careful not to sit on her long shirt. Amina and Zain came to sit next to him.

'It's so humid here, George. Hyderabad was cooler. Better for my bones,' Mir Saab's mother said.

'Our house is on a hill over there. Much fresher and it has lovely gardens,' Mir Saab said.

'The Nizam's wife joins me sometimes.'

That name was in his history book too: the Nizam of Hyderabad, one of India's richest men before the two countries divided.

'Have they changed much?' Mir Saab asked.

'The Nizam's hardly at home these days.'

'I meant the gardens.'

'Oh, the trees have grown. Nothing like here though.'

'You should try planting English oaks,' Mir Saab said.

His mother laughed. 'It'll be like foggy London on an autumn day.'

Her laughter faded away and she turned to Mir Saab. 'You should come back with me to India, George. Bring the family.'

Mir Saab only sighed and went to the chest to take out the roll of drawings of the boat. He flattened them out on the coffee table.

'Still planning your escape route, I see,' his mother said.

Hassan leant forwards to see what Mir Saab would add to the ship today.

'The more I see the greed and envy to which you're subject, the more I think the boat's a good idea,' she said.

'I'm worried about the water levels and the animals,' Mir Saab said.

'And your beloved forests.'

'The government's making trouble again,' Mir Saab said.

Mir Saab's mother took a long inhalation of her cigar. 'What is it this time?'

'The factories.'

'What?' Smoke erupted from her mouth. 'Your father should have been stronger.'

'Father did his best to keep Harikaya independent,' Mir Saab said, as if reciting from a book he'd read a thousand times. 'The state was too big to be stuck in the middle of the new country.' Mir Saab bit his lower lip and looked down at the boat plans.

'I do wish you'd stayed the ruler,' his mother said.

'Those days have gone, Mother. War or merge into the new state: that was the choice I was faced with.'

'You were only eighteen when your father died,' Mir Saab's mother said.

The cigar was smoking on its own again. The smell seemed sweeter now, more bearable.

'The school principal told me in the middle of the night that he was dying,' Mir Saab said.

'And you left immediately.'

'On the ship for three weeks.'

Everyone in the region had been given a small bowl made out of the local stone when Mir Saab had been crowned the new mir. Hassan's mother still had it somewhere.

'I was too late; Father died before I got back,' Mir Saab said.

Mir Saab's mother sucked on the straw again. 'And now you're just a symbol.'

Mir Saab looked down at the ship. He took up his pencil and started to draw.

Mir Saab's mother turned to Maryam. 'You have such pretty eyes. Take your glasses off for a moment, will you?'

Maryam obeyed.

'Yes, I was right; they're beautiful,' Mir Saab's mother said.

Hassan glanced towards Maryam. Her eyes were big but that was all.

'She should use the forest honey so she won't need glasses.'

'Hassan's going to look for it,' Maryam said.

The others stopped playing to listen.

'Why are you going to look for it?' Mir Saab's mother's eyes grew wide.

'I'm going to look for the beekeeper. He'll help me find the black honey for my mother's eyes,' Hassan said. 'She'll lose her sight if I don't.'

She put down her glass and said, 'My husband and son met the current beekeeper's father a few times. They were both touched by his magic.'

'When are you going?' said Maryam.

'If Mir Saab allows it'—Hassan looked at Mir Saab—'I could go before I start school here in Karachi.'

'There's a new law now.' Mir Saab's voice was quiet.

'So?' his mother said.

'I can't allow a child to go honey hunting. It's dangerous enough for the adults. That's why I passed the law. The forest is forbidden.' He sounded irritated, as if he had had this conversation with himself a thousand times.

Mir Saab's mother huffed. 'That's not the real reason.' She lit another cigar. 'The trouble is, George, you've become jaded.'

'What do you mean, Mother?'

She sighed. 'It all changed when you started school. If only you'd found the beekeeper again.'

'I tried.'

'I know.' Her voice was kinder now. 'The truth is, he didn't want you to find him.'

Mir Saab's body began to sag.

'You wanted to protect the forest, make it grow – the most important thing in the world for you. But there was also a part of you that doesn't want anyone else to find him, isn't there?'

Mir Saab looked too weak to argue with her.

'The bees,' he said. 'They never forgave me.'

'That's what you believed,' she said. 'And as revenge you stopped believing in them. In their medicine.'

'Mother, that's not…'

His mother waved her hand as if to signal that any protest was useless. 'That boy, who has come because you chose to help a poor village boy, has come to help you.'

Mir Saab was staring at the floor. Hassan felt his heartbeat start to race.

'He has the same hunger in his eyes as you had, George,'

she said. 'You've got to let him try, at least. Let him go.'

Maryam stood up. 'If he goes, I want to go too.'

'Why don't you all go?' His mother looked serious.

Mir Saab slowly started to look up.

'All right.'

Hassan couldn't believe it. There was a rush of blood to his head. He wanted to go over to Mir Saab and take his hand.

'Mir Saab, thank you,' he said. 'I will find the beekeeper.'

Mir Saab was scratching his head. 'We will all go back, on one condition. Hassan must go to find him alone.'

There was a hush.

'If he allows you to find him, then the rest will follow,' Mir Saab said.

'When will we go, Mir Saab?' Hassan asked.

'In a few days. Yes, we'll all go in a few days by plane.'

'We have to come back before I go back to London in twelve days,' Maryam said.

Mir Saab's mother raised her glass and looked straight at Hassan. 'Well, that's a good result, isn't it?'

Hassan could breathe freely again. Things would be all right. Amma's eyes would be all right. There was a warm glow in his chest that was getting stronger. He decided to be this woman's loyal admirer for the rest of his life.

'I hope you do better than he did in the forests,' she said, nodding in Mir Saab's direction.

Everyone laughed and Mir Saab's mother looked at her son for a few moments and sighed.

'He's different, George; that's what you meant, didn't you?'

'Yes,' Mir Saab said.

Nothing more was said for a few moments until Mir Saab's mother clapped her hands. 'I want to play bridge,' she almost shouted.

'Now we can stay up all night,' Zain said.

'And watch films too,' Amina added.

The night was lost to play. Maryam, Zain, and Amina – and even Hassan – stayed up with her, watching films, playing bridge, and laughing as she smoked cigars and drank whisky. Not even Begum Saab had authority over Mir Saab's mother. Mir Saab stayed around her for most of the time, except when he was praying or sleeping.

'Stay a while, a few weeks or months,' he said to her in the morning as they all went to sleep for a few hours.

Afternoon came with no reply to this request. Mir Saab waited like a child by his mother's side.

And she talked to Hassan as much as she did to the others.

'Special eyes,' she said to him.

She didn't say any more and they picked up their cards again, but Hassan could only think of his promise to his mother. Maryam tapped his shoulder and said, without moving her head, 'Your turn.'

His attention was back on the cards.

'You two are friends,' Mir Saab's mother said.

The smile that passed on her lips showed Hassan that she thought there was nothing wrong in that. And there *was* nothing wrong with it. He smiled back at her.

Mir Saab's mother picked up her glass and went for her

lighter. 'My son lived away from his parents too.'

Hassan wanted to say that Mir Saab had been further away from his parents than he was, but he stopped when he saw Mir Saab's mother's face. Did his own mother look like that when she thought of him?

The next day she gave her son an answer: 'I would stay, George, but it's too humid here.'

Late in the afternoon, she said goodbye to each of them in turn in the hall and when she got to Hassan, she took his chin and held his head high. 'It won't be easy in the forests,' she said.

At the door, Hassan had to look away when Mir Saab's mother took her son's hand and Mir Saab became the small boy again left at school in England. They all followed her out to the car. She turned around at the car door and hesitated. Hassan held his breath, but she got in, lowered her window and blew her son a kiss. Mir Saab stepped back into the house.

The car drove through the first set of gates. The leader of the show had gone and a great space had opened up in her absence. Hassan raised his chin a little higher even though he wanted to cry. The previous night and this afternoon had been like a dream, no, a film, and the ending brought Hassan back to earth. He would never forget her.

He shielded his eyes in the haze of the sun. He had been here for what seemed like an eternity now. He felt a longing to be with the bees again. He wanted to feel them again, to feel their love. It was Maryam who touched his elbow when the others had left and it was she who guided him back into the shade.

'I'll meet you at the other side of the wall,' she said.

Chapter Eighteen

Hassan crawled through the hole in the wall to see Maryam standing under a tree. She had beat him there. A bee flew into her face and she brushed it away, jumping to the side. Hassan stopped himself from laughing.

'I've been dying to speak to you about the bees,' she said. 'I still don't get it.'

'It's hard for me to understand too,' he said.

'Not everyone's like you.'

'I'm not special.'

'Then what makes you able to do what you can?' she asked, a small frown on her face.

He shrugged his shoulders.

'Come on, let's get out of the house while they're making the preparations.'

He glanced sideways at Maryam. Her curls bounced. Her glasses were always smudged but she didn't care, and her eyes were awake to everything around her. They walked side by side on the path that he knew so well by now. She wasn't just 'the girl', as the cook had called her. But she was also not the kind of girl Hassan would want. He thought of Sami. Harikaya was far away now; too much had happened. The truth was, he didn't want anyone. No, that kind of thing wasn't for him. Maryam looked at him, her mouth curled up with mischief.

'Let's race,' she said, 'up to the old pool.'

Hassan followed her; it was a close finish.

'I won,' she crowed.

Hassan laughed, still out of breath. They both leant on the wall.

'Are you seeing your stories?' he asked.

'Not mine, yours.'

His eyes roamed the tiles on the floor of the pool. Underneath the leaves were whole, broken, and chipped pieces.

'I'm seeing you when you were little with your father,' she said.

Hassan leant further over the edge, his heart beating fast.

'Did he tell you about the black honey?' she asked.

'Yes.'

There was a loudness to her silence. He looked over to her.

'The stories help me feel less alone,' she said.

'In London?'

'At school.'

The sun was hot now but they stayed there, both of them holding onto the edge. They squinted at the tiles together until a cloud passed overhead.

'It's so quiet here; the house and the city are so far away,' she said.

'In Harikaya, when it's quiet the crickets sound very loud.'

'I can't wait to go there.'

A few car horns sounded in the distance but apart from that even the crows were quiet for a minute or two. Hassan thought about the trip back. Mir Saab had to fix a date soon.

'They're making preparations in the house,' Maryam said.

'What are the preparations for?' he asked.

'Don't you know? It's the birthday of a holy person from the olden times,' she said. 'He was twelve when he disappeared.' Maryam thought for a few moments. 'They say he gave a talk and walked into a cave and was never seen again.'

Hassan pictured the boy walking with his back to the people into the entrance of the dark cave.

'Was this a cave with no ending?'

'Maybe,' she said.

'Is he in this country?'

'No, silly, he's everywhere. Like a spirit.'

'Do you think his body just vanished?' he asked.

'I think he must have turned invisible. Look, I'm invisible.' She started to walk away. 'I'm going to hide.'

'I'll count,' he said.

'Not yet.'

Her footsteps were moving away and he turned in time to see some tall leafy bushes wave and then he started to count. He looked down at the pool again. All its stories had gone now and without them, it was nothing more than an old pool with smashed tiles and weeds on its floor. But losing stories made room for new ones. The masjid had lost its old story to become the temple of the bees.

A crow screeched. It sounded like a scream and Hassan counted out loud, 'Ninety-nine, one hundred.' There was no sound from Maryam.

'I'm coming!' he shouted. He ran into the forest, moving branches and leaves as he went. 'Maryam, where are you?' He stopped trampling the ground to listen but it was taking too long. He walked in circles for minutes, his heart racing more after every turn he made. 'If this is a joke, please stop now.'

Had she left? Was she hurt? Thickets and thorns scratched his ankles and feet but he walked on, sweeping bushes aside. 'Mar…y…am!' He wanted to shout more, wanted to tell her that he wanted her back now.

Suddenly, she jumped out from behind the leaves, like a ghost from another world. He wanted to rush up to her, to check she was all right but he stopped himself, a mere foot away from her. Her voice was quiet and she was watching him closely. The longing to touch her stopped his breath for a second, but the longing was only on his side. She was calm. Too calm. He didn't know what to do with the leftovers of the feeling that hung around his chest.

'I was playing,' she said.

He dared not look at her face.

'You have a lot to think about, don't you?' she said.

'Yes.' He let the longing dissolve; it was pointless here.

'Have you been to the jungles of Harikaya before?' she asked.

He thought quickly. 'I can't remember,' he swallowed. It was the closest to not lying that he could think of.

'So you might have been when you were younger?'

'Yes.'

'It's getting dark, Hassan.'

They started to head back.

'I'm going back to London on the fourteenth of September. That's twelve days away,' she said. 'That'll make my uncle hurry up. You'll be in the forests soon.'

'When will you come back?'

'I don't know.'

Why not? The question pricked him inside. He thought of Harikaya – the days spent wandering the streets on his own ever since his father had left. All those times when he had tried to look like he was going somewhere, doing something, to stop people noticing his aloneness. They walked, he and Maryam, in the fading light, side by side. And now she was leaving too.

'You'd go into the forests in Harikaya on your own, wouldn't you?' she asked.

'Yes.'

'It would be nice, though, to...' she said, grasping his elbow, making him stop. Her eyes sparkled.

'What?'

'To see you do it.'

'*If* I can do it.'

'Will you go again as soon as we get there?'

'I have to get back there. I have no other choice. My mother's eyes...'

She clapped her hands. 'Ha, I knew it! So, you've been there already. Why didn't you get the black honey then?'

She had tricked him, but that was all right. He was too happy that he was going back.

'I'll explain one day. It's a long story.'

They had reached the wall of the house again. She carried on while he went around the back and slipped through the hole. By the time they were together again in the courtyard, the sun had nearly set. They stood by the wall of the servants' quarters. She was panting; she must have walked fast through the darkness. He wished he didn't have to leave her to go round the wall by herself.

Just then, a man came out of the open gate that led to the back of the building. It was the cook, whispering something under his breath. He hadn't seen them and Maryam was looking in the direction of the house.

A woman came through the gate behind the cook; she was hurried, with bare feet and loose hair. 'Wait!' she said.

Hassan took a sharp breath. It was Kulsoom. She hadn't seen them in the shadows but Maryam saw her now. Hassan put his hand over his mouth to signal to Maryam to keep quiet. Kulsoom had her back to them as she gave up the chase and the cook walked away. She walked to the washing line in the corner and began to take the washing down, her mouth snapping and growling curses as she did so. The swearing became louder. She barked until her throat was dry and then she gulped. The gulp broke into a sob from somewhere so deep and dark that Hassan walked away. Shock squeezed his chest.

He waved his hand for Maryam to follow, but Kulsoom must have heard their footsteps and her sobs shut down. Hassan turned in time to see the gate click; she was gone.

As soon as they entered the house, the activity cooled his head.

'You'll stay awake the whole night,' Amina said as she passed them in the hall, carrying matches.

Hassan followed Amina and Zain and Maryam up the stairs and into a candlelit world.

They walked from room to room until they settled in the prayer room. They waited to see if spirits would appear as they were said to on this night. Hassan was drawn in, even though it was all new for him. They huddled together as Zain told stories, full of heroes and adventures. The candlelight became the normal light that night, for their bright eyes reflected each other's faces. Flames danced with the wings of night creatures that watched and listened too.

After several stories, Maryam spoke.

'Maybe he's here,' she said. 'I saw a light.'

Was it just her eyes? No, he thought he'd seen the light too. But later, Maryam changed her mind.

'They were just shadows,' she said. 'It must have been a trick of the light.'

Battles with eyelids started in the early hours. Sleep gathered force in the room, but Hassan watched the walls while the others slept and the candles shrank. It was like in the city of bees, in the hive, except that there the magic was all over and around him and in him and he forgot who he was and how to think or doubt.

In the morning, he woke to the sound of footsteps and

creaking doors. His dreams had been full of shadows and hidden lights.

'Begum Saab wants to take you all to the bazaar to buy some clothes,' Muhammed said. 'Hassan, you too.'

They shot up, still charged with the presence of magic and went to eat and prepare themselves. As Hassan got dressed, he thought of Kulsoom's sob. It made him cold. One thing was now clear; he understood why the cook knew so much.

The bazaar was packed even though it was morning time. They entered the indoor market that sprawled like a miniature city with unending aisles lined by stalls, both large and small and packed with cloth, furniture, bangles, and food. The driver stood behind their group, ready with a note or coin every time someone stretched out a hand.

Hassan had never seen anything like this but every time he lifted his camera, someone stopped right in front of him to haggle with a stallholder. A fortune teller sat cross-legged on a mat and a woman went to sit in front of him, holding out her palm while her family peered over her shoulder to hear her future. Hassan walked on with his camera ready. People shouted, fighting with numbers as buyers and sellers arrived at their final price. Everyone wanted to be the winner. They passed a man with glassy eyes who squatted over a basket. In it was a coiled fat snake. He raised his camera. At last, a picture.

The others stopped in front of a stall stacked with bangles. The shopkeeper stood behind a mix of different colours.

'I like those,' Maryam said, pointing at the yellow glass ones.

'Try them on,' Zain said.

Her hands squeezed through them like rubber.

There were too many pictures that needed to be taken for Hassan to stay in one place. He took a few steps away from the others. He saw families talking, people cutting through on their way to work, a few men dressed as women, children shouting and playing amongst the hustle and bustle.

Hassan scanned their faces. His gaze landed on a profile. It took him a few seconds until he was sure. It was him. It was the cook, standing at the bottom of the lane, his head jumping from person to person as if looking for someone. He started to move away, holding onto his shoulder bag as he walked. Hassan followed, keeping a few yards behind, weaving through the people.

The cook was looking around at the stalls, the vendors, and the goods as if all this was new to him. He stopped to look at a stall which was more like a shop, with glass-fronted cabinets containing jewellery. He pointed at a chain but the shopkeeper shook his head. He was not going to open the cabinet for the cook. The cook kept on pointing, but the shopkeeper waved his hands. The cook looked around and Hassan ducked to the side of a stall. Copper and brass pots and kettles hung all around, shielding him.

The cook began to argue with the shopkeeper, both their voices rising above the general din, until the man opened the case and the cook picked up the chain. He held it close to his eyes and looked as if he was going to eat it. He gave it back to the shopkeeper and pointed at another piece.

The stallholder came to stand next to Hassan and stopped to look too.

'Do you know him?' Hassan asked.

'He comes here sometimes,' the man said, using a duster to swipe at the hanging kettles.

'What does he do?' asked Hassan.

'Nothing much, looks at the jewellery, buys a piece now and again. Why?'

'Oh, no reason. I don't know him.'

The cook was already slipping away, weaving through the people crowding around the huge open gates of the market. Hassan followed, almost running to keep up until, not far from the gates, the cook stopped in front of a pair of glass doors that led to a small hotel. Hassan stood diagonally across from him in a doorway. The cook was facing away from Hassan as he took out a cigarette and lit it. People went in and out, past the smoking cook who took out a folded piece of paper from his bag and opened it up. Hassan squinted. It was Mir Saab's plans for the ship. Hassan raised his camera and pressed the button.

His first instinct was to run up and grab the paper but a man and woman approached, stopping a few metres away. The cook nodded and they came closer. Without any words, the cook handed the man the paper and, in exchange, took a bundle of rupees. Hassan took another picture. The man and woman turned and hurried across the road. They got into a rickshaw that sped off to the end of the street and turned a corner to join the city traffic on the main road. The cook stood for a few seconds, his smile hardly visible but definitely there.

He walked off in the direction of the rickshaw, his steps slower this time, before he dissolved into the city too.

Hassan returned to the others, slipping behind Maryam, Amina, and Zain.

'Hassan, you look tired,' Maryam said, as she turned to him.

'I like those,' he said, pointing to the bangles that Amina was carrying. It worked; they looked away again.

So many things were churning inside his head. The bundle of money. The ship plans. He had to let Mir Saab know. But the cook would find out and tell Mir Saab who his father was. The bangles shone and glinted; the voices around him blurred and were replaced by the sound of dogs barking on the street outside his house. He pictured his father jumping over the back wall. Hassan held onto his camera more tightly. There was only one thing to do. He had to speak to the cook himself.

Begum Saab joined them with Ali Noor by her side, loaded with bundles of silk on his outstretched arms. 'They call me Aunty now, not Bibi anymore. Do I look that old?' she asked, shaking her head.

Chapter Nineteen

Back at the house, Hassan ate lunch with one thought in his mind. He finished before the others and excused himself from the table, avoiding eye contact with Maryam. He walked through the dining room, then the passageway, and pushed through the door flaps of the kitchen to stand in the middle of the room. His arms were folded under the camera which still hung at the end of the strap around his neck. The cook turned to him from the pots on the stove as if he were greeting an old friend.

'So, you've had a think, have you?' he said, stirring the pot and dropping the lid with a crash on the worktop. 'I knew you'd see sense.'

'Yes, I've been thinking,' Hassan said.

'They want Chinese food this evening.' The cook continued stirring.

'I'm not working for you.'

'Then what do you want?'

'I want to know more. What do you sell?'

'Are you trying to trick me? If you try anything, I'll get Mir Saab on your father before you can pick up your broken teeth.'

'What information do you sell and who are you selling it to besides the newspapers?' Hassan asked, sweating. The cook came nearer to him with the long wooden spoon in his hand but Hassan didn't move. He could feel the heat coming from the cook's body.

'You think you can come in and talk to me like that, do you? You think you're one of them now, better than me. You're wrong. You'll never change who you are.'

The cook sprayed water from his mouth as he spoke but Hassan stayed where he was.

'Your father thought he could do better too than what he was. He went to work at the newspaper in Harikaya. Thought he was special. Got ideas of equality. What rubbish. He was nothing more than a drunken loser. Both of you are nothing but losers. I'll tell them you gave me the information. You'll never go back now.'

The kitchen doors flapped. It was Kulsoom.

'Come to help, have you?' the cook asked her.

She scowled. 'What are you doing?' she asked, looking from the cook to Hassan.

'We were just talking,' the cook said. His arm stretched out to stroke her cheek. She jerked back. The cook wobbled but steadied his legs.

'Where were you last night?' she asked him.

The cook grew bigger and a darkness passed over him. He took a step towards Kulsoom. Food dripped off the spoon in his hand. Hassan's whole body hardened and his fingers tightened around the camera.

'Enough.' The cook waved the spoon. 'As long as I come back, what's it to you?

'Tell me where you go,' she said.

With one shove of his free arm, the cook sent Kulsoom to the floor. Hassan rushed between them and received the blow meant for her. His ear drum rang like a siren and his jaw screamed but he held onto his camera with both hands.

'Get out of here, you son of a bitch!' the cook shouted at him. 'You're as bad as your father. That bastard.'

Kulsoom was standing up, holding onto Hassan. Her hands were hot on his shoulders. She pulled him away and screamed at the cook, 'Leave him alone!' It was a raw, desperate scream at some wild animal about to spring. She pushed Hassan through the door, following him to the dining room.

'Hassan, he's a dangerous man. Stay away,' she whispered once they were in the dining room.

Hassan felt blood on his face. 'Why didn't you tell me you were…?'

She looked up at him; her eyes were haunted. 'Go now,' she said.

'I'm going to get him,' Hassan said. He ran through the hall and out of the door, ripping his sleeve on the handle. He was powered by a heartbeat that set his body on fire. The hot sun made him raise his arm to his face. His sleeve was ripped and his mouth was wet. That taste again. Ink and oranges. Blood. He made for the gates. Exhausted, he leant against the wall out of sight of the snoring guards.

Where are you? a voice whispered in his mind. He put his hand in his mouth so he would not scream from the pain in his jaw. *Where are you?* He thought of the beekeeper and his father. His eyelids drooped. His knees were weak. 'Where are you?' The voice was clear now and loud; it was outside his head. There was a blur of noise around him, warm bodies; he was surrounded by the others.

'Where were you, Hassan?' Maryam asked him. 'What's happened. Your face, it's bleeding.'

'I fell,' he said, straightening up against the wall.

'That must have been some fall.'

They gave him water and he drank most of it. It was cold. It eased the pain and he found he could stand without the aid of the wall. He washed his face with the rest of the water and spat out blood. He had no memory of them walking to the pool.

'I can manage,' he said, when Zain took his elbow.

Zain picked up a stick and pretended to draw it out of a sheath in his belt. He used it to draw an imaginary circle on the sandy ground around Hassan. Then, he drew a line that pushed out and away from the circle.

'A path for you,' he said to Hassan. 'Walk, kind sir, for you are free.'

Hassan took a slow step forwards and Maryam and Amina followed along the line.

'Bend on one knee, Hassan.' Zain spoke in an American accent now, copied from the films. Hassan let Zain place the stick on his head.

'My sword makes you a Knight of Bee City.'

Hassan stood up and Zain handed the sword to Maryam.

'You may draw the first shape,' he said to her.

Maryam drew a hexagon as big as the circle.

'Please step inside the bee's cell,' Maryam said to Hassan. 'You've set forth on a magic island. The power of darkness comes to you, Knight of Bee City. You will walk alone through the forest, day and night, with no fear.'

'As King of Bee City, I command you, Amina,' Zain continued, 'to draw your shape.'

Maryam then handed the stick to Amina who stepped forwards.

'This is the perfect hexagon,' Amina said.

They all spoke with solemn voices.

'Your horse waits outside. But only after the magic shapes are finished, can you go and do your duty,' Zain said to Hassan, 'to find the beekeeper and serve the Queen. Now you must draw the perfect hexagon around me. It is your first test as a Knight of Bee City.'

Hassan stepped out of his circle and drew another hexagon. The corners of his hexagon overlapped with Maryam's.

'It's the code,' Zain said.

'What code?' Hassan asked.

'The code for magic identification,' Zain replied with a dark tone in his voice. 'Each of us is one of these hexagon shapes.'

Maryam took the stick again and drew another hexagon and then Amina. Zain followed.

'A comb,' Hassan said.

'The link between us and the key to Bee City,' Zain said.

'This magic identification is our entry to Bee City,' Maryam said.

Hassan poked a spot in each small hexagon. 'The first stage is nearly over. The young bees are growing.'

'What's the second stage?' asked Amina.

'That comes when Hassan goes to the forest,' Maryam said.

'Now we'll go and find water; the lake is near.' Zain jammed the stick into the ground below the hexagons. He closed his eyes and concentrated. 'The lake will reveal itself to us when we're ready. But first, there's a lot to do.'

Hassan closed his eyes and imagined a lake, a large one surrounded by trees, by the forest. When he opened his eyes, they were all in shadow; the light had disappeared behind a rare cloud.

'Come on, the first task is to ask for guidance; we need to know the direction of the lake,' Zain said.

'The beekeeper will live near water,' Maryam said.

'Draw circles and hexagons everywhere. Find your swords and make the cells,' Zain said. 'Work for guidance.'

They made more overlapping hexagons, working hard for guidance until the cloud disappeared and they felt the heat.

'We need to go back. Mother will be doing the gathering soon,' Amina said in her usual voice again.

'We'll come again,' Zain said, 'tomorrow, to find the lake together.'

It was perhaps the use by Zain of the word *together* that triggered a flash. Whatever it was, a path of electricity was set in motion through Hassan's brain. The others set off into the forest but Hassan hung back with the shape, his stick in his hand and the dust still settling around him. Only Maryam turned her head and stopped but he was stuck. Her form became hazy and turned into a shadow, coming towards him and stopping on the edge of his hexagon. Hassan stabbed his stick into the ground and leant on it but the images in his head didn't stop. The cook's arm, raised above him. The wooden spoon growing bigger. Smash. The pain. His mind cracked.

Hassan held his stick in the air and saw a body on the floor. The cook. He raised the stick higher with both hands and brought it down in one swoop on that body.

'Die! Die! Die! Die! Die!'

The word wouldn't stop.

'Die! Die! Die! Die!'

'Hassan!' It was Maryam's voice. But his was louder, so loud that it broke through to him and he stopped. The earth below him was covered in holes, holes coming closer, so near his face now... Hassan fell to the ground. A hand was on his shoulder. It touched the outer shell of his mind. Through the dirt, the blood, and the tears, he saw Maryam's face.

Chapter Twenty

The family ate dinner earlier than usual that evening, still tired from the previous night. Maryam's gaze was following him. She looked as if she had a million questions but he had no answers, not yet.

'That was quite a fall you took on the stairs,' Mir Saab said.

Hassan raised his hand to cover the bruises. Mir Saab had his drawings in front of him at the dining table and was trying to draw but after a minute he muttered to himself – something about the factories and *charity* – and got up to pace the room. Then Mir Saab stopped at the table, drew something on the boat drawing, and started to walk around the room again. It kept happening until, finally, Mir Saab sat down and picked up the newspaper, still neatly folded on the tray that Muhammed always brought in the morning. Mir Saab froze as he read. On the front page of the newspaper was a photo of him. His eyes shone with disbelief, moving over the article; he let the newspaper drop to the floor.

'What's happened?' Zain asked, picking up the newspaper. He read the headline out loud: '"The Mir of Harikaya's Plan to Build an Ark".' He read on. 'The mir has a passion for animal life. It has been reported that the mir favours animals above humans.'

'The government's eaten my dream.' Mir Saab covered his head with his hands.

Zain continued reading, '"This kind of fantasy-driven attitude in today's society is dangerous. We, the government, are now working to take over the responsibility of the factories of Harikaya for this reason, to safeguard the people who work there."'

'Tell the police,' Zain shouted, throwing the newspaper on the table.

'What can they do?' Mir Saab had tears in his eyes.

The government had trapped him again, stamping on his dream. No, they had stamped on him. Breakfast sat on the table untouched.

'I give up,' Mir Saab said.

'Baba, no, you must fight back.' Zain stood up.

'Fight back?' Mir Saab said. 'I'm not entering into a war with gossip columnists or the government.'

'Who do you think leaked the news, Baba?' Amina asked.

'It could have been one of the servants,' Zain said.

Hassan's jaw hurt now even more. He excused himself and left the room.

'You didn't tell me what happened to your face.' It was Maryam at the bottom of the stairs. She had followed him.

'I fell.'

'Tell me the truth.'

'Maryam.' Her name sounded out of place amongst his hard thoughts and he stopped. 'Not now.'

Hassan ran up to the first floor, round the landing, and up the second flight, past the room where they had evoked the jinn and round again to the floor where the attic rooms were. He climbed the few steps to the door to the roof. It was bolted and only opened with some difficulty, creaking and breaking through a heap of cobwebs as it did so. The air was cooler outside now.

He wasted no time walking over to the generator which buzzed quietly in the middle of the roof. He walked all the way around until he found what he was looking for – a flap. He opened it and there was a small space, cool and dark and big enough for his camera. He took off his waistcoat with the comb in the pocket and wrapped the camera in it before he placed it in the space. It was not visible even if someone lifted the flap and it was safer here than in his room.

He tiptoed down to the bottom step and turned the corner behind the banister. 'Maryam, you're still here.'

'Where have you been?' she asked.

'On the roof. I was looking for something.'

When his father had come back from his adventures and his mother asked him where he'd been, Hassan had learnt then that the best way to lie was to tell a part truth.

'What happened to you, Hassan?' Maryam was not satisfied as easily as his mother had been.

'Maryam, I can't tell you. Not yet,' he said. 'There's some business I need to finish now.'

'What?

'I can't tell you that either,' he said. 'I have to ask you for one thing.'

Maryam nodded.

'I'll need somewhere to hide.'

'Who from?' She grabbed his wrist.

'The cook.'

'Why?'

'Please trust me,' he said.

Maryam's face was so familiar now. He wanted to trust her too. It was hard to believe she would be leaving soon. She let go of his arm.

Hassan left Maryam and went down to the kitchen. Quick steps. Determined stride, in case he changed his mind. The cook was alone in the backyard, sitting in front of a fire with a metal mug in his hands. Smells of fried food hung about the place. The cook was startled to see him.

'The prodigal son returns for more,' he said. 'Enjoy your dinner?'

'Yes.'

'Why are you here?'

'I've been thinking about what you said. About us working together.'

The cook continued looking at the fire and drank from the mug. The liquid splashed as he brought it down again.

'What do you want me to do?' Hassan asked.

'What made you see sense?' the cook asked.

The cook seemed to be laughing behind his words but Hassan had to go on.

'I'm not one of them. I never will be. Our types have to do what we can,' Hassan said.

'How do I know you're not setting me up?'

'I know what you'd do if I was.' So far it was working.

The cook stood up. 'Meet me when the sun has set at the main gates by the road,' he said.

'What are we going to do?'

'I'll show you how I work. If you pass that test, I'll show you more. I'll tell you where your precious father is.'

Hassan kept his face calm. He couldn't leave without asking one more question.

'Why do you hate my father so much?'

The cook's eyes betrayed the bitterness inside him.

'Why do you love him so much? He still hasn't been in touch with you.'

'That's because...'

'He doesn't care.'

'Where is he?'

'I'll tell you after you help me.'

Sunset was only an hour away but it was still too much time to wait and too much time to think. This was a risk. Did the cook believe him? If this 'errand' gave him the information he wanted, then Mir Saab would have justice. He had to take that risk. He made his way back to the servants' quarters and reached the bottom of the steps but then changed his mind and stopped. The crow with the white spot on its wing landed at his feet and he knelt down.

'I have no more gulab jamun,' he said.

It leapt backwards and took off, flying over the two-storey building in the direction of the forest. Hassan took off too, making sure no one was around before he slipped behind the building and through the hole in the wall. The pain in his jaw stayed with him as he entered the temple of the bees.

Here he was safe again. Warmth was spreading from the nest. The cluster of bees around the hive shuddered. Baba had said this was what happened before the swarming. When the colony shuddered, they were keeping the nest warm for the cells which were getting ready to hatch. And then they would swarm, find a new home and the cycle would start all over again.

The colony was working together as the shudders rippled across the surface of the nest. It felt like a celebration. He had been in Karachi for a week now. It seemed much longer. And the family would be going back to Harikaya soon, and Hassan would go with them.

The crows screeched outside. Even they were joining the celebration. Hassan wanted to stay, wanted to enter the hive, but he had to meet the cook. He shivered, out of fear this time. What if the cook was lying? What if he had no idea where Baba was? That was likely but he had to meet him, to take that chance.

It was hard to leave, but there was no other way. Cold fear spread through his body. Danger was also a dance. *This* was a dance. His departure from the stirrings of birth was a dance. He'd come back soon. Their energy would see him through what was to come. However far away he was from the hive, there was an invisible line that would bring him back; it worked for the bees and it had worked so far for him.

He stood at the doorway and whispered, 'Let me get back for my mother's eyes.' He had never prayed in his life before.

Chapter Twenty-One

The rickshaw stopped in a narrow street outside a greying corner building with its shutters closed.

'I'll wait for you here,' the cook said. 'Once you've knocked, someone will open the door and you give him this.' He pulled out a cloth bundle from the pocket of his trousers.

Hassan was holding onto the seat of the rickshaw to stop himself from running away. Everything smelt of lies but he had to do this, for Mir Saab's sake. He trod over piles of rubbish left in the street and his feet were wet from the sewage. He walked a few steps and looked back at the cook. There was venom in his eyes and Hassan nearly ran. This was a big mistake.

'Go on,' the cook hissed, waving his hand in the direction of the door.

Hassan reached the pavement and made his way to the flaking door. He knocked once. There was no answer and he looked back at the cook who had his fist in the air. Hassan knocked again. On the third knock, he heard footsteps. It opened slowly onto a dark gloom, out of which a man appeared, holding a long rifle. He had eyes like those of the children Hassan had seen on the streets. The smell of acidic sweetness came out of the house from behind the man and made Hassan want to sneeze. He gave the man the bundle, turned and took a few steps back towards the rickshaw.

'Where's the money?' the man shouted and Hassan looked back. The man had unwrapped the bundle and a bunch of papers was drifting to the floor. The man took his rifle in both hands, raised it to his shoulder and stepped out of the house, pointing the gun at the rickshaw.

'You son of a bitch. Sent a kid to do your dirty work,' he said calmly. The man fired.

The cook laughed and the driver took off down the street. Hassan ran around the corner and dived into the gutter between a car and a concrete pavement. His arm was touched by the spray of bullets and his head and shoulder hit the pavement when he dived. Hassan squeezed under the car with a fist in his mouth to stop himself from screaming from the pain that was burning inside him. The smell of sewage was all around him.

The man ran around the pavements near the car for several minutes. His footsteps came close and stopped by the car, his foot right next to Hassan's eyes. The man's feet stayed by the car for a minute, maybe more. In that time, Hassan tried to force his eyes to stay open but they kept closing; his lids were unbearably heavy. If this was his time and place to die, there was nothing to do but accept it. He had tried to trick the cook but the cook had tricked him. Everything was over.

Eventually the man left. Hassan waited until he heard the door of the house shut and the locks turn before he pulled himself out and retched. He was sick by the side of the car and his clothes were heavy and caked with the mud of the sewer. They stank.

The street was dark; there was only the light that came through the cracks from behind the closed shutters. Without thinking, he started to run, numb to everything. He had to get away, had to find his way out of this warren of streets. He reached the end of the road and, with no idea of where he was going, he ran over rubble, into dead-ends, and back again through streets that all looked the same. He nearly tripped over sleepy addicts huddled in corners. The stench of the drains was normal here and his feet splashed through puddles of sewage and old rain water. All he wanted was to get as far away from that place as he could, as far away from that man with the gun as possible – and fast.

The sound of it still throbbed in his ears as he ran. He came to a square that swam in a haze of hashish and the smell of incense. He had reached a shrine, much bigger than the one in Harikaya. Crowds had gathered everywhere but there were no poets. He missed the poets. A few more steps and he hit the ground. Two children loomed over him. One of them said something, but only their lips moved. The pain drowned out the noise; it was all over him. He fought to keep his eyes open. He had to get back. Back to Maryam, back to Mir Saab. Two women were above him now, both with long, straight hair. No, they were men. They were women. Who cared? They lifted him up and carried him in soft arms. He was put down by a small fire; it was warm but the pain wouldn't stop. Other people, women or men, he wasn't sure, sat around. His eyes were too heavy now. One of them put a cloth on his skin. It was warm and wet and she wiped his face.

'I am Maya,' she said, taking his hands and wiping them clean. She sang a lullaby and his eyes closed. He heard the tune. It was one his mother had sung many years ago. Sometimes she still sang it. The woman wiped his feet. That felt good. Then she removed his clothes, leaving his pants and wiped down his body, all the time singing a lullaby. His body burnt with pain but the lullaby was making him sleepy.

During the night, he opened his eyes and her hand was on his forehead. For a second, he thought she was his mother. He tried to rise but he fell back on the blanket underneath him.

'Where have you come from?' the woman asked him.

He mumbled something.

'Are you a man or a woman?' Hassan asked.

'A bit of both.' She shrugged and Hassan lay back again as she started to sing that lullaby again.

During the night he woke a few times and Maya was always there.

'I must get back. My mother's eyes,' he said and Maya nodded as if she already knew everything.

Another time when he woke, sweating, he saw her form, holding a wet cloth on his head. 'Amma,' he said.

He dreamt that he was standing at the side of a great wooden sailing boat, moored with a thick rope. The moonlight reflected on the water. Men were carrying on board beds, tables, chairs, and wooden chests for Mir Saab's cameras, balancing along the plank connecting the ship to the silent harbour. Hassan went too into the wood-panelled ship. The men and women inside worked by the light of small oil lamps positioned every few feet along the wooden floor planks.

Hassan was checking everything was placed in the boat according to the plan he carried. He remembered Mir Saab's words, 'If this got into the wrong hands…' But the workers were coming too quickly and the piece of paper in his hand was getting crumpled and frayed. Hassan looked at the sheet but the pencil marks were fading.

And now animals started to come aboard. Goats with shaggy hair and horns that twisted round and round to scrape the ceiling. A snow leopard growled as it too boarded the ship. Its pale fur turned black and he could see its white teeth. The growls became deeper, more menacing. Someone was hiding inside the boat behind the open door but whoever it was vanished by the time Hassan got there.

And then he heard the shots. They were outside the boat. He dived down onto the wooden floor but the shots still rang out. He heard footsteps on the plank. It was that man with the gun!

Hassan opened his eyes; he was panting. Where was he?

'It's all right,' Maya said. 'You're safe.'

He fell asleep again, and the next time he woke up, she was still there. It must have been early in the morning because people were dotted about after the night, lying on blankets like him. A few walked around like ghosts. The fire next to him was still going.

'You're very lucky,' Maya said. 'The bullet only got your flesh, but you have some bad cuts. What happened to you?'

The warmth in her face and the way she sat, so relaxed and accepting, made Hassan's words come forth. The story poured out and there were no questions from her or signs of shock, or even opinions. She just listened. He talked about his mother, the honey, and his father. He talked about the boys, the doll, the dog, and the train to Karachi. He spoke of Maryam and Mir Saab. But when he talked about the cook, his voice was small and his throat felt dry.

'You showed courage,' Maya said. 'You wanted to help Mir Saab.'

'The cook paid me back for that.'

'But what he did was... There has to be more. Why did he want to hurt you so much?' she asked.

'I wanted to prove his guilt.' And yet he agreed with Maya. There had to be more. Perhaps some debt the cook wanted him to pay back on behalf of his father. He sank back on the blanket.

'Your father was snatched away from you too soon,' Maya said.

'It was stupid of me to go with the cook,' Hassan said.

'We can't always know what we're meant to learn when we suffer.'

'Do you believe we always learn from suffering?' Hassan asked.

Maya just looked back at him.

The next time he woke up, children were playing in front of a shrine. The sun had risen. Everything from the night before came back to him in pictures. The cook, the rickshaw, the shots. If only he could remember the name of the street. He sat up. Maya stirred and smiled as soon as she saw him up.

'You're better,' she said. 'What's your name?'

'I am Hassan. Do you live here?' he asked.

'Yes, we have the house over there.'

She pointed to the corner of the square to a three-storey house that was waking up too. Some of the shutters were open, some women with the arms and hands of men were looking out of the window.

'You can rest there,' she said.

He managed to walk to the house with her and he was grateful when the door to a room on the ground floor opened. It was a simple room, just a bed made out of bamboo, like the one he had at home. Maya left him and he lay down and drifted in and out of sleep, cushioned by the comings and goings of people on the stairs and through the front doors and even by the stomping up and down the stairs.

She came in to give him some food, a plate of rice and yoghurt, and some water. She asked him again where he lived and he tried to remember the name of the street where Mir Saab's house was. The most he could do was picture the sign on the wall.

Stomping turned to creaking and Maya had to stop curious people from entering the room. It was really time to go. The pain was still there but now it was bearable. He stood up; he could walk without hobbling. It was as if he had been reborn into a new life. A second chance. He pictured Maryam's face. He did not want to spend another night away.

He sat on the bed. He tried to remember but the name of the street was gone. He thought of the house, the courtyard. The guards. The masjid. He'd been away a night and it must have been late afternoon now. He pictured the nest, how it had shuddered just before he left. He heard their humming again. The sound was filling his head.

It took him back to the first day he arrived in Karachi. Kulsoom had been in the car with him as they whizzed through the city, through the traffic to the house on the street which was lined with a wall. Yellow, like so many in Karachi, but this was a long wall. The paint on the wall was flaky, showing the undercoat in parts. The car was approaching the gate. The car slowed before it turned and that was when he saw the sign. Shiny metal. Two words. Yes. Harikaya House, Mistra Road.

The next time Maya came in he told her where he lived and she hugged him.

'My aunt works there,' he said.

Maya stood by him like an old friend saying goodbye, hopeful that the next time wouldn't be too long. Both of them knew that there would never be another meeting. She gave the rickshaw driver some rupees before he drove off with Hassan at the back. When he reached the bottom of the street, he turned and there she was: the woman-man who had saved his life and, even though she was one of the poor, the unnamed and untouchables of Karachi, she had handed over her money for him. He waved and she raised her hand. She blew him a kiss.

Chapter Twenty-Two

It was evening by the time the rickshaw drove up to the inner gates of the house. When the guards saw that it was Hassan inside, they started shouting, 'He's back. Tell Mir Saab.' He stepped out to more greetings from the guards who stood around with guns held vertically against their arms. He walked through them and into the house straight to the kitchen. The humidity made Hassan's clothes stick to his skin. He found the cook through the doors in the backyard, sitting alone on a low stool by the stove again. Hassan walked straight up to him. His shoulder hurt and his legs ached but the pain made him angry enough to keep him standing straight even when the cook looked at him as if he was a rat climbing out of the toilet.

'You tricked me,' Hassan said. 'You wanted me dead.'

'You tried to trick me.' The cook flicked the ash of his cigarette onto the ground.

'You knew that man had a gun. That's what you wanted from the beginning, to kill me.'

'Now you understand.'

'Why do you hate us so much?' Hassan asked him.

'"Us" is the right word,' the cook said. 'You're not as stupid as you behave.'

'I'll tell Mir Saab everything about you.'

'A threat,' the cook smirked. 'What about your beloved father and everything I know about him?'

'You know nothing.'

'You'll see. This friendship you two have. *Mir* and villager. It means nothing.'

The cook laughed – a crazed laugh. He picked up the flour and began to dust a wooden board with it. He scooped the dough out of the bowl and dropped it onto the board. He began to knead the dough with his knuckles and it became coated with the flour, growing drier with every press and stretch. The pain in Hassan's shoulder throbbed.

'Where is my father?'

'Your father's in prison.'

Hassan kept his fist still. The cook was lying. He had hesitated for a moment too long. 'How do you know that?'

'I have friends.'

'Why…?'

'Don't blame me. Blame your father, blame the country. When there's no other choice, what can a man do?'

The cook was speaking in riddles. His laugh had a sense of hysteria in it. A force out of control. It stopped too suddenly.

'I'll tell Mir Saab everything,' Hassan said.

The cook looked straight back at him as if he'd already

won the battle. 'You're not supposed to be here.' He smiled as though he had come to a realisation. 'Who'll believe a kid anyway? You'll get put away for dealing in opium and selling information. That's what I'll tell them about you. And then what'll happen to your poor mother? She'll have no choice anymore. She'll have to agree.'

'To what?' Hassan took a very slow step back.

The cook looked ready to pounce from some very dark place in the past and that place involved his mother.

'Agree to what?' Hassan asked again, his voice trembling.

'You ask too many questions.'

The cook lurched up to a standing position but then wobbled. He'd been drinking.

'And kids get tortured in jail, especially kids who betray their mir,' the cook said.

Hassan turned around and re-entered the house through the kitchen. The cook followed but drink slowed him down. Hassan ran all the way along the corridor into the dining room. He slid along the marble floor and turned the corner into the hall. Maryam was there like a ghost in front of him. Startled, he stopped short.

'Hassan,' she said. 'Where have you been? We've been worried sick. We called the police.'

'The cook's after me,' he whispered. He took off his sandals. There was no time to lose. He heard footsteps in the dining room, careful and predatory. Maryam ran to the front door. The cook would never dare hurt her, and so he flew up the steps, pausing after the first flight to see Maryam open the front doors and bang them shut.

After a few steps, Hassan stopped. The cook was in the

hall, but he had stopped too; he had to show manners to Maryam, no matter what. He asked her where Hassan was and Maryam said, 'He went that way,' pointing to the front doors. They swung open and closed again as the cook launched himself outside in pursuit. Hassan went higher, round and round to the top.

Hassan panted as he hauled himself outside onto the flat roof into the darkness of another power cut. The generator would soon whirr into life and the world would be lit up again, but for now he needed this darkness. He put his sandals back on and went to the place where he had hidden his camera and the honeycomb. They were safe, and he hung the strap around his neck and put on his waistcoat. He tapped the honeycomb in his pocket; it felt like his father was with him again. His breath relaxed to a steady pace and he listened out for the cook down below. He was safe up here, for the moment at least. The top of the house was out of bounds to the servants unless Begum Saab was with them on a cleaning mission.

He squatted against the wall that bordered the roof until his eyes became used to the lack of light. He tried to gather his thoughts. But the clash of metal and horns from the city streets beyond the grounds didn't allow this. They pounded on his ear drums until he wanted to shout 'Shut up!' at the top of his voice.

He stood up and looked over the wall. A guard walked across the yard, rifle in hand, towards the back of the house. The door to the roof clicked behind him and Hassan dropped to the floor behind the wall, in the shadows.

'Hassan.' It was Maryam.

'Over here.' He stood up.

'Why was the cook…?' Maryam began.

'We can't talk here. He might see us from below.'

'Come on.' Maryam went down the stairs in the dark with care and Hassan was happy to follow her, through her bedroom and out into the back corridor. At one end of the corridor was a glass doorway that led to the stairwell at the back of the house.

'Is that door locked?' he asked.

Maryam checked; it was. They crept down the long corridor lined with smaller rooms. At the other end, they entered another bedroom and off this was a bathroom.

'I'll go and tell my uncle what's happened,' Maryam said.

'Not yet,' he said. 'I need to think. Please just wait till I'm ready. Please.'

The truth was that he didn't know what to do.

'The cook's hanging around,' she said.

'He'll never find me here. Maryam, I'll tell you everything in the morning.' He was exhausted and she saw it too.

'You can sleep here,' she said, pointing at the four-poster bed in the middle of the room.

She was about to leave but she stayed beside him, both of them looking at the bed. It was draped with heavy curtains tied to the posts. Two folded sheets lay on top of the bed and the mattress was so thick it looked like a ship.

'My uncle knows that you're back,' she said. 'I'll tell him that you're asleep.'

'I need to give you this,' he said. He held the camera tightly for a few seconds. It gave him a feeling of some kind of permanence, however fleeting, and he needed that now. He handed it to her. 'The film inside is important. It's best if you keep it. I'll explain in the morning.'

He started to make the bed when Maryam left. There was no lightbulb, but a candle lay on a plate on a side cupboard with a box of matches. It was in the semi-darkness of that one candle that he created a nest for himself, protected by the impenetrable world that belonged to Maryam and Amina.

He went over to the shutters, closed by day to shut out the heat. He opened them to let in air now. He went outside and stood on the balcony which was shielded by the mosquito mesh affixed to the teardrops and swirls of the wooden framework. He remembered his first time here when Maryam was telling her stories. That felt like so long ago that it was like another life, but he still tried to imagine the people of her stories through the mosquito mesh. He moved closer to it and put his hand up to rest on the ledge.

He leant forward and his hand slipped through the gap where the netting joined the wooden frame; the gap was bigger than he remembered. It had made him stumble the first time he was here and he imagined Maryam's hand on his elbow, steadying him.

He looked out over the courtyard, the gates, and the dry land that lay like a carpet up to the boundaries of the world outside. He thought of taking a picture but it was too dark and anyway, his camera was with Maryam now. Mir Saab had spoken of night lenses that he had used in the jungle. They'd work for the jungle of Karachi too, he thought. His mind went back to Maryam. He refused to think about the fact that she was leaving soon. They would be going to Harikaya any day now. Mir Saab had promised.

The power cut ended abruptly and the city lights came back on. The lights made the sky brown, the colour of the river Indus flowing through Harikaya in the rainy season.

There was movement down below. A foot appeared from the doorway of the servants' quarters. Hassan stepped back into the shadows of the balcony. The whole body was there now – in the courtyard. It was the cook. Someone came out behind him. Hassan's head was stuck to the meshing, pressing it forwards to see who it was. It could only be Kulsoom. Her shirt and trousers shone in the dark as she walked behind the cook, who turned around and hid her from view. What were they doing? Hassan stepped back into the darkness but he could still see them.

The cook was drawing aside Kulsoom's scarf and bringing his face down to her shoulder. Her head was back; perhaps she was looking at the stars. Hassan stepped forward again, this time with his hand pushing out the meshing so he could get a better view. It was a mistake. The meshing rattled and the cook looked around and then up. Hassan jumped back and stood still. A few seconds later, he heard footsteps and peered over again. The couple were walking off towards the gates.

Hassan felt sick. How could Kulsoom stand that man? He went to lie on the bed, fully clothed.

He shifted restlessly about, too hot with his clothes on but too tired and tense to take them off, even his waistcoat. He checked the clock by the bed. It was midnight and his body was beginning to settle. He lay flat and felt sleep begin to wrap around his body, but just as it did, a door creaked. It had to be the glass door that Maryam had checked before. His own door was not completely shut and he heard footsteps, tripping lightly across the floor.

'Son of a bitch.' It was the cook's voice.

Other doors were opening along the corridor. The cook was checking the rooms. Hassan had to get out.

He seized his sandals then crept towards the balcony. The shutters had to be quiet. He had to be quick *and* quiet. That hole, where was it? *There*. The outer ledge was thin, almost too thin, but he held on tight to the frame as he tucked in the mesh again. Once the hole was invisible he turned to face thin air. He thought he could make the tree branch. He had to risk it; he couldn't stay here, no matter what. He jumped and grabbed hold of it, swinging from there to the ground. A silent drop.

The balcony shutters were opening. He hid behind the tree and the cook stood behind the mesh. The cook's breathing was heavy. He risked a great deal going up there to find Hassan.

The cook vanished. Hassan ran to the back of the servants' quarters.

The cook had to be coming down, but if Hassan was quick…

The hole. There it was.

He was on the other side.

He ran.

Chapter Twenty-Three

There was no moonlight, only a cloudy sky that no stars could break through. Snakes and lizards didn't matter; he just wanted to reach the bees. His footsteps remembered the way in the darkness. His feet and arms held back the branches instinctively.

Inside the masjid, Hassan paced the chamber like a caged tiger. Should he go back or stay? He stepped outside. All was quiet. The cook would never think to come here. He went down the steps and stopped at the bottom to look at the city sky, pretending it was full of stars like in Harikaya and that the distant traffic were reeds in the wind that snapped as people rushed past on bicycles along the track back to the village. Snap, snap, snap. He was there again, even if it was just a story in his head unfolding on that track. He imagined walking in the opposite direction to all the other villagers, through the fields under the starry night, nearer the forest now. The smell of the rains was stronger. It was a sweet smell.

The trees stood before him under the moon, and a silhouette with a silver outline. His father? He ran to greet him but the form became clearer. The man's hair was long and matted. The beekeeper. His body was thick and strong. His eyes stared at Hassan and changed colour as the night sky moved through them. Hassan was about to speak but the beekeeper's form dissolved into the darkness of the trees behind him.

It was time to go back into the masjid and he turned to climb the steps but then stopped. He heard a distinct rustling; someone was moving in the leaves. Then all was quiet. Someone was watching him.

He counted, one, two, three… and then he turned suddenly and jumped onto the first step and then stopped. There was the beating of wings and he turned around to see the crow. *His* crow, with the white spot. It landed on the top step with a worm in its mouth. Hassan crouched down. 'You followed me, didn't you?' The crow swallowed the worm. Both of them were silent for several seconds. It was good to know the bird was with him. 'I have to go now.' Hassan looked back as he opened the door and stepped inside. He bolted the lock behind him.

Something stronger than his own fear had made him stay: a wall of invisible power that exhausted him the more he fought against it. He sank down against the pillar cradled by the humming of the bees in their nest. The city of combs looked majestic. The bees accepted his presence; he was one of theirs.

The humming was a great wall of sound and he noticed that there was a new tone to the humming. The births of the drones must have happened and he had missed it. He had missed the first stirrings of the newly born from inside the nest. The humming touched him out here on the floor. Young bees. Workers, drones and the queen. He leant back. The bees were busy with their young.

He sat thinking. He would wait here for now, with the bees, and sneak back to the house in the morning where he would find Maryam to work out a plan. Maryam... his stomach leapt. The cook had got so close to Maryam and Amina, but he could do nothing to them. Not to the mir's daughter and niece. Playing with Hassan's life was one thing, but playing with theirs was another thing altogether. They had to be safe.

The floor was not as soft as the bed he had just come from, but he was soon asleep and when he opened his eyes again, daylight was pouring onto the floor. He was greeted by the humming, but there was a markedly different feeling about the nest.

He unbolted the door and went to the forest to empty his bladder. As soon as the water left him, his throat felt dry. He swallowed a few times. There were puddles of rain on the ground but he wasn't thirsty enough to drink from there. There must have been showers overnight. That meant the rains would be coming soon in Harikaya, if there were already signs here. He had been gone one night and now another. As soon as he got out, he would explain everything to Mir Saab and they would go Harikaya – any day now.

His chest lifted, yes, there was hope.

There was always hope. His stomach rumbled. There was no water but it was still too early to go back to the house; the cook would be prowling around, waiting for him. He went back inside.

On the floor was a dead bee, its body empty of life. He knelt down. The others were at work; not even death stopped them. Bees were arriving back from the early morning journeys to flowers, carrying yellow drops of pollen on their legs, food for both young bees and adults alike, as well as those just out of their cells.

Hassan sat down to save energy. He would leave, just not now. But his stomach roared and, worse, his thirst was growing. The floor swayed under him and he put his hand on it to steady himself. He would make it, he told himself, but it was hard to fight the dizziness that was coming over him. The humming was growing louder, as if competing with the sounds of his stomach.

A cluster of bees broke off from the bigger nest. They formed a ball that approached him and stopped in front of his chest; their humming penetrated the emptiness inside him.

He drifted in and out of sleep with the bees close by, feeding him with their energy until they left again. They must have sensed the presence of another human, for when they left, there was a knock on the door. Hassan stood up, as if in a dream, and went to stand behind the door.

'Hassan.' It was Maryam's voice. He unbolted and opened the door in a flash. She was alone, carrying two bottles of water and some chocolate. She came in but stopped after just a couple of steps when she heard the humming, which was growing louder and more intense.

'It's all right,' Hassan said. He led her by her arm to the pillar across from the nest. Another human was here to share their temple. He offered her his place in front of the pillar and took the water that she gave him, drinking a whole bottle in one go. He wanted to run up to her and wrap his arms around her, thank her a million times for coming, and tell her how scared he was. Instead, he sat down on the floor in front of her.

She was looking at the bees with wide eyes.

'The bees are friends,' he said.

The humming grew steady again. Her gaze moved slowly from him to the nest and then back to him again.

'They've been teaching me,' Hassan said.

Here, in the temple of the bees, Maryam was like a human queen bee. Everything, even the curiosity of the bees, revolved around her. Two or three bees approached her and she stayed still. More came near to her, getting very close. Her stillness was tense but they felt no threat from it.

'The rains are coming,' he said. 'Did you see the puddles outside? We'll need to speak to ask Mir Saab to book the plane tickets today.'

'What happened? Why did you leave the room?' she asked.

'The cook found me. I had to run here.' He grasped his shoulder. The pain rushed through his nerves like ants crawling inside his skin.

Maryam didn't react and her expression was serious.

'What's wrong, Maryam?'

'Tell me what's been happening.'

'I told you.'

'How did the boat design get in your room?'

'Boat design?' It took a few seconds. 'Oh yes. I found it on the floor in the living room. I forgot to ask Mir Saab if I could have it.'

Her stare was like a glass knife.

'Why, what's wrong?' he said. 'Mir Saab had thrown it away. I liked it.' It was then that he understood. 'You don't think I…?'

'The cook found the paper in your room this morning. He used it to accuse you.'

'They think I leaked the information to the press?'

'Yes.'

'Mir Saab too?'

Her silence made him tense. He stood up and paced the floor.

'Maryam, everything I've told you is the truth.'

'But not the whole truth.'

The sound of humming cushioned his pain, in his body and in his heart. The water was more than good. Only sips but it was heaven. The chocolate eased his pain like the humming. He chewed slowly until it melted.

'Before I came here, my father took some black honey from the forest.' Another swallow. His face was hot and his hands soaked in sweat. 'He fell from the tree and the beekeeper saved him.'

Maryam's mouth opened.

'Yes,' Hassan nodded. 'The beekeeper is real.'

'And you kept it secret.'

'I had to. Mir Saab's guards came at night but my father escaped.'

'You were worried that my uncle would start another search for your father,' she said. Her voice was quiet.

'The cook knew everything. He threatened to tell Mir Saab about my father.' Tears dropped that he brushed away angrily. 'The cook wanted me to get information from Mir Saab. He said he would find a way for me to get back to Harikaya in time to save my mother's eyes. I only told him that Mir Saab likes animals. I thought it would be harmless. I was desperate.'

Maryam didn't react.

'When I realised he was the thief, I decided to play a trick on him to prove he was guilty.'

'And it didn't work.'

'I nearly died,' Hassan took a breath. 'He knows some dangerous people.'

'He's hurt my uncle too.'

Hassan touched the honeycomb in his waistcoat pocket. Safe. And his camera? He stopped.

'Do you have the camera?'

'What?' Maryam asked. Her attention was with the bees again.

'My camera. I gave it to you last night.'

'Yes, you told me the film was important.'

'The market,' he said.

'The market?' Maryam said.

'He was there at the market. The cook was there. I have a picture of him.' Hassan stood up, both fists in the air.

'Maryam, I saw him with two people. He swapped the plan of the boat for money.'

'And you took a photo?' Her voice was hopeful.

'Yes.'

'And it's in the camera?'

'The evidence,' he said. 'Where is the camera?'

'I gave it to Ali Noor this morning. I asked him to have the pictures developed urgently. Mir Saab knows a place that can do them quickly.'

Hassan paced the floor. 'This is my only chance.'

Maryam looked at the bottles and the chocolate. 'Ali Noor will be going to pick the pictures up soon. I'll go with him. I'll make sure they don't get lost. You wait here.'

He was at the door when she reached out for the handle. He put his hand there first.

'Maryam, I need to get back to Harikaya. The bees are about to swarm here. That means they will swarm in Harikaya soon.'

She looked around the temple, saw the urgency of the bees, heard their changing tones. She took it all in.

'I won't be long. I'll knock and say my name when I come back.' She stood up. 'Do you think the beekeeper's waiting for you?'

'I don't know. Sometimes I think he is,' Hassan said.

She went to leave through the door and some invisible force rose from his body and it flew to her. She turned around.

'I've forgotten what my father looks like,' he said as she looked back.

~

Hassan set about watching the bees when Maryam left. The activity around the nest seemed slower. A few bees, workers no doubt, were taking a rest, hovering around the cluster that clung to the nest on the outside. More emerged from the inner depths. They were waiting for something. Despite their slowness, there was urgency. Hassan remembered his father's words.

'The bees need to find a new home for the new queen and the colony before the rains.'

'Why?' he had asked his father.

'It's hard to move through the storms. It takes too long and the food can run out,' his father had replied. 'The bees will send scouts to look for the new place.'

More bees joined the hovering ones, and they were all now moving together in a specific dance. These were the scouts, and the bees that were still dancing were sending them off to look for a new home.

One of the scouts left the group and Hassan followed its movements upwards, higher and higher, past the spiralling tiles. On its way, it stopped in a beam of sunlight coming through one of the holes in the rim. It hovered for a few moments in the warmth before it moved towards the hole and out into the air. Another bee followed, and soon all the scouts were leaving.

He ate the chocolate slowly. Where was Baba now? The cook had said he was in prison but Hassan knew that was a lie. Ansari Saab had said he had been seen in a musical band. His father might be travelling from village to village now, playing the instruments that he'd found or made.

Hassan stepped outside, just for a minute. It had to be

midday by now. Inside again, he paced the room, taking sips of the water. He had known Maryam for little more than a week but he trusted her and he would do anything for her. Did that mean he loved her? No, love was for films. Romantic love, at least. But was this another kind of love? Was it possible to have different kinds of love that he could measure or compare? And what about his love for the bees? Was that what he felt when he was inside the nest? Yes, it could be his imagination but that didn't matter anymore. The love in their home filled him with longing. When he was there between the walls of honeycomb he knew what he wanted: to be closer to the queen. In those moments he would do anything to be near her. Was this love?

He paced across the floor. Where was Maryam? Should he try to find her? What if the cook had followed her and what if he had hurt her? Hassan couldn't bear to think about that. He reached for the door and nearly opened it but turned around and paced to the other side of the floor again. He did that five times, stopping himself each time with his hand on the bolt.

The fifth time, he noticed the bees again.

Fifty or so scouts had returned and they were all dancing around the cluster for attention until there were just a handful left dancing the same dance. Their discovery seemed to be the most popular. Then they stopped too and, in one fell swoop, they dived into the colony. They had won the battle outside the nest but there was more work to do inside. The bees there had to know the news too.

The sound of humming grew quieter until the whole nest shuddered again and sent out a warmth which reached Hassan too. There were some sharp tones in the humming now, like horns, but higher pitched. The whole nest shuddered again and this time it glowed. The bees had agreed on a new destination.

They were about to swarm. The hive shuddered again, a compact ball of energy. Outside the mass, scouts darted up and down, left and right, about to lead the way. The cloud of bees began to move, changing shape from a ball into a cylinder. There were thousands, about to leave.

He heard a knock at the door, sharp and short. Hassan was there in a second, his ear on the wood. Footsteps on the soft sandy ground outside had to be Maryam's. There was more knocking on the door, but it was hard to hear against the humming from the hive. He had to be double sure; his hand was on the bolt and he waited for Maryam's voice. Nothing. He put his head to the door again and waited. She said she would say his name. Had she forgotten? Was the humming too loud for him to hear her? He began to pull at the bolt. Then the banging started and he froze.

Hassan rounded his mouth and puffed. The bees grew quieter for a few moments and then began to stir, moving upwards a little as one cloud. They understood the language.

The beekeeper's face was in his mind again, his lips moving, making the sounds. Hassan copied the shape with his jaw and lips – movement and sound – grunts, puffs, clicks, and a deep-throated roar until the formation of bees became a force, hovering at the door near him. Their humming, now more of a growl, entered his heart.

The column was spinning, like a mini tornado. Hassan was there in Harikaya, the flatlands spread out around him, the shrine in the distance, the drumbeat, the desert sands, the warm air, the night sky all spinning at once, blurring into one mix. The energy of the bees was his energy. All became sheer energy, expanding, a glimpse of the universe within him.

He raised his hand to the door. The bees inched closer, and he pushed the lock and pulled the door. The bees were quick through the open gap.

The cook waved his hands as thousands of bees surrounded him. He screamed and slapped his head and face as he scrambled about. The bees were only warning him; they would not hurt him. That was not Hassan's instruction.

Hassan thanked the bees and ran, leaving the cook to fight and swat as best he could. They would give him enough time to run back to the house. A car was pulling into the courtyard and stopped in the carport.

The door crashed open.

It was Maryam. Hassan leant back on the wall of the servants' quarters to wait for Ali Noor to go inside. Hassan was there in a few seconds. Without a word, Maryam took his arm and guided him into the hall.

'I have them,' she said, taking an envelope out of her shoulder bag.

They sifted through the photos together. His time in Karachi slipped through his fingers until they found the three photos of the cook, the journalists, the plan, just as he remembered. Maryam pointed to the living room. There was no time to waste.

Mir Saab was on the chair with the television blasting news. He turned his head slowly; a tiny light passed through his sad eyes when he saw Hassan.

'We've got them,' Maryam said.

'Where is he now?' Mir Saab asked.

'At the masjid,' Hassan said. Maryam must have told Mir Saab everything.

Maryam turned to Hassan. 'But, how...?'

'It's all right. The bees trapped him,' Hassan said, 'but we need to be quick.'

Mir Saab rang the bell and Muhammed appeared. Mir Saab told him to send the guards to find the cook and then, when it was just the three of them, he turned to Hassan. 'The cook said he found plans for the boat in your room.'

They stood face to face, a foot or two apart.

'There are very few truths in life. One of them is nature. The other is friendship. I still believe in that,' Mir Saab said. 'Forgive me for doubting you.'

'I doubted you. I thought you would send the guards again to look for my father.'

'What do you mean again?'

'You sent them for my father.'

'What are you talking about?'

'The forest fire was his fault.'

Hassan wanted to go on but Mir Saab was shaking his head.

'What are you talking about? I never sent any guards.'

'The guards that came to my house in Harikaya. Amma saw their uniform.'

'That's not the first time I've heard a story like that. Someone must have paid them.'

The truth hit Hassan like a punch in the stomach. Everything had been a lie. Hardly able to breathe, he staggered. The cook had done all this. He wanted to run out and find the cook himself, but the thought made the pain in his arm stronger. His vision became a blur. A gentle grip took his elbow. It was Maryam who led him to the couch.

'What about Baba? Where is he?' The question played over and over in his mind while they all sat in silence. Something was wrong. The clock chimed from the study. It was taking too long.

Muhammed came in, panting. 'We looked everywhere,' he said. 'Must have escaped into the city.'

'Inform the police,' Mir Saab said.

Hassan left them after a few minutes and returned to the servants' quarters.

Chapter Twenty-Four

Kulsoom's door opened by itself when he knocked. Hassan remained in the door frame. She was lying on the bed in the dark, airless room.

'Who is it?' Her face was still creased by sleep.

'You thought I'd be dead by now, didn't you?'

'What?'

'You've always been jealous of my mother, always happy when things went wrong for her. It must have been good to take her son away too.'

'She begged me.'

'You knew what the cook did. You knew he paid the guards.'

Kulsoom sat up on the bed and sighed as if she had expected these questions.

'Give me my ID card.'

She looked confused for a second.

'Give it to me now.'

She reached to the cupboard by her bed and opened the top drawer. She held it out to him. He came into the room just enough to take his card back from her.

'Why didn't you tell me about the guards?' he asked.

'What would it have changed?'

He swallowed. She looked weak. In her way, she had lost everything too.

'Why did the cook hate my father so much?'

'Your mother was a beautiful woman. She had a choice between two young men, one who loved bees and the other who only loved money.'

Hassan sat down on the floor in the doorway.

'Your father tricked your mother with poetry. With song. With forgotten promises. My family paid a dowry for your father and he gave it away to the needy, to anybody who asked him for it.'

His father's ways had been hard on his mother.

'He never worked hard in his life,' Kulsoom said. Her expression was blank and her voice carried no emotion.

'He wrote for the newspaper.'

'Writing a few articles that got him into trouble. Call that work? Your mother did the work of two people.'

Hassan knew where she was going now. Baba had often gone off for days. Adventures, he had called it. He had always come back, with poetry and presents.

'So, when your father left, I said nothing.'

Kulsoom had forgotten about one thing, the one thing she didn't seem to have ever known. Love. What about his father's love for him? She hadn't cared about what losing that would mean for a child, for him. She had known the cook, known what he had done and kept it secret. He wanted to scream at her dishevelled form. Instead, he sighed. She had never known love.

'He never loved me,' she said, guessing his thoughts. 'I know that now.' She put her head in her hands. 'He loved your mother. I always knew that. But who was worse? Your father or him?'

She had loved someone so imperfect, someone who hurt her. She had been ready to sacrifice her own family for this love. No, this kind of love was not love, but she had held onto the cook's false love as if it was her own heart itself. Everything she had done made sense in a sad way.

She looked up at him sharply. 'And your mother loved him too, once. But your father got her.'

'That's why the cook hated my father so much.'

'I took what your mother threw away. I always came second.'

An expression crossed her face that made Hassan almost pity her. A lost child, forgotten by her family.

'He doesn't like to lose. In his own way, he still loves your mother. He needed revenge. He was eaten away by it. When he saw your father come back from the fields, he had the idea of going to the guards. They were friends of his.'

'You mean he paid them off.'

She sighed.

'What did he pay them with?' Hassan asked.

'What do you think?'

'Opium. And my father, where is he now?'

'The guards told your father to stay away or they would—'

There she stopped; she looked broken now, shrunken and ten years older.

'What?'

'Or else they would kill you.'

Hassan managed to get up to his room somehow, in a cloud of silent anger. He had blamed the wrong man. All this time.

There was a screech at the window. It was the crow and it was quiet again, waiting for Hassan to say something, to make the first move.

'I'm going to leave you,' Hassan said to the bird, getting up close to it. 'I'm going back home.'

Chapter Twenty-Five

Hassan was glad to be at the dining table and eating again. It was lunch time but it seemed like much later. He ate with his hands, breaking the bread to scoop up the daal and vegetables. The bread was soft and warm to touch. The rice was easy to mould.

'They think I'm a fool,' Mir Saab said.

'Who does?' Zain asked.

'The Prime Minister's cabinet. Everyone. I'm a laughing stock.'

Hassan stopped eating.

'My manager spoke with my contact in parliament,' Mir Saab said. 'They've all seen the article about the boat.'

'They can't use that against you,' Maryam said.

'They are,' Mir Saab said. 'I told them my plans about the charity. But they're discussing a new bill now.' He coughed, his eyes watering. 'Charities are to be state owned. They're voting tomorrow to try and pass it.'

Hassan passed him a glass of water. 'Everyone wants to win,' he said.

'And nobody cares about anyone else,' Mir Saab said.

'There must be a way,' Maryam said.

'When are we going back to Harikaya?' Hassan asked. 'The rains will start soon.' He was thinking of the puddle he had seen that morning outside the temple. 'We still have time before Maryam returns to England.'

'Baba can ask his estate manger to book the plane tickets,' Zain said.

'For today,' Maryam said. 'Or tomorrow.'

Hassan dug his fingers into the seat. He wanted to fall backwards and hide his joy behind the cushions.

'You'll find the beekeeper,' Maryam said.

'When you find the beekeeper, Hassan, what's the first thing you'll ask him?' Amina asked.

'Where the black honey nests are,' he said.

Mir Saab sat down. He turned a pencil round and round in his fingers. Hassan's fingers were sticky; he really wanted to lick them, like he did at home.

'It'll be better in Harikaya,' Amina said.

Mir Saab was mumbling to himself. He picked up the newspaper and stared at it for more than a minute. 'We're not going,' he said.

The clock ticked as each of them absorbed this information.

'I'm going to parliament tomorrow. Some of them might vote against the bill if they see me in person.'

'But bills can take months to pass,' Zain said.

'I have to convince the neutral ones. The sooner the better.'

'But the black honey...' Maryam said.

Mir Saab turned towards Hassan. 'We'll go as soon as this business is sorted.' Mir Saab tried to sound calm but his voice trembled.

'The rains are starting soon,' Hassan said. 'I'll go by train.'

'But the trains run once a week,' Zain said. 'And the service has stopped for the festivities.'

'Baba, please.' This was Amina.

Their voices were becoming a blur to Hassan.

'I have to go and stand up for the people.'

Mir Saab was trying to save a world that was breaking apart. Hassan looked down at the clouds in the marble floor. The sound of the looms grew louder in his mind, blocking out all the words that had been spoken. The women were smiling. He was dancing again. He twirled like one of the villagers at night when the moon and the flames of small fires were the only light. One by one, the looms crashed to the floor. Darkness. Ink and oranges. His mother's eyes; they were growing worse.

'I need to prepare. The estate manager's coming in the morning,' Mir Saab said. He stood up, somehow stronger. 'We need to act fast, like sand cats, running into desert caves away from the men who've heard that their skins are good luck.'

Hassan pictured the sand cats hiding in the deep cracks of caves, too dark for human eyes. Mir Saab shuffled off to his room. The others left the table to go to their lessons. Hassan dipped his hands in the water, wiped them dry and went to sit on one of the chairs. The study door was open; Mir Saab lit a candle.

The fan was creaking overhead. Endless creaking. He wished he could get up and switch it off but his limbs were heavy. He was sinking into the cushions of the seat. What would the bees do? This was the question, and he had to have the answer. Mir Saab was at his desk in front of the golden hive, lighting candles around it.

'What would the bees do in your situation, Mir Saab?'

Mir Saab gestured for Hassan to sit down. 'The bees? I used to think about that when my father gave me the factories.' Mir Saab continued lighting small candles under the hive. 'Departments are like hives, working side by side. Workers care for their own work and their neighbours' work. That's the spirit of community.'

'And you were the queen,' Hassan said.

'No, that wasn't my job. The queen is all of them put together. A united intelligence.'

Hassan nodded. It was the feeling of the queen that mattered, the presence behind the hive.

'The factories provide the workers with purpose as well as survival,' Mir Saab said. 'Without them, migrating to the cities will be the only option.'

The golden hive structure glowed now. He took another match to light a final candle.

'Mir Saab, in the masjid, the bees showed me inside their nest.'

'They're letting you in?'

'Yes.'

'Go on.' The match was still burning. The flame reached Mir Saab's fingers, and he shook them immediately and blew it out.

'At first I saw lights… flashes. Then the comb and the cells. And then I saw the welcoming platform.'

'Where did you learn those words?'

'My father… I… From books—' Hassan stopped. There was no need to lie anymore. 'My father loves bees.'

'They're taking you in, step by step.' Mir Saab's breath was quick.

'I feel joy when I'm in there, as if they've been expecting me.'

Mir Saab looked as if he had solved the last pieces of a puzzle. 'I've been trying for so long and I was never allowed to cross the threshold into their world.'

'I don't know why it's happening,' Hassan said.

'Sometimes it's best not to ask why.' Mir Saab put the spent match away. There were six lit candles under the large hive structure. 'At least I've met the one that the bees have chosen.'

'For what?'

'For their teaching.' Mir Saab shook his head. He sifted through the drawings. He picked out the one with the black honey and looked closely at it. 'And then what, I don't know.'

'But I only want the black honey for my mother's eyes and then I want to go to school.'

'They may be your school.' Then Mir Saab asked, 'So, do you know the answer to your question? About what the bees would do?'

Hassan stared at the hive on the desk. Humming, darkness, flashes of light. The hexagons turned and merged into the real wax cells that he saw in his mind – honeycomb, fresh honey. Its taste was in his mouth. What would the bees do? The humming was growing louder. His eyes were open, but he was in two worlds at the same time. One where Mir Saab stood by the hive he had created, and another where flickers were fast, where sound and light darted and flashed. The humming left him. He was back in the room.

'The bees would call for change. They would hold a conference and dance until they reached a decision,' Hassan said. 'A peaceful revolution.'

'Revolution. Yes, that is what the bees would do,' Mir Saab said.

'Why don't the people march for change?' Hassan asked.

'For people to claim their power, they need to come together, to believe in themselves and their equality. Use their voices. The government is splitting them. It's pointing out their differences. They've already made certain sects illegal.' Mir Saab shook his head. 'The people need to learn that freedom is their birthright. But to do that they need to wake up, to take their life in their hands. There's still too much fear for that.' Mir Saab dropped his head.

Hassan remembered his father surrounded by the crowd, and their loyalty to Mir Saab. His father had only wanted peaceful protest, and for the law to be changed. Only one man had stepped forward. What was needed was the whole village to step forward, to act as one, like the bees. Hassan looked over at Mir Saab. The truth was that the people were scared of him. They were scared of this man with his thinning hair and woollen cardigans, because he stood at the front of a long line of ancestors on horseback. Warriors who had built forts and claimed land. This was not just about the fear of one man. It was the fear of everything that stood behind him and was still standing behind him. But for how long? That was how civilisations started and ended. This man before him, the mir, was part of that cycle.

'The bees are suffering too. You and my father have both said that their numbers are getting smaller. The bees can't do anything about that.'

Mir Saab looked up. 'No, but humans can. There has to be hope.' He started to pace around the room, coming to a halt in front of the clock on the mantelpiece. Life was pouring back into him.

Hassan understood now: a new era was being built on an older one.

'I discovered the best way to fight is not to fight but to remain still,' Mir Saab said. 'The bees taught me that too.' A tiny light began to flicker in his eyes. 'I'll talk to parliament, see what they say. There have to be good people there, people who understand.'

'This is what the bees would do,' Hassan said. A tear worked its way out of his eye and dropped onto his cheek. Mir Saab had made his choice: the factories over his mother's eyes.

Mir Saab began pacing the room again, scratching his chin. He was fighting for his people.

Hassan's breathing was slow. His father had needed coconut spirit to stand up and speak to the crowd. It would be difficult for Mir Saab in front of the government. The politicians had no loyalties, only their own desires. Hassan looked hard at him, puffed up like his father had been. He thought of the plans for the boat, the waves beating its walls. Where was that now?

Hassan stayed in the living room for the rest of the afternoon and the evening. Begum Saab was away for the evening seeing relatives and the others had gone with her. The study door was open and Mir Saab flowed through the movements of prayer, his forehead touching the small stone slab at the top of his prayer mat between each round. Over and over. When he finished, he knelt on the mat.

'Things will be all right,' Hassan told himself, but the belief was weighed down by a dull ache all over his body. It was not only his pain but the pain of those in Harikaya and beyond that would be affected. Everything was coming apart. Mir Saab's plan had to work tomorrow.

Hassan sat in the room as darkness fell outside; the candlelight grew weak, threatening to fade at any moment. But, instead, the light became steady and, after what must have been hours, the study glowed with what could only be something more than candlelight. It was the same glow that came from deep within the hive.

A lizard darted up the wall across from him, the first one he had seen inside the house. And then another. The door from the dining room opened and Begum Saab walked in. It must have been late.

'You're still here,' she said, looking towards the study. Her gaze went to her beads on the long sofa. 'Go to bed,' she said and walked away.

Mir Saab's back looked small and weak as he walked into the government buildings with the estate manager the next morning. Hassan waited with Ali Noor outside in the car. Mir Saab came out a few hours later; he was walking fast. His head was up and he was smiling. Yes, he was actually smiling. Ali Noor and Hassan looked at each other.

'Things will be all right?' Hassan said.

'The talks are promising,' Mir Saab said. 'They seem to be listening to me.'

They went back after lunch that same day and the same happened, but Mir Saab seemed even more hopeful. 'I've asked them to throw out the bill.' Mir Saab was smiling when he came out. 'We'll be off to Harikaya soon.'

This is worth it, Hassan thought.

The next day, they ate lunch late in the morning, a simple rice dish because they were about to go to parliament again. Hassan could see Ali Noor moving around in the courtyard through the open shutters. He was probably preparing the car.

'This might be the day it's decided,' Mir Saab said. 'They might throw out the bill altogether.'

Hassan heard the sound of someone clearing their throat. He looked up. The estate manager was at the living-room door; he held his head like a rag doll.

'Urgent news,' he said.

Mir Saab followed him out to the drawing room and Amina, Zain, and Maryam crowded with Hassan at the open door. The manager had his back to them.

'Those villains!' Mir Saab exclaimed. 'Parliament was about to throw it out.'

Mir Saab's face was grey and his fists were clenched.

'They quoted exceptional circumstances. I don't know how they've done it,' the manager said, 'but they've passed the bill without a vote. We have to stay here in Karachi and fight this business.'

Mir Saab rocked forwards. Ancestry fell backwards, thrones toppling over like dominoes, mir upon mir.

'No.' Mir Saab's word echoed through the room.

'But Mir Saab, we have to do something.'

Hassan stepped into the room and the others followed.

'I've walked into a checkmate situation,' Mir Saab said.

'If all the villagers voted, what would the government do?' Zain asked.

'Perhaps, this is what I must ask for,' Mir Saab said.

'Yes, yes,' the manager said.

But Mir Saab was sinking again. Hassan didn't think; he went up to him and led him to a seat.

'It's all my fault,' Mir Saab said. 'I should have known something like this would happen. He was always out to get me.'

The government was ambushing him, running him into a corner like a hunted hog. Like the cook had done to Hassan.

'And now he's the Prime Minister,' Maryam said.

'There are small birds in the forest that appear feeble. They've discovered a way to gather energy from others by sucking the blood of bigger birds. By the time they've noticed, the bigger birds are too weak to do anything.'

'We have to ask the bees what they would do,' Hassan said.

'It's obvious what they would do,' Mir Saab said. 'They

would organise themselves, take a collective decision, and then act on it.'

'Just like my father wanted the people to do when you made your new law.'

Mir Saab looked at him. 'He could have come to talk to me.'

Mir Saab still didn't understand what it meant to be a villager.

'The people should demonstrate,' Mir Saab said.

'But the government doesn't listen to people in Harikaya,' Hassan said.

'Not unless there is persistent activity.'

'Or unless they don't give up,' Maryam said.

'My father said it's the people who make the change.'

'But what about when people get hurt by the ones in power?' Maryam asked.

Hassan thought of the people at the shrine. Most of them had been too scared. 'I was scared of you, Mir Saab,' he said.

'I would have listened.' Mir Saab was tapping his finger on the table. 'We've got to make them realise they have a voice.'

'Most of the bees are women,' Maryam said.

'Most of the factory workers are women too,' Hassan said. He thought of the women who went to work in the mills, on the fields, never missing a day so their children could be fed.

Mir Saab was pacing again. 'Without the women, we're nothing. The government doesn't want us to believe that or they'll lose their power.'

He stopped in the middle of the room.

'The society of bees does not ignore the women – far from it – it's the same with all animals.'

'Except us humans,' Hassan said.

It didn't take long for Mir Saab to decide what to do.

'I'll go to my people.' Mir Saab stood up and looked towards Amina and Zain. 'Call your mother. There's still time to catch the afternoon plane.'

Part Three

Harikaya village in Harikaya state

Sindh Province, Pakistan

Chapter Twenty-Six

'If one plane crashes at least there'll be one heir left,' Zain said.

Hassan sat next to the window. Maryam sat between him and Zain. Amina had taken the first plane out with Mir Saab, Begum Saab, and the manager.

'You'll do it before the rains,' Maryam said.

She must have been reading his thoughts but that wasn't too hard.

'I have to,' he said. 'I want to do it before you go back.'

'You will. And you can give me a little black honey too.'

The flight was ninety minutes long and they were already halfway there. The air hostess brought cucumber sandwiches made out of white bread with no crusts and sprinkled with salt and pepper.

The land he could see from the plane window was flat. Sand-coloured earth was planted with green, yellow, and brown vegetation – rice, cotton, and wheat – in rectangular, overlapping patches like the ones in his mother's weaving. Then came the bigger fields, laden with date palms. Green, spiky-headed giants, standing in line, army-like in their formation and ready to protect the land.

Bold and graceful, muddy waters of the river Indus flowed down the middle. The land looked freshly soaked by light showers but the irrigation channels that framed the fields were still dry.

Bright cloths and brown flesh dotted the landscape as workers, men and women, bent down to sow seeds. They looked up at the sky as the plane flew over.

The village appeared in the distance, a mere cluster of buildings. His breath steamed up the window pane which was cold against the tip of his nose. Would his mother be at home or in the mill?

'When will you see your mother?' Maryam asked him.

'I promised I would go back with the black honey,' Hassan replied. The glass of the window clouded over and he wiped it with his sleeve; the village was gone. That was when the pain started.

'Why are you covering your ears?' Maryam asked.

His ears felt like they were going to explode.

'Suck on this.' Zain gave him a sweet, and the pain had disappeared by the time they landed.

Mir Saab's manager met them outside the plane. Someone had put Hassan's bag, a soft plastic box bag with handles, on the trolley with the others. It was floppy and old on top of the suitcases and chests. But still, he was walking with them and people would think he was a brother or a cousin, or one of the many distant relatives of Mir Saab's family who lived in the fort.

No. That kind of thinking was the old him. His cheap bag, his old sandals, and fraying waistcoat were part of him. He was Hassan, who had helped his father home from the jungle, who had been in a Karachi gutter with a bleeding arm, and who was here now, a villager with his new friends.

He was home. A wide smile spread across his face. Maryam saw it and smiled back.

Outside, the midday heat was like a bread oven compared to the humidity of Karachi. The smell of rain was in the air and the cool air inside the car was a relief.

'That's where my mother works,' he said to Maryam, pointing at the factories and cotton mills.

Her forehead creased. He didn't want to see Maryam worried. It made things even worse.

The road narrowed and bamboo lined the path. There was so much to tell her about his life, about how he had lived. He and his father had hidden in those reeds from this very car.

The car slowed down to almost a stop. An old man was in their path, ahead of their slow-moving car.

'He's one of my neighbours,' Hassan said.

The man shuffled to the side of the road and bent forwards, ninety degrees from the ground, holding his cupped hand to his chin. Hassan shrank back into the seat when the man looked through the window as the car made its way past.

They drove along a high wall and through a set of iron gates, opened by a guard.

'Zain, you never told me you lived in a palace,' Maryam said, climbing out of the car.

The palace was the colour of red fire. Amina was waiting for them in the shade under the arches as they got out of the car. The doors of the palace opened onto a great hall. Paintings the size of a village house hung around the walls.

'Ancestors,' Zain said.

In a corner was a swinging seat with big red cushions on it to which Maryam and Amina both ran.

'Hassan, have a go,' Maryam said, moving closer to Amina to make space.

'No Bibi, it's all right.'

She asked again but he said no. He looked around, pretending he had made the right choice when he suddenly felt a strong push and he found himself landing on the seat. It was soft and he gave in to the laughing. The rays of the sun fell on his face from the windows in the sky.

'Come on,' Zain said, pointing to a door in the far corner behind which there was a maze of rooms and beds and wood-panelled walls.

'Who's that?' Maryam asked, pointing at the painting.

'Jinnah,' Amina said.

The face of the man was thin, his eyes kind and he wore a narrow black hat.

'The founder of the country,' Zain said.

'I know that,' Maryam said. 'Why is it there?'

'Baba put that there when he came to stay.'

'1948, to be precise, a year after partition,' Zain said.

And so on, room after room, each with a painting of a new Prime Minister that had visited. The final painting was a landscape.

'The future,' Zain said.

There was no picture of the current Prime Minister. The last door led them along a corridor that opened onto a dining room with a long wooden table and about fifty wooden chairs. Maryam ran to the other end.

'Pass the salt!' she shouted.

Outside again at the front of the building, Amina, Zain, and Maryam were no longer behind him but their voices echoed in the dining room; they must have found something. Hassan looked out onto the gardens. When he was back with his mother, he would bring her here one day. Mir Saab was by the arches, talking to the manager and a second man with the same long, curly moustache as the manager. The men were still and quiet.

Hassan went closer, his camera ready. He stopped a few feet away. The button, there it was, under his finger now. Would the scene stop and turn into just a picture? Mir Saab had given him no advice about how to take a photograph. Hassan pressed.

'Arrey!' The cry from the new man cut through the stillness.

Hassan took the camera away from his face and let it hang around his neck.

'Chalo!' the man said. 'What are you doing, taking a picture of Mir Saab? Go! Go quickly, get out of here.' He waved his hands at Hassan.

Although his tone was harsh, the man's face was tired. Hassan stayed where he was.

'Stop that,' Mir Saab said to the man. 'How dare you?' His voice was loud. 'That boy is called Hassan. He is a human being.'

The managers bowed. The rough heat of shame on the man's skin was dark and blotchy; the man bowed again, this time to Hassan, and both of them left.

'The constitution talks about equality but things will take a long time to change,' Mir Saab said tensely.

They stood for a while, facing the gardens. The breeze was gentle but there was that familiar smell mixed in with it that signalled the imminent arrival of the rains. They had to be coming soon. Hassan took a deep breath in. Mir Saab deserved the truth. He turned to Mir Saab who turned to him at the same time.

'I'm going tomorrow,' Hassan said. 'Alone.'

'Yes, I know.'

Late afternoon, with his shirt sticking to his skin, Hasan sat in the back of the jeep with the others while Mir Saab sat in the front with Ali Noor. They bounced and jolted over the uneven sandy ground. The jeep hit a bump in the road and Maryam flew up off her seat and crashed down again. She scrunched up her face and rubbed her head.

'At night, that's where the hogs go to drink,' Zain said, pointing to a drinking hole.

The trees grew denser, less spindly, and bushes became more ragged and competed for space. Animals looked up as they drove past, surprised by the jeep and the clouds of dust that followed it. A flock of geese noisily flew upwards and a flock of ducks made angry noises. They slowed down as they approached the edge of the forest and the dirt track stopped at a sign: Harikaya Nature Reserve. Hassan had never been this way before but he decided then that it would be his path tomorrow.

They walked in single file under the forest canopy, picking their way through thicket and weeds and came to a small hill with a hide perched on top, lined with bamboo reeds and large leaves.

'My main concern is the hog,' Mir Saab said. 'Make sure you're absolutely quiet in there.'

Ali Noor lifted some of the reeds off and Hassan went through the entrance with the others into darkness.

'I'll wait for you here,' Mir Saab said, lifting his binoculars to his face.

Inside, Ali Noor took out a strip of the wall leaving a thin slit, about a metre long and five centimetres thick. A few feet away from the shelter was a tall bush. On one side of it was a deer and on the other, a hog, each with their head down, munching at the grass. The deer picked at the grass, delicately pulling it out with its teeth; the boar chomped with its huge jaw like a machine.

Hassan started to sweat. He'd heard too many stories about boars that had charged into people, either killing or maiming them. It looked peaceful now, but everything could change if the hog decided that the deer was dessert or if it heard them. It lasted a few minutes longer, and when Ali Noor signalled for them to leave the hide, Hassan was drenched in sweat. All of them stayed quiet on the forest path along which

Ali Noor and Mir Saab led them. They carried on for another hour but then Mir Saab stopped and turned around.

'Can we keep going?' Hassan asked.

'No, the sun will set soon.' Mir Saab reached for his shirt pocket and opened a box. He held what looked like a metal ball in his hand. 'This compass might be useful.' He opened the lid and Hassan saw that the arrow inside was vibrating.

'The arrow points north. The fort is to the west,' Mir Saab said.

For a moment, he was back to his old self, the one who fiddled with cameras and talked about nature.

'Thank you, Mir Saab.'

Mir Saab gave it to him and he held it tight. It would fit in his waistcoat pocket alongside the piece of honeycomb.

Hassan dropped back to the end of the line of people. The canopy was full of birdsong and the light was fading. There was no fear now but would it be the same in the morning when he would be here on his own? They reached the track again and he jogged to be level with Maryam.

'Do you think the beekeeper knows you're coming?' she asked him.

'Yes,' he said, looking down at the compass.

Together they walked behind the others. He tripped on some thicket and Maryam steadied him. This time, for the first time, his body stayed relaxed.

In six days, she'd be too far away to touch him.

~

That evening, they drove from the palace to the hill fort, to stay there for a few nights as was the family tradition when they were in Harikaya. The great iron doors of the fort, with short spikes running all over them, opened and the car just got through.

'Invaders used to come on elephants and they couldn't fit through narrow doors,' Zain said.

'Now they come with wedding invitations,' Maryam said.

The jeep slipped through the gateway and stopped in a small courtyard, surrounded by walls.

'This is the first stage of entry into the fort,' Zain said. 'Invaders could never get further than this.'

A heavy iron door opened and they all walked into a much bigger courtyard surrounded by arches. It was like the dance platform of the hive. Servants appeared and took suitcases out of the car.

'You're still wearing bright colours,' Begum Saab said to Zain and Amina. 'Come with me.'

Amina turned to Maryam and Hassan. 'Explore,' she whispered before she disappeared through one of the arches.

He followed Maryam through to a great terrace that crawled around the fort and was bordered by a wall. Maryam went over to the wall and stood in front of it; it came to her chest.

'I've never seen stars like this before,' she said.

A man below the fort at the bottom of the hill rode a bicycle, in no hurry and singing to himself. He cycled past the huge marquee outside the village wall.

'That's where the gatherings are,' Hassan said.

The rhythmic tones of a slow drum beat rose up from inside the tent while a steady stream of villagers was going in.

'My mother used to go,' he said. 'The bread she brought back was special.'

A tear dropped onto his cheek before he could stop it. He wiped the wetness with his hand but it was too late.

'Why don't you go to see your mother?'

'I promised I'd find the honey first and bring it to her.'

As the drum beat played, melodies rose up in the thin night air.

'Can you see the alams over there, shining in silver?' Maryam asked.

A line of poles with thin metal tops shaped like hands were being carried into the tent. Each one was draped with long black cloth. Garlands of roses and silver thread were hung over the cloth.

'Why do people cry at the gatherings?' Hassan asked her.

'Don't you know the story?' She looked at him and laughed. 'You don't know anything about different stories, do you?'

'I was too busy,' he said.

She laughed again. 'Two hundred years ago, the governors of a town asked the ancestors to come and help them govern. The ancestors came and set up their tents outside the town on the banks of the Euphrates. But it was a trick.'

'A trick?'

'That's when the ambush happened. The ancestors didn't want to fight but they had to go out and ask for water for the children and the sick. The rulers of the town attacked them. Three days it took before each man, one by one, met his fate.'

'Why did the governors do that?'

'Because the ancestors had magic and that was forbidden.'

'Why?'

'The rulers were afraid of magic, but the ancestors only used it for good.'

'What kind of magic did they have?'

'It was the magic of the earth and healing, the magic of love and ancestry, a magic that understood the stars. After it was all over, the people of the town came out and saw what had happened. They gave the children and women food and water.'

'Why were they afraid of their magic?' he asked.

'Those governors didn't realise that magic is everywhere – that they had lost touch with it.' Maryam shrugged. 'The women suffered a lot. They were the ones left behind with the thirsty children.'

Hassan thought of Harikaya, of his mother, of the women working in the factories and on the land. They were the ones who suffered most. Below, the drum beat continued. The chant had stopped and now he missed his mother.

'We have to do something. It's the women who will suffer the most.'

'If the government got the factories and closed them?'

'Yes.'

'We could organise a march.'

'My father tried. They wouldn't listen.'

'What if we write leaflets? They can't shut leaflets down.'

Hassan laughed. 'It's worth a try.'

They stood together looking upwards. For a few moments, Hassan felt some space around him. He was home.

'Hassan,' Maryam said.

'Yes.'

'Do you want to come back with me to London?'

The question was a great wave that came without warning and he had to hold onto the top of the wall to stop it carrying him away.

Chapter Twenty-Seven

Hassan looked round for his waistcoat in the room with stone walls. It was the first time he had slept in a bed with a real mattress – that time in Karachi didn't count; it had only been for a few minutes before the cook—

He stopped himself thinking and walked over to the window – no meshing, no crow, just an opening. The sky was empty of vultures; it was too early for them now. He slipped on his waistcoat and tapped the pocket; the honeycomb was safe. He opened the heavy wooden door and made his way to the terrace and looked out over the wall.

The fort overlooked the ancient forest and desert flatlands that were dotted with craggy rocks and rolling fields. Sand seeped into irrigation channels that lay parched in the fields.

There was a shout from behind him and before he could turn around, footsteps arrived by his side. They stood face to face and he laughed. Maryam stretched out her hand with a cup of white milk that had pistachio nuts floating at the top.

'You're early,' he said.

'Sharbat,' she said. 'From last night.'

He drank it down in a few gulps. It was sweet and good.

'You have white lips now,' she laughed.

They were both silent on their way to breakfast. While he waited for her to say something about London, his head raced with thoughts. There was no way a village boy could go back to London with her. People in the village dreamt of visas to London all the time. There was a family on the street where his house was. One of the boys had left, made it to a city, paid for his sisters to follow him, yet every time they came home to visit their mother, they only talked about going to London. It was an out-of-reach desire that swallowed their daily lives. He knew Mir Saab had taken Muhammed to London a few times, but that was as his servant. Mir Saab could manage that kind of visa easily. Hassan would never go anywhere as a servant. Maryam was still silent as she went through the door. Perhaps it had just been a wish, nothing more. And anyway, Amma needed him to be closer than London.

He ate with the family in a room with high white walls and windows framed by mosaics. Afterwards, Amina and Zain left with Begum Saab. Maryam stayed with Hassan and Mir Saab at the table.

'Remember the honeybird,' Mir Saab said.

It was time to tell Mir Saab more. After all, he wasn't the one who had sent the guards after Baba.

'I saw the beekeeper less than a month ago. He saved my

father from the fire.' Hassan imagined his father's face, his creased forehead, his pain after the fall. The golden hive in Mir Saab's study in Karachi shone in his mind and, just at that moment, the sun's rays reached the floor through the windows. The light was bright.

Mir Saab chuckled and shook his head; his eyes widened and he let out a big laugh.

'That's it!' he shouted. 'That's it. That's why the bees in the masjid were preparing you.' His face was alight and he brought his fist down heavily on the table and bent over. 'What did he say to you?'

'Nothing. He spoke to the bees.'

'The beekeeper recognised you. I don't know how, but he recognised you.' Mir Saab rocked as if a current of energy was shooting up his body. 'The link you have with him is important.' He was speaking fast. 'You're connected to the bees, like him,' Mir Saab said. 'You're connected to their knowledge.'

They sat for a minute, maybe two, in silence as if they were waiting together for some kind of message.

'You will be another holder of this knowledge,' Mir Saab said. 'Your journeys into the hive, what do you think they were showing you?'

So many things, he thought, but all he could say was, 'The queen bee. I never reached her.'

'She only appears to a very few.' Mir Saab got up and paced the room. 'You have more of a chance than I ever had.' Mir Saab stopped. 'I left too soon.'

'Do you think the queen is the gateway to their knowledge?' He thought for a moment.

'Reaching her is part of knowing that,' Mir Saab said, 'or at least the presence of her. Her energy. You need to reach her energy centre. I wasn't sure of that until now. Yes, the hive revolves around her energy; it's a great responsibility. But you know all this.' Mir Saab walked to the window.

With his back to Hassan, Mir Saab said, 'Go now to the jungle. The beekeeper is waiting.'

Birdsong burst from the forest which was only a few metres away now, but he needed to rest for a moment. It had been a long walk and the sun was hot this morning. He stood in the shade of a fig tree and a red drop fell on his finger. He looked up. A fig was open, rich and ripe, and ants were streaming over its pink flesh. He licked his finger. Just then, a bee buzzed high in the tree. It flew higher and higher until he lost sight of it. Another bee hovered at a lower level, testing the flowers on nearby bushes. It carried bright-yellow balls of pollen on its legs and flew from bush to bush. He followed it into the forest.

He stood still, silent, searching for the sound of the bee. None came. The forest was watching and listening to his every move. There was no clear path to follow but he kept walking and the canopy of the forest grew denser and darker. His eyes began to get used to it and sunbeams shot down through the trees to point the way.

And Hassan followed.

Thickets and thorns scratched his feet.

He sat down on a fallen log and picked off sticky cobwebs from his long trousers. Ants, in their own world, marched in a line in front of him. Was this all worth it? The forest was huge and the beekeeper could be anywhere. The last time Hassan had been here had been with Baba. If only he were here now, then this would be easier. It would have taken a day to find the honey and he'd be back with Amma by now. It could take forever. But, Maryam was leaving in—

Something moved through the undergrowth in the distance.

The outline of a man. The beekeeper. It had to be him. Hassan stood up. The figure glided through the forest and Hassan ran after him, barely keeping up over sandy mounds, hurtling past overgrown shrubs, flinging his arms through low branches and bushes. But the form vanished and he was lost. The leaves rustled and he looked around but saw nothing. It had happened again.

The sun was directly above now, but he kept going.

He came to a pond and his feet got stuck in shallow swampy ground. He stepped out of the mud, bending to pick up his sandals which were now caked. He would have to carry on with them like that. They squelched with every step, but such was the violent heat that he could feel the mud drying already under his feet.

Mir Saab had said that bees gathered by the water. Leaves rustled again and he lifted his head. Vultures were standing around the pond like aged beings from another planet. They stared at him, their heads moving slowly and their black wings shining in the sun.

There was something in the way their wings were poised that made Hassan take a few steps backwards. The birds stood like guards and kept their eyes on him. If the beekeeper was somewhere in that part of the forest behind them, Hassan had no chance, at least not today. The vultures left the forest in search of food in the early morning; that would be the best time to come, earlier. Later, in the evening, the deer and hogs would be moving to the drinking holes. He had to keep moving. He would try again tomorrow, skip breakfast and come straight away. But he only had two days before Maryam left for Karachi; he couldn't afford to waste any more. He looked at the birds and their menacing eyes. He would do it, even if they pecked at him. That idea made him turn around.

Back on dry land again, he took the water bottle from his bag, had a few sips, and leant against the tree, sliding down to the ground. He rested with his head on his knees. His legs and feet felt heavy. This was an impossible task. But Mir Saab thought this was his path. Maryam thought he had some kind of special magic. And he had seen the beekeeper.

'The beekeeper is waiting,' Mir Saab's words were in his head. He couldn't give up now. His mother would be waiting. Maryam was waiting. And Baba. Hassan had to wait for him. He tried to ignore something else that stirred quietly now at the bottom of his mind. Maryam's question. He tried to stop the thoughts but they were too strong. Plane tickets were expensive. He had heard visas were difficult to get. Maybe she had a plan.

He took a few more sips from his water bottle and rested his head back against the tree trunk. The roughness on his scalp brought him back to the path in front of him. If he went with her, he would have to be dependent on her family. That would be wrong. Baba would think that was wrong. Maryam was kind but it would never work. His jaw tightened. No.

Even if he could get a visa, and even if Maryam had been serious, the bees had allowed him to enter their world.

Hassan's crumpled form started to unfold against the tree trunk and he raised his head. He had to go on. All this thinking was slowing him down. All that mattered was Amma's eyes. Until then, he couldn't go anywhere.

Footsteps. Someone was walking behind the bushes and leaves. Footsteps came closer.

'Hey!' Hassan shouted. 'It's me.' Hassan moved towards the figure but the man was faster. 'Remember me?' he shouted again. The man must be deaf. The figure disappeared.

Hassan was breathing hard and he stopped to rest on a hilly mound. A stray sunbeam touched his head and poured gentle light over him. He had seen the beekeeper; it had to be him. Just then, there was a sudden rustle of leaves below him but no movement. He was ready to go on again when a snout and eyes poked out of the undergrowth. He scrambled up. A large hog head, joined to a much larger body, emerged. Its snout pointed in his direction and its squeals and grunts came closer. The hog began charging up the hill towards him, like a bomb bouncing over the forest floor. Hassan picked up a thick log, high over his head, and he roared.

He squeezed his eyes shut to wait for the collision. The squeals and grunts were loud, a fire rushing between the trees.

'Aaaah,' he screamed, rocking backwards.

He opened his eyes. The hog had just missed him and was moving away. He dropped the log, jumping back as it fell by his feet.

This was enough. He had to head back now. Snakes came out at night. A line of low-flying parrots screeched above him as he checked the compass. His legs ached but he marched down a path with thickets, trampled earlier by his own feet, until he came to another small clearing.

Small animals like wild dogs were digging their long teeth into a carcass which looked like the bloody remains of a long mongoose, fresh and still largely intact. Jackals, sharing a feast. They spotted him, flesh hanging from their mouths. They wouldn't hurt him; they already had food. He edged around them, searching for a stick just in case. They were smaller than the hog; he could manage them but his heart beat fast even when he was well away and back under the canopy of leaves.

Something was there, and he pulled back behind a tree. A deer with a white face and antlers like antennae looked up and stared, its head turned at a right angle to its body.

'I'm here to find the beekeeper,' Hassan whispered to the deer.

The deer continued to stare. Hassan went closer. The deer blinked. Hassan blinked. Another step. The deer didn't move.

He was barely a couple of feet away from the animal now, its muscles flexing and its breathing steady. His own breathing slowed down too and when the deer leapt, he followed. The deer ran with playful steps. They zigzagged together through the forest until the deer stopped, waiting for him. Not for long. It leapt into the air again and Hassan ran with it.

Stopping and starting, he followed it deeper into the forest. Scrambling and leaping and stopping, the deer was leading him somewhere.

He had to watch and anticipate; the deer's next move was Hassan's entire focus. Ready, alert. His arms, his legs, his senses. He could do it. It worked, and he kept up through bushes, bramble, and trees, young and old, thick and thin. Until the deer suddenly slipped away. It had let him keep up, tricked him into believing he had a chance but there had never been any chance.

He was panting and he bent over to catch his breath. The animals, the beekeeper, the forest, and most of all the bees, were playing with him, with his life. He scrunched his face and fists and shook them in the sky until his arms hurt and he sat down on a log.

A bee hovered by a blue flower, silent. Other bees also fell quiet, each near a flower. All took a deep breath in together and then each one dived into the centre of a flower. Nothing was more important. Each came out again loaded with nectar and pollen. Some of the bees took off back to their homes. Smaller bees worked on, slower than the others, new to the searching work and the language of colour. Others stayed behind because they wanted more. Each of them was part of a greater whole, all pieces in the jigsaw, as Baba had said.

All the bees grew heavier and, more and more took off on their journey back. Mir Saab had said the bees always took the most direct route back home to the nest. There was one bee in particular, new and slow, weighed down by pollen. Hassan waited for a pause in its humming.

'One, two, three,' he counted, 'four…' He was ready to run. 'Now—'

He stopped.

The sound of breathing, steady but loud, came through the trees. A giant bulk of a figure shuffled forwards into view. Hassan dashed behind a clump of bushes.

'Who's there?' the voice echoed off the trees.

Hassan couldn't move. Opposite him, the form started to break up into separate parts: a dead wild boar strapped to a log, carried on the shoulders of a man, was placed on the ground. Drips of dark boar blood formed a path onto the dusty floor behind him.

The beekeeper.

Hassan had waited so long for this moment and now it had come and he was hiding behind a bush. The beekeeper stood still in the centre of the trees a few metres away. His eyes were like flames, the same amber colour as Hassan remembered. He stood up to face the man.

'What are you doing here?' the beekeeper asked.

His voice was a low growl. It made Hassan think of sand cats and dark endless caves.

'I've been looking for you,' Hassan said.

The beekeeper stayed still for several seconds. There were still the lines and creases in the skin of his face but his hair seemed longer, even more matted and darker.

The beekeeper's face hardened.

'They let my father take a little last time. It worked on Amma's eyes. Please, I need to take her more…'

'Even I don't touch their honey. Why should you?' It was a simple question.

'I won't take more than they give me. I'll be careful, but I can't do it by myself.'

'You,' the beekeeper said, 'you were with your father. The fire.' There was a deep recognition in his eyes that told Hassan that there was something more to it than that one meeting. The beekeeper was somehow showing Hassan that the visions he had had when he needed this man – when he needed to communicate with the bees – had been real.

'I need to find the black honey,' Hassan said, 'for my mother's eyes...'

The beekeeper took a deep breath in and shook his head.

'Please... I stayed in Mir Saab's house in Karachi. There were bees there.'

'Mir Saab?'

Hassan had said the important words. There was a faint smile on the beekeeper's face and a flicker of recognition before his head turned to the boar on the ground. He picked up the hog, held it with both hands on each side and swept it over his head, back onto his shoulders. 'I found this one dead.' With his hands placed on the log and the great hairy boar behind his head, he began to walk.

'Come with me. Tell me your story.'

They walked through the undergrowth until they reached the watering hole on a dry path that Hassan had not seen the first time. The vultures saw the beekeeper and didn't stir.

'Sit,' the beekeeper said, pointing at a low fallen log. He placed the hog on the ground. 'For the vultures,' he said, 'and then the jackal and the hyenas.'

The beekeeper was still, looking straight ahead as if he could see through the trees beyond the pond.

'Were you waiting for me?' Hassan asked.

'You're asking the right questions.'

'I'm Hassan. What's your name?' Hassan asked him.

'I forgot my name long ago,' he laughed. 'Call me beekeeper'.

'I only have a few days left to find the honey,' Hassan said.

'And your father?'

'He had to leave.'

It must have been the way the beekeeper asked the question – or was it his silence? Or was it the unending birdsong behind them or the stink of death that lay in front of them that made Hassan's tears drop?

'It was my fault,' Hassan said.

'How?'

'I asked him to go to the forests.'

'Why?'

'For my mother's eyes and because I was curious.'

'Curiosity isn't a sin.'

The rhythm of the beekeeper's breath was like the drum beat at the shrine, regular and constant.

'That man made the guards threaten my father.' Hassan's chest tightened. 'They told my father they'd kill me if he came back.'

He didn't hide his tears in the middle of this ancient forest; there was no need. Ants paused in their work; songbirds listened to this melody of human sadness. Even the munching of the hogs grew softer as they felt the air chime with this release.

The beekeeper said nothing to comfort him. His presence was enough.

'I'll climb the tree like Baba did,' Hassan said. 'Please help me find it.'

'It's time to leave,' the beekeeper said.

'Leave?' Hassan was trembling. 'It's still only afternoon. What if my mother goes blind?' Everything had been a waste of time – all those hours and hours in the masjid and this day in the forest. 'It's all useless.' His voice was breaking and a sob stuck in his throat.

'The bees have to agree. It's your will or theirs.'

'I'm running out of time.'

The beekeeper came nearer, placing a hand on Hassan's shoulder. A stillness spread through his body.

'You expect me to say everything will be all right. That you can stay and the bees will obey.' The beekeeper shrugged. 'Let's see what happens. If it's their will, the bees will teach you.'

There was nothing more to say. They walked back together in silence, but inside Hassan's mind the question played over and over again: *What if it's too late?*

The beekeeper stood up and raised his head to the trees around him. 'Come back tomorrow, after sunrise. I'll meet you where the vultures drink.'

Hassan had another question before he left. 'How can I get the bees to agree?'

'You can't. The bees agree very rarely. They let your father take some and that was a good sign. You can only try.' The beekeeper sighed. 'But for them to agree involves a sacrifice.'

'What kind of sacrifice?'

'Service. Your service.'

'Mir Saab wanted to give it,' Hassan said.

'He had another service to give. A service to his people.'

'And what if I can't give this service?' Hassan was thinking of Maryam. A great longing rose up in him that surprised him. He shuddered. 'Why do you stay away from humans?'

'I stay here to fulfil my service,' the beekeeper said.

'And to learn their secret?'

'Secret?' The beekeeper laughed. 'There is no great secret. You'll learn one day.'

For a second Hassan was too stunned to say anything – and yet, somehow, here in the jungle, faced with the man who had been in his mind so much, the idea of there being no secret seemed to make sense. But how could he think that? Mir Saab and his father had made this secret their passion. And here was this man throwing their dream away.

'Why did you never let Mir Saab find you?'

'His service to the bees was meant to come in other ways. Meeting me would have confused him.'

'Who are you?'

'Who I am is not important,' he said. 'What's important is that we are here.'

The beekeeper only answered the questions he chose to answer.

'Until tomorrow.' The beekeeper raised his hand to his heart and headed off, gliding through the forest.

Hassan felt his hunger now. Baba had told him of hyenas in the forest that came out if they were hungry. Hassan began to run. He panted but he didn't stop. The compass was becoming like a trusted old friend. After an hour he reached a different exit point, the same path he had walked with his father. As he emerged, he discovered that the sky was still bright; it was probably still only late afternoon, by the angle of the sun. Time was different in the forest. It expanded and shrank at the same time. It no longer had any meaning.

His legs were heavy all the way up the road to the fort. He slipped through the small door in the main gates, opened by a guard who hardly looked up. In the courtyard a servant rushed past. They didn't talk to him up here, the in-betweener.

Hassan didn't knock when he went to the library. Mir Saab had finished his prayers and was kneeling on his mat.

'The beekeeper said—' Hassan began.

'You found the beekeeper!' he exclaimed in wonder.

For a few moments Mir Saab looked into space as if a thousand images were running through his mind.

Chapter Twenty-Eight

Hassan's whole body ached but he made it to the dining area where Maryam and Amina were finishing their meal.

'You're back already,' Maryam said. She stood up and went over to him, taking him by the arm and guiding him to the table. 'Have you had a chance to think about London yet?' She gave his arm a secret squeeze on the way.

He shook his head.

'We're all going to my little house in the jungle soon,' Amina said.

'But you're not an adult yet. How do you have a house? Is it your dowry from Mir Saab?'

They both laughed at him.

'Dowries are so old-fashioned, Hassan. I'm not a vill—' Amina bit at her lip.

Maryam stopped and her hand fell away from his arm.

'It's all right,' he said. 'Yes, you're not a villager and I am.' It didn't matter anymore. He was different and that was that.

This time, he guided Maryam to the table. It felt easy to be close to her.

'Baba gave the house to me as a birthday gift,' Amina said, her voice more serious now. 'He liked the idea of it being in the jungle. Will you come with us, Hassan?'

'I'm ready,' Hassan said.

'Some of the clan are coming for tea first,' Amina said. 'They wrote the leaflets for us.'

It was then that he noticed a pile of leaflets, each about the size of a book with neat Sindhi writing.

'Hassan can give them out at the gathering this evening with me,' Maryam said.

Amina picked one up. She translated the text. '"The factories are in danger. We need to march peacefully for our right to keep them open. This is your chance to have your voice heard. We will meet together after the festivities on the twenty-seventh of Sha'ban." That's the fifteenth of September.'

'I'll be gone by then,' Maryam said. Hassan could feel her gaze on him. It followed him as he moved to sit down.

'They'll be here soon.' Amina put the leaflet back.

'They live in the towers around the fort,' Maryam said. 'I thought the towers were used to watch for invading elephants,' she said, taking a biscuit and passing it to Hassan. He put all of it in his mouth at once.

'That was two hundred years ago,' Amina said.

The distant family came in, one by one in a line, each wearing a chiffon scarf hanging loosely over her hair and smiling and giggling like schoolgirls without a teacher. Once seated, the head of the line said, 'Dupattas off.'

They removed their scarves and all of them smiled until one of them screamed, 'There's a boy in the room!'

Hassan nearly choked on a biscuit – his third.

Elbows bumped into other elbows as chiffon was flung back over hair. Giggles squeezed through multi-coloured veils. Heads were lowered and raised again to sneak a look at him.

'Why are they…?' Maryam began.

'Whenever there's a boy…' Amina said.

Hassan started to cough. 'I'll wait in the library.' He picked up a leaflet and waved at them before he slipped through the door, dodging the shower of giggles behind him.

Mir Saab was busy with his books at his desk. 'I thought you would have all left by now,' he said.

'Soon,' Hassan said.

Mir Saab got up and went to a cabinet. He took out a thick book and came to stand next to Hassan.

'Look out for the goshawk. They're around at this time,' he said. 'There, that's it.'

Hassan took the book in both hands. The bird looked like an eagle, but smaller. It had a lightly striped chest and a darker striped tail. Its long claws grasped onto a thin branch and its face had the same proud stare as an eagle. Its wings hung on either side of its chest like a dark cloak.

'They see everything up there in the sky.' Mir Saab took the book and slapped its covers shut. 'I never forgave myself for making the wrong choice.'

'You had to follow the path you did so that you could do your duty to the people.'

'Yes, I had to stay in a world of systems and society.' There was a scowl on Mir Saab's face.

'But the bees' world is a world of systems and society too,' Hassan said.

'Systems that are millions of years old. They're in harmony with nature, with its flow, with life around it. Humans are like children who think nature is there to serve them.'

'But it's the other way around,' Hassan said. 'That's what the beekeeper said.'

The scowl on Mir Saab's face disappeared. He looked like a boy again, the one that had made the decision many years ago. Or had the decision been made for him?

It was different for Hassan. The decision was his to make. The bees and his mother or Maryam and a new life. Perhaps it was easier than he thought. A life with Maryam would be easier than in Pakistan, even easier than in Karachi. That was why everyone wanted to go to London, wasn't it? People became richer. They travelled where they wanted. They were safer. People from Harikaya wept when they tried and failed to go to London. He could study there, earn more and help his mother more. He'd pay back Maryam's mother one day too.

He could help the bees from there. The beekeeper talked about service to the bees. The bees served each other. He could serve them by studying, being successful. He laughed out loud at that. It was him who needed their help now and they were taking their time.

'What?' Mir Saab said.

Both of them broke away from their own thoughts.

'Maryam and I have a plan.'

'Yes?'

He took out a leaflet and showed it to Mir Saab.

'Just be aware that there will be spies amongst the crowd.'

Ali Noor was steering with all his strength around as many potholes as possible, but the road became steeper, narrower, and bumpier as they came off the main track and went through the fields and into the beginnings of the forest. Hassan held onto the railing at the back of the jeep as he bounced one more time off the seat.

'This is the land around the house,' Amina said.

They drove past wildlife that was normally left in peace. Ducks waded through tall reeds that stood in marshes. Beautiful birds posed on grassy verges that led into the jungle, some with spindly legs.

'They're migratory birds,' Zain said.

Only the geese objected to their presence and a flock burst screeching into the air.

'That's what they always do,' Amina said.

They stopped at a large pond laced with white lilies and rimmed with golden-brown rushes which was about a hundred metres away from the house, a one-storey building with a flat roof.

'Buck deer,' Zain said, pointing at a herd with curly horns and white bellies and legs that was drinking from the pond on the other side. The deer looked up but stayed where they were.

'Yes, I know them,' Hassan said.

A pheasant-like bird danced over to them.

'A jacana,' Amina said. 'They walk on lilies. He might do it now.'

They waited but nothing changed.

'Let's have a camel ride,' Zain said.

Hassan preferred the bumpy ride on the camel's back around the house to being in the jeep, but Maryam was groaning.

'That's enough,' she said, holding onto the hump of the camel.

After a couple of circuits, Amina said, 'Tea on the roof. Go up, we'll sort it out.'

Hassan followed Maryam up the stairs and onto the roof where there were four chairs and a table. It must have been around seven o'clock; the sun had not yet set. Hassan was used to being alone with her by now but somehow it felt strange. They sat down. Their seats faced each other but he moved his so that it was alongside hers and they both looked out onto the jungle. There was enough noise from the birds to allow them to sit in silence for a minute or so. It started with one or two butterflies and then a few more came until there was a shower of butterflies that flew all around them. Dozens of white butterflies.

'Where did they come from?' Hassan asked.

'It's a sign,' Maryam said to Hassan, her voice quiet.

'Of what?'

'You tell me,' she said.

'That we still need to talk about time,' he said.

She laughed.

'How can time be the ruler?' he asked.

'*"How?" the lover asked, tired that she had just resigned herself to watching his nails and hair curl and twist,*' Maryam replied.

'Until the day they stopped growing,' Hassan said.

'Because he died?' she asked.

'No, because she did nothing but watch him in the bubble of now. And her fear diminished until there were no more words for her or him to paint the scene with.'

'Was that enough to make time stop?' Maryam asked. 'For her to simply watch?

Hassan nodded and started to recite:

'She learnt by listening to what she heard from deep
in the oceans.
The wind's spirals carried a strange language of
silence to her ears.
Songs of great sea creatures became clearer as she
became truly still.
Sounds arrived at her ears without any sound at all
And joined with the spirals inside her body
To dissolve borders and slow down blood flow,
Until the cycles of moments ending and dying
stopped,
And only one moment was left that never stopped
expanding.
The two lovers joined together.

Two circles, two dances that merged into one.
One circle and time grown still,
With their love at the centre and all around.'

Maryam clapped. He laughed. The butterflies vanished and all of life was perfect. Her eyes were cat-like now and, to Hassan, she was simply magnificent. This was the right path – with her. It had to be.

'Have you thought a little about London?' she asked.

'Yes,' he said.

'You could come back during the holidays,' she said. 'You could meet the beekeeper regularly and your mother.'

Hassan sat back in his chair. Her words came out fast, breathless. He felt dizzy, as if he had drunk the coconut spirit. Doubt tiptoed in his belly and crawled around his skin, like the ants in the jungle – only these were invisible ants. Even Mir Saab had not managed to have both worlds at the same time, but when Hassan looked at Maryam again and her happy face, he slipped that thought into the drawer of unthinkable thoughts. Service to the bees could be possible. He would make sure of it when he came back in the holidays. He had travelled further than Mir Saab into the hive and he had found the beekeeper. England and the bees, both of them were his destiny.

'You'll learn to speak with an accent like mine, Hassan.'

'Oh no… Maryam, if I did decide that it was the right thing, how would it all work?'

'My mother could arrange a visa for you.'

'I have no qualifications. I'm just a kid.'

'My mother could tell them that you're studying. She would pay for your life there. You wouldn't have to do anything while you study.'

Maryam was speaking fast. Her eyes were dancing. She could see the plan working and he smiled.

'Why would your mother do that for me? Why would she let me live with you? She doesn't even know me.'

'It wouldn't be a problem. She'd be happy that she could provide someone from the village with…' She slowed down now and looked at him. 'An education.'

Hassan looked upwards and shook his head. This would never end. He would always be an object of charity.

'Hassan, I didn't mean…'

'It's all right.'

'I just want you to come back with me. I like you. I want you to live with me – as a brother.'

'Once you've gone, you'll forget me.'

'I'll never forget you. If there's a chance that you can come, why not try? My uncle could even write a reference for you. You could get a student visa.'

'I know so many who would die for this opportunity. But…'

'I understand. It's difficult. I'm just being selfish but I can't help it.'

Hassan took her arm. 'I do feel the same as you.'

She let him hold her arm. 'What do you feel, Hassan?'

He felt warm. His hand was trembling. 'I like you too.'

An owl screeched from deep within the forest – or was it from somewhere inside of him? Was Baba in the forest?

Somehow, he could sense his father drawing closer. Perhaps they could sense each other, now that they were nearer again. His heartbeat quickened. A knowingness squeezed through.

Hassan couldn't wait any longer. It was late, nine o'clock already, and he had run down from the fort in the dark after they got back from Amina's house. Most people were already at the tent or getting ready to go to there. Faint music greeted him when he knocked on the front door.

'Amma,' he called.

No one answered. He pushed the door open. Nothing had changed apart from that there were a few more plates on the shelf and two chairs by the table. No one was in the house.

He went through the back door. His mother had his back to him, and she was sitting on the carpet of bamboo leaves next to a tray full of white roses and an oil lamp. A gramophone stood on a small table in the far corner of the courtyard – a dark wooden box with its brass horn speaker playing Indian classical music. Amma picked up a rose from the tray and threaded it onto the garland on her lap. She finished one garland and placed it on an empty tray. Loose petals fell onto her bare feet.

Something moved in the corner opposite the gramophone, probably a lizard under the leaves. There was no more movement until the bamboo shook again. The leaves lifted, and then stillness. More leaves lifted and the head of a snake peeked out. It was three metres away from his mother and its long body began to slide over the leaves – towards his mother. She had started another garland.

He didn't think. He just grabbed the broom next to him and lunged forwards. Smash! He brought the broom down on the head of the snake. And again, this time on its body. It went limp.

A rose fell onto the floor out of his mother's hand.

'Who is it? What's happened?'

They were facing each other.

'Who's there?' she asked again.

He let the broom drop and ran to his mother and they clasped each other, both crying.

'Your eyes,' he said, 'the doctor said two months.'

'Yes, it's been quick.' She put her hands on his shoulders. 'I can still see you. My eyes are much worse in the dark. You're blurred but I can see you.'

He put his head on her lap. 'I should have come back straight away,' he said, 'I wanted to find the honey first.'

'Do you have it?' Her voice was hopeful.

'Not yet.'

She nodded and squeezed his hand. 'You'll find it.'

'How do you manage, Amma?'

'I'm fine. The neighbour's girl comes every day.'

'Sami?'

'Yes, she stays with me after school. She just left.'

'How is she? Is she all right?'

'Yes, I give her some money, now that—' She stopped.

'And Baba…?'

'Nothing.'

'I found the beekeeper and I'll go again tomorrow.'

The lines on her forehead smoothed out and her lips relaxed. He stood up and pushed the snake onto a bamboo leaf with the brush and took it out of the house. If he had been a minute later… He didn't want to think about that as he took the snake to the bottom of the street. The dogs and cats would eat it. He came back inside and sat down at her feet. He told her about the forest, about the bees and about the beekeeper.

'Mir Saab sent the gramophone as a gift when he heard about my eyes,' she said, 'just a few days ago.'

That must have been when he had told Mir Saab about her eyes. Amma felt for a rose on the tray and carried on with the garlands. Her remaining eyesight along with her sense of touch worked well together.

He had wanted to tell her about London, ask her what she thought about Maryam's idea, but instead he said, 'I missed you.'

'How was Karachi?'

'You were right. I learnt a lot there.'

'And you will continue to learn a lot there. I'm happy you're settled. Don't worry about me.'

It was true, she had someone to help her. But her eyes were much worse. It was taking too long with the bees. A restlessness began to creep up his feet and into his legs. He tried to shake it out but it would not leave. It became stronger every time he looked at Amma. He had to find the honey.

They sat mostly in silence as she made the garlands. After an hour, he started to stand up.

'I'll be all right, Hassan,' she said.

She seemed to understand.

'When are you coming back?' she asked.

'Tomorrow.'

Poetry was rising from inside the tent. Mir Saab was ahead, about to go inside with two guards. Hassan went over to the family's car as Maryam was stepping out and joined her behind Amina and Zain. Ali Noor followed them.

'How is she?' Maryam asked him.

'Her eyes aren't good.'

'Will the honey still work?'

'I hope so,' he said.

'Do you want to stay with her, Hassan?'

He had thought of nothing else since seeing his mother but now, when he was with Maryam, he was not sure. He shook his head. 'I don't know, Maryam.'

Inside the tent, they made their way to the side. Around them were distant relatives of Mir Saab as well as his staff and family friends. Maryam started to walk around the women's side, handing out leaflets. Hassan walked amongst the men, slipping leaflets into raised hands. They were like messenger bees bringing news of the whereabouts of flowers. People took the leaflets and glanced at them and then dropped them to the ground where they sat. Hassan wanted to pick them up and make them look again. Some of the villagers looked at him longer than they did at the leaflets. That's when he shrank into his own bubble. He wanted to shout and tell them to look away but the priest started speaking and it happened by itself. The priest was the storyteller in this tradition.

The storyteller's voice was quiet as he began the story of

the ancestors who were tricked into leaving their homes. 'Come and be our advisors,' the leaders of a neighbouring city had said to them. But once there, with their horses tethered by the river Euphrates, and their tents providing shelter for the women and children, they were left without food and water. After three days, the men were told to come out one by one to fight for water. And one by one, they died. The women and children were made to begin the long journey home on foot. The long hair of the women blew over their faces in the desert winds.

The villagers of Harikaya cried for these women, for their children and also for themselves. Mir Saab had brought them together for these gatherings for this very reason. Hassan understood now. This was about bringing the people together as a community, allowing them to let out the grief that had been carried down through generations and which spread out now, understood by each of them. Hassan thought of his mother and a tear dropped from his face too. What if he was too late? And Baba, where was he?

The sobs grew quieter as the priest finished. The gaps grew bigger between the cries until there was a welcome lull. The villagers rose together for a love that had lasted hundreds of years, a love that touched a place in all of them. Hassan stood with the others. The leaflets lay around on the floor.

A melody broke free over their heads – a voice from the speaker that rose out of the tent through the skies. Their grief was free again and there was a feeling of relief. People clapped their chests.

Perhaps there was still a chance. He'd got this far; the black honey could still work. Mir Saab's words dropped into his mind: 'You are the next holder of their secret.'

The humming was in his ears again behind the poetry of melodies around him. He followed Mir Saab and the others outside and looked up at the moon, which was around two-thirds full. He had to find the honey soon.

Maryam had her head turned upwards as they headed back to the jeep.

'I wish I could see the view more clearly without my glasses,' she said. 'Will you give me some of the black honey when you find it?'

'I will.'

She took off her glasses and looked up again, her eyes growing wider.

'What do you see without them?' he asked.

'Over there I see an eagle emerging out of snowflakes. Yes, I see it clearly now. It has a hooked beak and small eyes that stare straight at me. Its wings are open and it's about to take off. Don't you see it?'

He searched for the eagle but Maryam spoke again.

'And look over there.' She pointed to the right. 'I see a mouse, but the eagle is looking the other way.' A smile was beginning at the corners of her lips. 'Do you see the roads in the moon?'

'Yes, I do.' Mir Saab's mother was right. Her eyes were beautiful.

'Look, see those stars.' She pointed with her arm outstretched. 'I think they look like a honeycomb.'

A man passed, leading a donkey loaded with bags of fried chickpeas. 'Channah!' he was shouting.

Hassan gave him a coin and took a small paper bag. He put a few chickpeas in his mouth. Maryam held out her palm. He put his on hers. It was warm.

'Channah,' she said.

Chapter Twenty-Nine

Mir Saab had his head in his hands when Hassan walked into the hall for breakfast.

'Why don't you do something?' Begum Saab asked.

'What can I do? The government passed the bill. They're taking over all charities.' Mir Saab sat with his arms on his lap.

'Bills normally take months to pass.'

'The bad publicity did it. They think I'm a mad eccentric who wants to build an ark.'

'You must fight them,' Begum Saab said, in between the prayers that she whispered as she moved her fingers around the beads in her hands.

'I fought so hard to have the factories made into charities. It'll be hard to reverse that in a hurry.'

'Try,' she said.

'How? Like a lone warrior with a sword? Warriors with weapons have no meaning anymore. They've trapped me. I'm losing this battle and for what? A shameful glory for them at the expense of the people.' Mir Saab glanced at Hassan. 'The jungle is the only refuge. At least the animals are free. The government will never have that. They'll never hurt the animals while I'm alive. Nature will always have the final word.'

'You must fight them. The factories belong to you,' Hassan said.

Mir Saab looked at him, moving his head slowly. 'That's what I used to believe.' He was thinking hard, his eyes blinking through his glasses. 'But I'm a steward. That's what I am, a steward for the people.'

'Mir Saab,' Hassan said, 'I saw my mother.'

But Mir Saab was muttering to himself, lost in his own world. 'That man, the cook, he wanted money and he sold my soul.'

'You've brought community to this place, Mir Saab. I think the people need more encouragement. Change is difficult when people are scared of what might happen.'

'Yes,' Mir Saab was present again. 'The energy of fear is powerful.'

'We can't let it rule our lives. The people have to speak.'

Mir Saab thought for a few moments. 'I'll have a conversation with the speaker at the gatherings. He could say something about a peaceful demonstration.'

'Yes,' Hassan nodded.

'That's what the bees would do,' Mir Saab said.

'Yes, the queen passes on the wisdom to the colony.'

He wished he was there now, deep in the wave of her sound. Ancient wisdom passed on an ancient sound.

'Let's see,' Mir Saab said, 'whether the speaker can pass on wisdom or his own fears.'

The black honeybees were still far away but there was something in the air, a charge that was drawing him close. Like in the temple in Karachi, the force that had pulled him in was at work here in the forest too. Today his steps were lighter, and he reached the watering hole of the vultures more quickly than the previous day.

The beekeeper was already there, sitting on the massive trunk of a fallen tree, its thick roots flying like frozen flames into the air. He was chiselling a wooden stick as Hassan reached him by the pond. The vultures looked up and stared. They did their job well, guarding the beekeeper.

'Teak,' the beekeeper said, chipping at the wood with his knife. He pointed to the ground. 'I finished that this morning.'

By his feet was a log which was hollow inside. Hassan picked it up and examined it. The inner surface was smooth.

'A hive,' the beekeeper said.

'It's the most beautiful thing I've ever seen.' His father would have loved it.

'Except for the real thing.' The beekeeper kept chipping at his piece of wood.

'When will the bees swarm?'

'The bees control their own destiny. Remember what you're dealing with.'

The beekeeper stood up and headed into the forest. Hassan followed with the new hive, which was much lighter than it looked. They walked down a well-trodden path that led to a denser area of trees and bushes, then through an area of long bamboo which was wild and overgrown. They waded through the soft reeds until they came to another wooded area and then finally out into a clearing.

'My father built it,' the beekeeper said.

The beekeeper's house was made of mud and straw, with a round thatched roof. At the top of the roof, the straw was gathered to an opening. On either side of the house were round trees with dark purple fruit.

'Mulberry trees. The bees like their flowers,' he said. 'Every part of those trees is medicine.'

Other trees stood a little distance away, in the sun.

'Those are rosewood,' the beekeeper said. 'Very strong.'

The rosewood was shaggier than the mulberry.

'Is that medicine too?'

'I use the twigs to clean my teeth. Good for firewood and furniture.'

'What do you do for food?' Hassan asked.

'Behind the trees is swampy ground for rice.'

The beekeeper pointed to a few palms behind the house. Bundles of dates hung from their branches. 'Nature gives us everything.' A mango tree stood on its own and the beekeeper picked a ripe mango off and passed it to Hassan. He bit the skin and squeezed the ripe flesh into his mouth; it was soft and sweet.

The beekeeper went over to the door and Hassan joined him, still with the taste of mango in his mouth. He wanted another one. A bee buzzed in front of his face, a curious one that held its ground before letting Hassan enter.

It was beautiful.

'My family,' the beekeeper said.

Honeycombs were everywhere: hanging from the ceiling, from the window frames, from under the beekeeper's bed, from the chairs, from the simple table that was placed in the room. Comb after comb. The air was filled with buzzing. It was another chamber just like at the masjid. There must have been hundreds, or perhaps a thousand bees, wilder and louder than the city bees.

The beekeeper was quietly laughing. Or was he humming? He was part of them. Like another bee, he crossed the room and clusters of bees parted to let him through. He knelt down at a box on the other side of the room and nodded to Hassan to follow.

Hassan took a step through the buzzing, moving through the air which was filled with the smell of wax and honey. His arms were ready to fly about but the beekeeper's stillness reached him through the haze. He had to cross the room through the activity. Workers and drones whirled around their homes, while pathfinders and foragers flew in and out through the opening at the top of the roof. He took another step. He was trembling and the bees felt it. The humming became more intense, their movements sharper. A cluster of bees rose in the air as if to tease him. He thought of the masjid, the chamber of bees, and his jaw became less tense and his arms relaxed. One step, then another. His movement became a dance, like stillness flowing, to the other side of the room. They had accepted him.

The beekeeper opened the lid of the box, and there inside was his father's smoker. 'I repaired it,' he said.

Hassan picked up the tool. His reflection was clear on its surface. He turned it around and saw the beekeeper's face, floating in the shining metal.

'Who are you?' Hassan asked him.

'I am a friend of the bees. Like you.'

'So, you have been waiting for me.'

'The forest has been waiting for you.'

Being outside again was like landing with a bump on the cold floor of the masjid.

'Bring the hive with you and put the smoker in it,' the beekeeper said.

They waded up to their knees through the swampy ground behind the house until they reached higher dry land and picked their way across the prickly forest floor, between tall, thin trees with thin branches that shot out like spikes and other shorter trees with white flowers and long leaves.

They walked on until they reached an area of acacia trees. Some of them had golden leaves and long, thick trunks that split off into different shapes. Others were rounder, with their branches starting about ten metres above the ground, and still others had wide, twisting trunks. Hassan recognised the area. The fire had not been so big. None of these trees were affected.

Then they came to a clearing further on. He froze. Skeletons of trees stood, tall and thin, over the area; dead flowers, charred remains, and hanging leaves. He took a step forwards, brushing the low branches of a grey tree and a bunch of dead leaves fell to the ground. The ground was soft, cushioned by a thousand leaves burnt to ash, but it crackled as twigs dissolved under the weight of their feet.

The area was dead – not even jinns observed them from behind the trees. The birds had stopped coming, even the vultures did not show their faces here. No life at all. No green. The trees, bare and raw, stood in poses of desperation. There was only grey ash and charred skeletons that all looked the same and still carried the fingerprints of flames.

They reached the tree that his father had climbed. It was a ruin. Hassan wanted to bury his head in shame, to hide, but there was nothing to hide behind. The beekeeper didn't speak as they progressed through the remains of the forest fire – an area as big as the square in Harikaya.

They left the cemetery of trees behind them and came to a new area, where colour came back into the world. The beekeeper pointed at a tall tree, a few metres away from the others, on its own.

'Their new home,' he said.

Steady humming floated down from the top. The branches and leaves were dense but he could see a black hanging nest and the cluster close around it. Hassan put the wooden hive down at the base of the tree trunk.

'What shall I do?' he asked.

'Climb.'

'Do you think I can?'

'Fear can have its uses but not with the bees,' the beekeeper said. 'Take your time.'

'I don't have time. You don't understand. It's urgent.' His head hurt. 'Can you climb it for me? My mother needs the honey.'

'This is your task, and yours alone. You know that.'

'But you know what to do.'

'If I do it for you, what's the good of that?'

'I need the honey today.'

'The black honeybees work with those they choose.'

'You're chosen too.'

'This is not my promise and they know that.'

He began to heave himself up with his legs and arms wrapped around the trunk, as he had seen his father do. The sound of humming was still quiet but getting louder as he got higher, like a motor that didn't stop. About two-thirds of the way up, he lifted his eyes and looked up. He was tired and hot and he was losing his grip. No matter how much he wanted this, his arms had no more strength.

'I need this,' he shouted at the bees, lifting his head again.

Waves of sound beat down from the nest, blocking him. The bark was slippery; his hands were sweaty. He dried them, one by one, on his clothes but it was no good; his clothes were soaked.

A black honeybee came near his face. Another landed on his forehead, loud and big. Hassan waved his hand. 'No,' he shouted.

More bees came down, buzzing louder. A bee touched his cheek, too close. He smacked his face. He pictured Baba on the tree, doing the same before he fell.

'Hold on,' came the beekeeper's voice from below.

'Hold on.' This time it was a quieter voice. One that was cool enough to quieten a fire. It was his father's voice.

Hassan's palms stayed on the bark. His heart raced. Palms and bark. Human and tree. Something was holding him and the tree together – a mutual force. His father's voice was in his head again: *Their will is stronger.*

Hassan stopped trying. He had been doing it all wrong. There was no need for victory. It was enough, just as it was. He began to make his way down the tree and the bees grew calmer. Then it happened: his father's face was in his mind. It was there, clear as day, *really* there – his smiling face, his shining eyes. The face stayed with him all the way down to the beekeeper.

Hassan sank down, his back against the trunk. 'I wasn't listening to you or to them. They're too strong to battle with.'

The beekeeper pointed to the nest, 'Do you hear them? They want you to make a decision.'

'But it's their decision to give me the honey or not.'

'I'm talking about your choice to stay or go.'

'I'm not like Mir Saab. I can do both.' Hassan went to pick up the hive a few feet away from the tree. His feet dragged over the ground. He didn't know if the words he had spoken were the truth anymore. What he did know was that he felt the same feeling here as he had done in the temple in Karachi. That feeling of love that emanated from deep within the nest. He bent down towards the hive.

'Leave it. The bees know it's yours now. They'll decide what to do with it.'

Hassan didn't want to leave it. Time was running out for his mother.

'My mother's eyes are much worse that I thought they would be. I hope they decide soon,' he said.

But now he felt the moisture in the air; its smell was changing too.

At the pond, the vultures were drinking there again, used to Hassan now. The beekeeper turned to him.

'It's your intention that counts. That is what moves you forward.' With that he touched his heart – the Sindhi salute – and said, 'You know the way now to their tree. I'll wait for you there tomorrow.'

'How did they know it was your promise and not the beekeeper's?' Maryam asked on the terrace that evening.

'They don't think like we do. They just know things. They can feel your heart language; all creatures speak that.'

'They'll let you go higher tomorrow.'

'This isn't about me anymore or my will or need.'

'And the hive at the bottom of the tree, what's that for?'

'They might nest there.'

'And then what?'

Hassan sighed and shook his head. A light breeze skimmed above an ocean of night crickets to touch his skin.

'I can speak to my mother, if you like, about the ticket.'

He didn't know what to say. He had been thinking. Karachi was one thing, but London was another world. Even if Maryam thought it was possible to come back in the holidays, it would be expensive. He would be building up a huge debt.

'Don't worry about your clothes. We'll get new ones there.'

'Why would I need new clothes?'

'The weather's totally different.'

'What's it like?'

'It rains quite often. Well, very often and sometimes it even snows.'

'Like on the mountains in the north of Pakistan?'

'Not that much.' Her hand was next to his on the wall, small and fine.

A bonfire was being lit down below. It grew stronger and people were gathering around it.

'Are there forests in London?'

'England's very different,' she said.

'Scones and tea,' he laughed.

'And Big Ben.'

'What about the forests?'

'We can visit them.'

'And bees?'

'We'll find them. I have a big garden. We can keep them there.' She laughed.

'First I have to get the honey here. I need it soon. The bees are taking their time and I don't have enough.'

'They'll let you do it. You've got this far.'

'I have no choice.'

What he wanted to tell her was that he didn't even have enough time to think. Going to London was a huge decision but for her it was easy. The night crickets were loud; they helped Hassan stop thinking.

Perhaps it was just him that was making everything so complicated. It would be stupid of him to refuse something that everyone wanted. He looked at her now. He did want to be with her. It could work. She was staring at the bonfire and her fingers tightened. She spoke at last: 'It'll be a big change for you.'

'You'll be there,' he said. He touched her hand and moved his over her closed fist. Their faces came closer. He was in flowing water, drawn in by the waves and now lost to their force. Their lips touched.

No, he would not change his mind.

'How many days are there left before the plane to London?' he asked her. He felt his jaw tighten.

'Four.'

Chapter Thirty

Mir Saab prayed before breakfast and Hassan sat and watched the incense smoke and listened to Mir Saab's whispers, floating in his mind to their rhythm. First to the kiss with Maryam. Then back to their temple in Karachi, on one of his journeys in the nest, surrounded by their hum. He bent his head; his shoulders felt heavy with the thinking. Maryam, the bees and his mother. Three loves. And he had made a decision.

Mir Saab finished and knelt on his prayer mat.

'Did you tell the priest about the demonstration?' Hassan asked.

'Yes, I sent word. Hopefully he'll announce it tonight.'

Hassan was about to leave.

'Wait,' Mir Saab said. 'Their sound will speak to you.'

Hassan waited for Mir Saab to say more but he only started to fold his prayer mat.

'Go,' he said.

Hassan ran out of the fort, down the hillside. They were calling him.

The trees and bushes were blurred greys and blacks, forming a tunnel around him. His feet barely touched the forest floor. Driven by a scent deep in the forest, nothing else mattered. He was the hog, charging. He was the deer, leaping and running. He reached the acacia tree and bent over double, panting. The beekeeper wasn't here yet.

A black honeybee buzzed close by; it hovered for a few moments as the sun disappeared behind a curtain of rain clouds that appeared from nowhere. The bee's wings drooped and the bee fell to the ground. Hassan picked her up with his cupped hands and blew warm breath very softly onto her back until the wings came to life again.

The sun came out again and the bee shook off the dust on her wings. She wriggled her lower body, turning around on Hassan's palms – a mini dance before she took off.

The grasses moved a few metres in front of him. Yes, a ball of grass was moving and then stopped. A nose poked out followed by a head. It was a porcupine, watching him, the stranger in the forests. Both of them froze at the sound of footsteps. The porcupine scrambled like a rocket back into the forest.

The beekeeper entered the area with another smaller hive that he placed next to the first.

'The humming's quieter today,' Hassan said, touching the

bark of the tree. It had been the same in the masjid before the bees were about to swarm.

Hassan settled the bag with the smoker and a knife over his shoulder and started the climb. With each pull of his weight upwards, the forces of sound and the will of the bees played with him, giving him strength. He was entering their sky, their home; even the birds and trees lived in harmony with them. He took a few breaths and paused a couple of feet below the nest. The humming was steady. It felt as if they were accepting him.

There was no great effort anymore – only balance between his body and the tree. A few bees came to explore his face, his arms. He went higher, close to the nest. Bees stuck to it like soft balls of iron clinging to a magnet. There were patches of honeycomb not covered by bees. With one hand, he took the knife out of his bag and brought its blade to a bare section of the comb. Some of the bees started to become unstuck from the hive, moving to cover the section, maybe ten or twenty of them. More joined them. It was no good. They had refused him again.

He brought his knife down and put it back in the bag and waited. The mass shuddered and waves of warm air wafted towards him. It was happening; the hive was readying itself. The hanging clusters were warming up. The new queen was ready to leave with her brood.

The bees sent out messages of joy, beating over him, in a steady song. A few bees arrived back at the nest – messengers that danced to give news of potential new homes.

'Please bees,' he said, 'please choose the hive we made for you,' Hassan whispered. 'I think I'm too late,' he called down.

'I wish I could have reached them before the queen was born,' he said to the beekeeper.

~

They both sat on the ground below the nest. Hassan was growing used to the beekeeper's ways of silence. It was a spacious silence.

'I know what to do with the hive,' Hassan said. 'If they agree to use it, they could live with my mother.'

The beekeeper smiled. 'If that is their will.'

'Did you ever doubt you were meant to be here, to live with the bees?' Hassan asked.

'I don't remember anything different.'

'Didn't you want to do other things? What about school?'

The beekeeper chuckled. 'As you can see, I am unschooled.'

'But you're schooled in the ways of the forest.'

The beekeeper looked into the distance. 'And yes, there were other things. I wanted to see the mountains in the north, to see the wild cats of the deserts and the dolphins in the rivers and sea.'

'You sound like my father.'

The beekeeper got on his hands and knees and started to pick up the dead leaves around them. 'Good for fuel,' he said. The beekeeper looked up at the nest. 'The bees are busy. Go to your mother. She's happy you're back.'

'Not for long.'

'I see.' The beekeeper's eyebrows joined together at the centre just like Mir Saab's.

'I'm going to London,' Hassan said. 'I'll serve when I come back.'

'It's your life. Your will.' The beekeeper's face grew stern now. 'Being with the bees is a responsibility,' he said. 'You have to make your decision.'

'What if it's the wrong decision?' Hassan asked.

'Each of us has the possibility of choice,' replied the beekeeper, standing up with his hands full of leaves, 'and if we make those choices in line with life, with nature, then we move with life. We understand it. I think you know this.'

'I'm beginning to learn this from the bees.'

'Yes,' the beekeeper said. There was a twinge in his lips. 'It's not always easy.'

'But why me?' Hassan asked.

'Sometimes all we can do is accept how things are.'

'And how we are,' Hassan said. 'I felt her presence up there. I could feel that the new queen had been born. They've allowed me so far. I'll just keep going whenever I'm back.'

The beekeeper started to gather up the dates from under a date palm nearby. He held one out in his palm and a crow swooped down and took it with its long, hard beak. The beekeeper did the same with another date. This time the crow flew to the ground with its date.

'Crows are my friends too,' Hassan said.

'We beekeepers have an affinity with them,' the beekeeper said.

The forest was quiet, a rare moment in between animal and bird sounds. He would miss this jungle.

He went to his mother's house that night. She was on the roof, lying on the bed, nearly asleep.

'I feel like I'm in the middle of everything here,' she said.

It was true. Even though the house was at the end of the village in its own corner near the boundary wall, they could see everything from the roof. He brought up the bed from his old room and stayed there with his mother.

The night was much cooler than the day but still warm enough and Hassan drifted in and out of sleep. He tried to keep his eyes open to look at the stars, and squinted to make his vision blurry but he didn't see the animals without Maryam. There would be snow in England. It would be like these stars in space, only the snow would fall from a blue sky. And he would write a poem about the snow and send it to his father.

Baba would come to the forest soon and Hassan would tell him that there was no more danger. The sounds of Harikaya at night time seemed louder – strays, crickets, footsteps of drunken wanderers. He was wide awake now. He would leave all this for Maryam, for a love between humans. But not before he got the black honey. He had to get it before he left. He heard his mother stirring from her bed, muttering in her sleep. She wouldn't be alone when Baba came back.

Tomorrow, he'd tell his mother that he was going. He'd call her from London all the time. He pictured her walking to the village telephone in the square waiting for the call that he would have arranged with her. He closed his eyes and his body grew still. The sound of crickets carried him inwards. Baba would come home one day. There was something growing in Hassan, a feeling of sureness. Baba was on his way.

He wasn't far away now and he'd be here before Hassan had to leave. Yes, that was the truth – he felt it.

In the early hours of the morning, droplets of warm rain woke him up. His mother was still sleeping and he stayed on his bed, letting them fall on his face and outstretched arms. Small droplets turned into big ones.

'Who's there?' His mother sat up and put her hand out to feel the drops.

'It's me, Amma. Only me.'

'Beta, I forgot you were here. My eyes are worse in the dark. But I see you now.' She touched his face and they sat on her bed together with the rain falling on them – a shower that lasted but a few minutes.

'This is good luck,' she said. 'The rains will be here in a day or two.'

Chapter Thirty-One

The next morning, Hassan returned to the fort. Mir Saab was alone, staring ahead, with a plate of food in front of him. Hassan felt like a silent predator. A jungle cat waiting for its chance to ask a question. Any question, to get Mir Saab to talk. Just as he was about to pounce, Mir Saab spoke.

'What about the black honey?'

'I climbed their tree.'

A light shot through Mir Saab's eyes. 'And the bees, how are they?' he asked.

'They're about to swarm.' Hassan felt his own heart leap. 'Come with me. It's a different world there.'

'You know I'd like to one day,' Mir Saab said.

'I'll be gone then,' Hassan said.

'Yes, when you come back for school holidays.'

'No. Maryam has asked me to go back to London with her. She says her mother can arrange a student visa for me.'

Mir Saab was quiet for a few moments. 'She might well be able to.' He picked up his fork and stabbed at a piece of meat.

'I haven't completely decided.'

'There's a lot to think about, isn't there? What about your father?'

'He'll come back.'

The sound of the metal cutlery hurt Hassan's ears.

'The bees have allowed you much further into their world than they allowed me. I could never be part of both worlds. Perhaps it's different for you.'

Hassan came to sit next to Mir Saab at the table. 'I don't know what to do. I keep swinging from one decision to another.'

'What would the bees do?' Mir Saab said.

Hassan closed his eyes. That was the problem. He didn't know. When he opened them, Mir Saab was sinking again into his own world. The fan above their heads was working hard but the room was still hot.

'And they warm up by shivering,' Hassan said. 'I've seen it.'

He was in the courtyard with Maryam, Zain, and Amina. They sat on chairs under the shade of the tree.

'What?' Amina said.

'By shivering,' Hassan repeated.

'That means it's time to go,' Mir Saab said, coming in. 'A cloud of bees leaves the old hive with the new queen in the middle of them.'

Hassan got up to give Mir Saab his chair but he refused.

'The cloud then hangs onto a branch like a beard for a few hours or even a few days,' Mir Saab said. Hassan remembered the way the cloud had hung from another part of the wall in the masjid. 'They cool down when they hang and become very still,' Mir Saab said.

'What are they doing?' Amina asked.

'They're talking to each other before the messengers go off to look for a new home,' Mir Saab said.

'And then they come back and the hanging beard has to agree,' Amina said.

'A conference of bees,' Maryam said, 'and their language is dance.' She stood up. 'I'm a messenger bee. The nest is too crowded,' she said, wiggling her body and her head and spinning round. 'New nests sighted. Come and check.'

'That's exactly right,' Mir Saab said. 'And when they've decided, they shiver to warm up again. By then, the new queen has grown and the cloud moves together in an exodus to a new home.'

'In a swarm, like this.' Maryam demonstrated, then bowed and they all clapped.

It was the first time Mir Saab had laughed in weeks.

'The plane leaves in two days,' Maryam said as he was about to leave for the forest.

'If they haven't swarmed by then, it won't be long. I'll follow you – by train,' Hassan said.

'That'll take ages.'

'I'll be there.'

Hassan could see she was trying to smile.

'My mother said she's got some woolly jumpers for you.'

'Woolly jumpers?'

'Get used to it. It'll be cold.' She laughed.

Hassan walked down the hill and made his way back to the jungle. He ran for the last two or three kilometres of the journey, stopping for short breaks to pant. Eventually, he arrived at the tree. If he went to London, he would see the different people, Maryam's home, be with her.

The beekeeper wasn't there. Neither was there any sign of a swarm.

Hassan squatted on the ground under the shade of the tree opposite the one with the nest. There was no beard, no conference, nothing. There was no point in waiting.

He decided to walk around, going beyond this grouping of trees into a denser part of the forest. There were more nests in these parts, with quieter, milder bees of a different species. He walked on; the trees provided a perfect balance here between light and dark. The birds sang warnings to each other as he went deeper. Flowers grew in abundance on the forest floor, whites and yellows.

Suddenly he stopped. Something was on the ground a few feet away from him. A man, his face partially covered with leaves. But Hassan already knew who it was. And he was still. He had to be asleep. He ran towards him. 'You came back!' Hassan shouted. 'I knew you would come back.' Weeds and flowers framed his father as he lay on the ground. His eyes were closed.

'Baba,' he said, shaking his shoulder.

There was no movement, no flickering eyelids. Baba was a light sleeper. Even on the ground, when Hassan shook his body – gentle shakes at first then getting more and more frantic – his father wouldn't wake up. His face was too pale, the colour of sand.

'Baba, I'm here.' The voice that came out of him was sharp like metal, aimed at his father's ears.

Squirrels and porcupines watched as he took his father into his arms.

There was no breath. His spirit had left.

Hassan looked up. He could see another nest at the top of a tree, writhing with Baba's beloved black honeybees. He had gone for them. There was a basket lying on the ground near his feet. Tears dropped onto the drying skin of Baba's face.

'Baba, I'm here. It's Hassan. I'm here.'

He saw nothing anymore as he rocked with Baba's head buried under his neck, and Baba's shoulders in his lap. There was a hint of movement, the flap of wings.

Hassan looked around; a smoker and a small pocket knife lay on the ground beside him. Baba had fallen from the tree.

'Why did you allow me and not him?' he shouted up at them. But he knew the answer to that. A cloud of bees left the nest in a cluster.

Baba had not stopped when they wanted him to. They hadn't wanted to hurt him like this. He had gone too far, taken too much.

Baba wasn't getting warmer in his arms, no matter how

much Hassan tried. He rubbed his chest, his shoulders; he stroked his hair. His body was cold but not too cold. He couldn't have been here long.

Hassan's body began to shake. There was a scream rising from deep within him; it cut inside him like a sword. That scream became a crack that was heard in the void of distant space. It caused a cosmic seizure, a spasmodic scream of birth that bounced back something that caught him by surprise – hope. A simple hope that he needed now to give him the infinite focus of a dream cradled in a nest of starlight that emitted a sound. It was that sound that brought on life.

'Baba, wake up.'

He held his father tighter in case his own warmth poured into the cold body.

'Baba, I heard that sound that you talked about. I heard it in their nest. They let me in.'

Hassan rocked his father.

'Baba, you knew where it came from. That sound that is carried on their hum. That's why you couldn't stay away from them, isn't it Baba? You wanted to be with them, in their space, to listen to the universe's drum. That was where your poetry came from, wasn't it? From a place before and after time.'

The creatures of the forest gathered to accompany this grief. The steady hum of the bees became a distant, deep drone, a call from the furthest star, and Hassan let out that scream through the invisible crack it had made in his body. It rang out into the universe. A scream of a pain without hope.

He heard footsteps behind him but he didn't turn his head. He sensed the beekeeper.

Everything was clear. There was no need for words.

The beekeeper carried the body back to the house and started to dig. Hassan watched for a few minutes before he too started with a great old spade to bury his father.

'Do you want to stay with him longer?' the beekeeper asked him.

Hassan shook his head. Before they lowered the body into the grave, Hassan checked his father's pockets. There was a folded sheet of paper in one of them; opening it, he saw his father's handwriting. A poem. He took it and placed it in his own trouser pocket.

They went back to the clearing together.

'Have they moved?' the beekeeper asked under the tree.

'Please, I'm running out of time. Please help me.' Hassan had had enough. He lowered his head onto his knees.

Sounds without words joined together around him, like a string on an instrument playing by itself. The beekeeper was singing to them. It was a language of the stars, for bees had to be from the stars. Baba had known that. When the beekeeper stopped, the bees were floating around the nest. Some of them moved downwards and circled the beekeeper. The beekeeper sang again, this time with his lips moving faster making the sounds vibrate more. The bees drew nearer to Hassan and began to circle him too.

'What was the song?' Hassan asked.

'I told them that you're a friend but they already knew this. And I told them that if they choose the log hive, it will be taken to your mother who lives not too far away.'

'What did they say?'

'They asked if you would be there too. I said no.'

'Did they agree?'

'They're still deciding.'

The beekeeper had told them all of this through song.

'All we can do is wait.'

It was a conference, just as Maryam had said; a conference of bees. The humming was loud now as the bees discussed the plans and, in his mind, Hassan travelled to the inner chamber of their nest to join them. The dance hall, the welcoming platform, the place where the speeches were being made. A conference had certainly been called. There were a few bees in a circle, like the poets at the shrine. He was aware of the queen's presence in the background, as she listened to vibrations of love, and the bees took turns to dance in the centre of the platform.

Hassan waited but there was no decision.

There were other messages – strong ones. They were clear in what they said. They were speaking about him. The image faded and he opened his eyes just as the beekeeper was opening his.

'They want me to stay,' Hassan said. They had given him no other option.

The beekeeper nodded.

'I will go to my mother now,' he sighed.

The people in the tent were standing. The claps of skin on chest, slow at first, gradually became a steady beat, gathering pace, a thousand hands playing a rhythm for the song being sung. In a simple chair, on a raised platform, the priest told the stories that had lived through generations.

The song finished. The priest waved the people down and he began again. They were surprised but they listened.

'Mir Saab needs your help,' the priest said, 'to help you, the people.'

Some of them stood up. 'What is it he needs?' a few asked.

'We must act as one community. We must forget our differences.'

The call was spoken with a soft voice.

'We will march next week,' one man said.

Hassan felt his father's spirit. He felt his love, clearer than it had been over these weeks.

Hassan left the tent with Maryam, Zain, and Amina. They followed Mir Saab, Begum Saab, and Ali Noor to a bonfire some distance away from the tent. People were gathering around but none of the villagers approached him now that he was with the family. Perhaps it was better that way. Maryam's glasses reflected the flames. He nodded to her and left the group to go to his mother's house.

Stray cats and dogs and a few people shuffled through the streets. Hassan kept his head low. He entered the main square and breathed in the smell of jasmine.

'Hassan!' a voice shot out from the edges. 'Is it you?'

He turned around to see his old friend heading towards him.

'Ansari Saab!' Hassan rushed to hug him.

'How have you been?' the poet asked him, holding him tightly. 'Your mother told me what happened.' The poet looked down at Hassan's clothes. 'A bit muddy, but good quality. Tell me everything.'

They walked around the square and Hassan told him about his plans.

'So, you're leaving the country now too. Just like I did.' Ansari Saab held his hands together as if he was praying. 'You'll come back and visit me, so I won't stop you. But I need to tell you something.'

'What is it?' Hassan asked.

'Your father's been seen again.'

Hassan took a deep breath. 'I found his body.'

'What do you mean?'

The two of them stood facing each other, man and boy, one straight and the other beginning to double over like the crescent moon in the sky.

'No,' Ansari Saab's voice was muffled by a sob that turned to great hard ones that shook his whole chest.

Time vanished as they stood together, in an embrace.

'A poet has gone to the stars,' Ansari Saab said. 'A strong man who loved you so much.'

Baba was everywhere now.

Chapter Thirty-Two

Hassan had spent the night on the roof with his mother but he still hadn't told her about Baba. He wanted to now but his mother seemed so fragile on the bed. He had to bring back the hive for her first. He left his house and met Maryam on the terrace. She was getting ready to leave for her flight to Karachi at noon that day.

'I'll see you tomorrow at Karachi Airport. Remember your passport,' Maryam said.

She came closer to him, a question in her eyes. 'I can't believe you're really coming. You know if you don't like it, you can come back. Your ticket will be ready for you at…'

'I'm not coming, Maryam.'

'What's happened?'

He swallowed. 'In the end, it was the bees who decided.'

He couldn't tell her about his father. The echoes of that scream had not left him. They never would. A voice came from the courtyard. It was Amina's.

Maryam seemed smaller now, but she stood tall. 'I understand, Hassan. Will you come to the airport to say goodbye?'

'I'll get the honey first and then I'll come.'

She looked worried.

'The bees will let me have it today. They will.'

'I'll wait for you there.' She tried to smile. 'You chose the bees in the end.'

'Maryam, I…'

'I thought you'd be able to do both.' Her lips trembled. 'And your mother too. I've been selfish.'

'No.' He took her hand. 'We wanted to be with each other.'

'I still do.'

'It wasn't my choice, Maryam. In the end, the bees made the decision.'

Amina shouted again. Her voice was nearer this time.

'Get the plane to Karachi. Ask Ali Noor to take you to the airport as soon as you're ready.'

'I'll be there, Maryam. I promise.'

She nodded. 'The bees knew all along, Hassan. They chose you because you are the last beekeeper.'

They hugged each other until Amina came and then she left him on the terrace, turning around one more time before she went through the arch and ran to the car. He headed to the gates, the space behind him full with invisible stories. Maryam's voice, her presence, her soft body. He closed his eyes.

~

'I don't know how long this will take,' Hassan said to Ali Noor before he went into the forest. The driver stayed by the side of the jeep.

Hassan sensed the bees stirring from far away. Like him, they were preparing themselves for their journey to a new home, wherever it was. When he arrived at the tree, the beekeeper was sitting on a log holding a long stick that he was chipping at with his knife. The log hive on the ground was still empty. Hassan sighed and went over to sit by him.

'They haven't swarmed,' Hassan said.

The beekeeper lifted the stick and pointed upwards. Hassan nearly fell backwards when he saw it. A brown and golden beard was hanging from a tree branch, hardly moving. There were very small shivers and a quiet humming.

'They're preparing to swarm,' Hassan said.

The swarm had voted yes. The first stage of swarming had been reached. The beekeeper sat with Hassan and they watched and listened as the bees made their final decision.

'It's time to climb the tree if you want the honey,' the beekeeper said.

Hassan got to about a foot below the nest when he was gasping for breath and had to stop. He tried again but the force against him coming down from the nest was getting stronger. He wanted to give up. Baba had lost the battle too.

'Stop fighting,' the beekeeper said from below in a clear voice.

Hassan could barely open his eyes but he moved a few inches further up the tree. His breathing became deeper. The force floated over his skin. It was not against him; it was against his fighting. Fighting for everything. Fighting to stop himself sinking.

The force was stronger than him but he let the sound lead him. It bathed him, entered him and guided him closer to them, making him and the bees one. The force from the nest that had stopped him was now lifting him. Their will was with his will. He felt lighter.

He went higher. The bees were fewer now that half of them had left the nest and he asked the ones that were remaining if he could use the smoker. The humming grew calmer and he took the smoker out of the bag over his shoulder. Smoke that smelt of forest flowers spread over the bees and they moved away from the hanging moons of wax. He brought out Baba's pocket knife, his knife now, and cut a piece of the honeycomb. This would do for his mother for now. He climbed down into what seemed like a heavier world on the ground.

The beekeeper nodded and Hassan placed the honeycomb in a jar in the bag and put the bag on the ground. He sat on the log again with the beekeeper and waited.

'What's happening?' Hassan asked.

'You tell me.'

Hassan looked straight up at the bees hanging from the branch.

'One of the bees is moving. I see her; she's beating her wings and moving from side to side. She's hovering near the others, telling them something.'

'What?'

'She's telling them that she's about to leave.'

Hassan saw the bee head downwards to the hive on the

ground. He held his breath. Another bee joined her, and then another.

'A few bees are exploring the log hive,' Hassan said, 'and now they're on their way up again.'

The returning bees danced outside the cluster and they all listened, shivering in a glorious golden-brown wave.

'They're thinking about the hive,' Hassan said.

As soon as he had said this, some of the bees started to separate from the cluster as if they were waking up. More woke up and the humming grew louder. The whole swarm pulsed again. Hassan remembered what Mir Saab had said. The bees shivered to become warm again. It was a sign that they were about to make their decision. The beard formation started to grow longer and thinner.

'They've chosen,' the beekeeper said.

'They're rising. They're rising in the air,' Hassan said.

The bees slowly became a spiralling cloud, undulating upwards as if this show were especially for Hassan and the beekeeper.

The bees paused for a moment, and then, as one heartbeat, the swarm leapt into the air and time stood still. Silence wrapped itself around Hassan as he watched the bees, together as one body, dive like a bird into their new home.

Hassan wanted to shout a thousand thanks but all he could do was watch as the bees explored the insides of the log hive. They covered the outsides too in hills and troughs, made up of a mass of single bodies. He felt an urge to wade his hand through them as he would through grains of sand but it was enough to watch. Each bee moved in unison with the whole mass. A stream of bees went in and out of the hole cut in the log by the beekeeper. It was no bigger than his thumb. He watched and forgot time. Thoughts fell apart in his head. It was just as Baba had said. Nature will speak when you listen. It was as if he had always been here with this constant humming from the timeless bees. Nothing was important anymore. Things, success, travel, becoming anything. They all made up a great big, fragile tower stuck together by lies that tumbled down now into an invisible pot to be stirred and transformed. Everything dissolved for him and he was left with a simple knowing. His and the bees'. A knowing that needed to go nowhere and did not change. He let out a laugh.

'I've been looking at this the wrong way,' he said. 'It's not about me. It's about nature unfolding its own truth.'

The beekeeper showed no surprise.

'Please ask the bees if they will come with me much further than they thought,' Hassan said.

The beekeeper bent down and whispered to the bees in the hive on the ground. He closed the door of the hive with a wooden latch. There was still a small hole for bees to come in and out. The beekeeper gave a slight nod before he picked up the hive and handed it carefully to Hassan. It fitted neatly in Hassan's arms, not much bigger than the width of his shoulders.

'Amma won't need this hive now. I'll bring her fresh honey from the nest,' Hassan said. 'I'll be back. First, I have to deliver this.'

~

Hassan walked with the hive and the jar of honey to the jeep. Ali Noor's eyes widened as he opened the door at the back for Hassan to climb in while holding the hive level. At his mother's house, his heart was pounding. He left the hive in the jeep and went inside the house with his bag. His mother was inside in the main room. She looked up when he came in.

'Hassan?'

'I brought you the honey.'

'I knew you would.'

He put the jar of honey on the table and went to get a stick from the shelf – the same stick she had used when Baba had brought the black honey back.

He opened the jar. 'Take this.' He gave her the stick, its tip coated with the dark honey.

His mother dabbed her little finger into it and touched the rims of her eyes.

'My eyes feel cool,' she said.

There was little time. Hassan closed the jar and kissed his mother's cheek. 'I need to go now but I'll be back tomorrow,' he said.

Before they left Harikaya, Hassan had one final task. He ran to the study where he found Mir Saab.

'Maryam wanted some black honey for her eyes. With a small hive, she'll have a constant supply. A letter from you for the airline could make it work.'

Mir Saab took a minute or so to grasp what Hassan had told him.

'It's worth a try. Why not?' Mir Saab wrote on headed paper. 'They might be able to find a cupboard to keep it in on the plane. I'll call some bee friends in London to let them know there'll be a special delivery. Good thing Maryam has a very large garden. Here, take this too.' Mir Saab took a card out of his drawer. 'My airport pass.'

Hassan sat in the back of the jeep, with the hive on his lap, his arms holding it steady. There was no time to think; the train left soon. That alone seemed a small miracle, or was this an example of how nature unfolded its everyday magic? Images flicked through his mind. The bees, the beekeeper, Mir Saab, his mother. And Sami – he would ask Mir Saab to pass on his scholarship to her.

His home was here in Harikaya. In the forest.

Hassan thought about the days he had spent away from home – this was a new life.

Workers, drones or queen.
And all because the bees listened to the stars,
Which listened to the sun,
Which heard the queen speak.

Yes, this was all how it should be. This hive sitting on his lap, over which he was so watchful, was his gift for Maryam. The black honeybees had agreed.

'Keep the hive closed,' Ali Noor said as they climbed the steps onto the train. They had missed the plane and this was the only train back to Karachi. Ali Noor was nervous. They took their seats on the bench at the end of a carriage with no glass in the windows. It was still empty apart from a young woman who sat at the opposite end. She stared at the hive in silence. Her red dupatta hung over her shoulders and her hair blew out to the side as the train chugged slowly out of Harikaya.

Karachi was miles and miles away. More passengers entered the carriage at the next stop, a small town beyond the forests. Some of them left the carriage as soon as they saw the hive to jump off the train and onto other carriages or climb up to the roof. The ones that stayed stared as they took their seats. Soon, many eyes, big and small, young and old, male and female, gazed together. Some of them whispered to each other but the humming was quiet and steady and even the most nervous of the passengers grew used to it.

Hassan handled the hive as if it were a sleeping baby. He kept his arms loose so the hive could gently move in time with the rhythm of the train. He would show Maryam how to do this when he got to the airport. The bees would disturb nobody and she could put them in her garden in London. The humming carried on and soon the whole carriage was taken over by a lull as the train made its way across the land. Ali Noor was relaxed too and stared out of the window at the trees and the rivers and the villages.

Everyone was under a magical spell that wore off each time a passenger arrived at his or her stop, when they shook themselves as if waking up and looked around to see if anybody had noticed how the bees had taken them away from themselves.

Chapter Thirty-Three

A horn blasted. The train entered into the open arms of Karachi train station. He hadn't slept the whole night and they were late. Things were different here. Hassan walked as fast as he could through the people all around him. It was hard not to disturb the bees. Ali Noor hurried to the exit to find a taxi, one that would fit them all in.

'What's the time?' Hassan asked.

Ali Noor checked his watch again but didn't reply until they were in the quieter and wider roads that led to the airport. 'We have forty-five minutes before she leaves.'

It was very close. The hive would make it easier to say goodbye to Maryam. She could keep it at the bottom of her garden. She wouldn't have to do anything. Mir Saab's bee friends in London would help her. If she took just a little honey, the bees would look after themselves. He looked out of the window and felt the bees stirring close to his chest. What he was giving her was part of himself.

Ali Noor waved Mir Saab's letter and airport pass everywhere they went in the airport.

'We need to take this to a passenger,' he told the people at passport control. 'She's leaving soon. The airline is expecting us.'

The pass worked like a miracle. A man with a large phone in his hand left the desk and walked with them. 'We might make it before they close the door,' Ali Noor said.

The hive was becoming heavier and the bees were restless. It was hard to keep up with the others but Hassan pushed himself, harder and harder. He walked through staring faces, across shiny floors, past people shouting down telephones perched on desks and past shops with bright lights until they reached a hall with glass walls and he saw the plane. Maryam's plane. The room was empty.

'The doors are closed,' a woman said behind another desk. She wore the same uniform as the man. Another woman joined her and then another. They all wore the same clothes.

'Please open the door. I need to see my friend,' Hassan said. He asked ten times, but nobody was listening.

They were staring at the hive.

'How on earth did he bring that this far?' one asked her colleague. They finally left him and Ali Noor alone to look at the plane through the window. Maryam was on that plane and it was moving, backing up before it turned and taxied along a paved section.

'She's on the runway,' Ali Noor said.

The plane stopped and then started again, faster and faster now until it rose into the sky.

Something touched his arm. Ali Noor's hand.

'Come, Hassan. Let's go back to Harikaya.'

Chapter Thirty-Four

You bring the sound that never dies.
Carried on thin notes through reed, skin, and string.

These words of Baba's poem came to him as he walked through the forest back to the tree with the black honeybees. It didn't matter if the beekeeper was not there. For the first time in his life, time did not matter. There was tomorrow and the day after that. Countless tomorrows to spend here in the forest with the beekeeper and the bees. He had been so close to leaving all of this.

He walked over the bracken and the muddy puddles, through bush and along moist paths. The sounds of the forest welcomed him. The humming of the black bees in his arms grew quieter. They knew they were going home. Perhaps they had known all along that they would come back. Just as he was doing now. Coming home. He had been trying so hard. It had never been necessary to make a choice between three loves. In the end it had been down to where he had been most needed, and that was with the bees and Amma. In truth, it was him who needed them more.

He stopped by the lake. Its water levels had risen. It had been raining here in Harikaya and soon the forests would be out of bounds. When the rains were over, he would come back and see the beekeeper every day and live with Amma.

Ducks flew down to the pond for water before the hogs arrived. Deer crept forward too and the geese flew up, flapping and screeching.

Maryam would have laughed at that.

She would have arrived at her home by now.

He felt a sharp pang in his chest.

They had stood together in front of an empty space full of potential on the brink of two cultures merging. Hers and his. So many had gone before him on the path that Maryam had offered him. A jasmine-winding path that bridged new worlds of culture.

Going to Karachi, meeting Mir Saab and Maryam and all that had happened to him, had been a passageway, through which the old forms of his life had been unhooked from his very being; the old stories had fallen apart. He smiled to himself and walked to find the beekeeper by the tree where the black honeybees nested.

'They were waiting,' the beekeeper said.

Hassan stood in the middle of the clearing opposite his father's grave. A stone slab had been placed at the head of the grave. The beekeeper must have put it there while he was travelling to Karachi. Words floated into his mind over the humming from the nest.

Only those who truly know the honey's worth may receive it.
For they only listen to the ones who love them.
And for this love, the bees reveal their secret.

Baba was part of everything now – part of the intelligence behind all life. Hassan waited in case more words came. He only heard drops of rain on the leaves of the low-lying bushes – quiet drops without a constant rhythm, like the words he was waiting for – nothing he could hold onto with his will. No more words came and he lay the small hive down in front of the slab. This colony would find their home whether on the ground or higher up. He looked towards the nest in the treetop, at the dark humming mass.

It had a soft blurry edge to it with a sharp, focused centre. His eyes shifted with ease from the outer edge to the centre. The leaves whispered around him. Birdsong faded in and out. The humming felt stronger. He stayed with it, wanting to go deeper into their refuge – the nest of the black honeybees. And for a moment, his mind began to float. The intensity of the centre of the nest was expanding. His knowing was merging into theirs, into the wails from an unseen depth that surrounded him. Flashes began in the darkness. They came and went, on and off, like a steady drum beat on the waves of the humming. It was a drum beat that was not made by human hands.

It is the sound of truth, a law, dropped to the earth.
It is no accident.

All was as it should be. His whole life had been preparation for this. He was back with his awareness on the ground again. The black honeybees had allowed him a glance, a feeling of that intensity. He held out his hands; it was raining.

'Come back when the rains stop,' the beekeeper said.

Mir Saab went to Karachi again and Hassan came back to the jungle after a month, and then every day just as he had intended, to listen to the nature around him.

He wandered with the beekeeper, gathering information about the whereabouts of the different nests. He began to learn about the wild flowers and the herbs. He became used to his life combining two worlds, returning to his mother by night and, after school, visiting the forest, still lush, alive and fresh from the rains.

The sounds of the forest became louder than the thoughts inside his head and the spaces between the memories of Maryam grew large enough for him to listen for that sound that Baba knew too.

Hassan began to write poetry.

Mir Saab returned to Harikaya when the rains stopped and asked Hassan to come to the fort.

'I gave the scholarship to Sami,' Mir Saab said from behind his desk.

'It's the right decision – she'll have more choices that way.'

'I'm going to create more scholarships,' Mir Saab continued.

Hassan nodded. More education would give the people stronger voices.

'How is your mother?' Mir Saab asked.

'Her eyes are stable. Thank you for helping her.'

'I thank you too, Hassan.'

'For what?'

'For bringing me back to what I was before I… before my…' He brought his hands together in front of his face as if in prayer. 'I was full of fear. In a mental prison. Stuck.'

They sat in silence together for a minute, maybe longer.

'And Maryam, have you heard from her?' Hassan asked.

'Yes. She asks after you and I'll be able to tell her now.'

Hassan took the pouch out of his pocket with the piece of honeycomb. 'Can you send this to her?'

Mir Saab took it. 'Easier than a hive,' he said.

They both laughed again.

'It was a strange time, wasn't it, Mir Saab? I believed anything was possible.'

'You and Maryam managed to get the people to march.'

The march had consisted of mostly women, with some men on the edges. They had walked through the rain, soaked by the downpour that had started as soon as Maryam had left. Hassan had walked alongside his mother.

'The plans for the takeover are still going ahead, but it's a beginning,' Mir Saab said.

He was looking at Hassan hard.

'Are the black honeybees letting you in?'

'Yes. Sometimes I want to know why. Why me and not Baba… or you?'

'That's like asking what purpose the stars have. Is there a real need for an explanation?

Hassan shook his head.

'Hassan, I've been thinking.'

'Yes, Mir Saab.'

'Take me to the beekeeper.'

the spaces in between one star's light and that of the other ones,
reaches my ears having travelled through the cracks
on the waves of codes that came down so our ancestors
could perpetuate their generations, not only to stand behind time's helms
but to obey these invisible laws that unfold under our sun

that help the queen bee plan the numbers of daughters to come
that help her plan from one generation to the next all those ones
born by the codes of unfolding, that also inform the spirals on this shell
which I put up to my ear and now thank
its etchings linked to the greatness of my grandmothers,
that will still exist even when time has slacked

I look to the line behind my back
time is not the keeper of these ancestors
it is the invisible code that is to thank.

Author's Note

THE STORY BEHIND THE STORY

I grew up reading Shakespeare, Jane Austen, Thomas Hardy, Agatha Christie, Anne Frank and more. I love them all. Later, I found Arundhati Roy, Michael Ondaatje and Ben Okri, who all inspired me with the lyrical quality of their writing. I adore Gabriel García Márquez. I love the way he combines history and magic to create universal stories.

For me, memories can be the seeds for stories. They grow into something unrecognisable and take a life of their own. My memories started on the plane journey to London from Karachi when I was two years old, as I was transported from one world to another with my parents.

When I turned forty in 2010, I had just finished my Master's in Art Therapy and decided to join a writing class. In the first lesson, the teacher gave us a quick exercise to do and the image of Hassan skipping across the courtyard of a Karachi house that I had visited as a child came to my mind. It was as if a seed had fallen into me and I had finally found the story I wanted to write. It wasn't until a few years later in 2018 that I developed the regularity needed to finish the novel.

A couple of years after that first writing course, I went on a sustainable beekeeping course at a charity called 'Bees for development'. I learnt that the bees in Pakistan, till around the seventies, were a species quite unlike the bees of countries to the west or east of Pakistan. This 'in-betweenness' of the bees of this region interested me. Pakistan also has a certain 'in-betweenness'. It's a young country with different cultures and identities – resembling the countries that lie on both of its sides, yet impossible to categorise.

On that beekeeping course I also heard that, in times past, bees were sometimes transported in hives on long distances. For example, bees were taken on carts from one town to another. There was even one story of someone transporting a hive on a train between towns. I had found the last scene of my book – Hassan transporting the hive from Harikaya to Karachi. From that moment, I decided to make bees the focus of the story.

I later learnt that there was a species of black honey bees in the area – Apis dorsata – rare in Pakistan today. I tried to imagine how these bees would have been when they were more prevalent in the region – a mind unto themselves, hard to handle by humans, and a source of rich honey that was prized by honey hunters. My grandmother actually went blind from glaucoma before she died in 1972. Treatment wasn't very advanced in those days and it was common practice to apply the forest honey of the Sindh to the lower rim of one's eyes to help with such conditions. My grandmother's story of her eyes and the practice of using honey as medicine became the inspiration for the book.

Poetry and storytelling are so key to the cultural backdrop of Pakistan and I wanted to convey this in the novel. After partition in 1947, many people came to Karachi from different parts of India. Many had come with hopes and dreams of a haven and had left behind homes and families and were traumatised. It was a hard and immensely sad time for everyone on all sides. My grandfather arrived in Pakistan in 1949 from Hyderabad in India with his family. He was a scholar and a poet who loved Rumi. His house in Karachi was a safe haven for poets who would gather in his courtyard garden and recite their spontaneous verses in the coolness of the night. My grandfather also carried on telling the traditional stories that he had told in India. Large gatherings came to listen from across the city and eventually from all over the country. These stories of loss and love were an outlet for the collective losses and grief of the time.

In England, my father would write poetry for himself and shared this love with me. I often heard him humming a tune of verse or saw him scribbling down lines. Poetry was read and sung by family and friends in regular gatherings as I grew up in Manchester. As a family, we visited India in the nineties. My father hadn't been back since he had left at the age of fifteen in 1949. We were walking somewhere outside Hyderabad and my father recognised a man coming in the opposite direction along the almost empty road. It was a poet he had known as a child, someone who had come to my grandfather's house in Hyderabad for the poetry gatherings there. It was an emotional encounter.

Around 1974, when the story is set, the change in the political atmosphere in Pakistan started to intensify. Private industries started to be made public as a result of reforms that swept the country. This could have been a progressive move, but unfortunately, many of those industries suffered from subsequent neglect by the government. It was an 'in-between time' and marked the end of an era. My aunt told me how she used to walk alone to her classes at the university in the late sixties and early seventies, something that became very hard to do as the seventies progressed. My grandfather died in 1973 just before this 'in-between' time set in.

I visited Pakistan for the first time after I left in 1981 when I was eleven. I had just started grammar school in Manchester, a world away from the Sindh province. I visited a nature reserve, not too far from a beautiful two-hundred-year-old fort that wound its way around a desert landscape, overlooking a village. That image became the backdrop for the story and Harikaya.

Karachi was full of layers upon layers of history and cultures. I saw crumbling colonial architecture, Sufi shrines, bustling bazaars, flats and sprawling suburbs standing side by side. I remember having my palm read in the square in front of a Sufi shrine in Karachi at night time. The fortune teller sat cross-legged on the floor amidst street sellers, singers and shrine visitors, with my palm in his hand.

He told me that one day I would write a book.

Acknowledgments

I'd like to acknowledge and thank my editor, Bethan Morgan, for her finely attuned editing, dedication, and support; Lucy Bennett for the beautiful cover; and all the superb team at One More Chapter and HarperCollins for the welcome they have given me as my publishing home and all their support for me and *The Last Beekeeper*.

I'd also like to thank Christina Petrie for her encouragement and support, and also Molly and Chloe. And to all the others whose names I haven't mentioned here but who have been there with me along the journey of writing this story. Thank you.

Baba's last poem

Here on the sand, I look to the line of ancestors
staggered at my back
I hear the music that is still played by the very
first one
and my vision trails through brother, father,
grandfather
on and on – great-grandfather, great, great, great ones
great grandmothers too until there are blanks
and the stories that my grandfather told are mingled
with other realms

of silken cloths made from worms brought over on a
ship's helm
to lands where fires burnt only at night and
people sat,
singers, poets, people of the melodies that sung of
their ranks

that go back to times when snakes first emerged from oceans
to follow trails set out by other creatures into the sun,
worms, lizards, and greater beings that became our birds

all of them with a line in time behind their backs – of ancestors
and I, who walk this beach and take a shell,
trace its spirals etched by each of the elements,
and sketched by mathematicians with incessant lacks
that drove them to discover the codes behind the patterns on each one—
shells, fossils, flowers, ferns, unfolding shapes, and most of all the blanks

the spaces between lines on the shell in my hand, unnoticed until I sink
myself, a clear product of the paths of all my ancestors,
and bound by the line of time that reminds me of where I am from,
until I sink myself into that sound beyond perception by any sense
that rises from the spaces between the lines, between the tracks
that the mathematicians explore with a finite number of sums

beyond which the sounds of stars and all the blanks—